ROTTING IN VAIN

LADY KILROY

*To all my RBF girlies
and the men who told us to
smile.*

Taunting Death Series: 1

Rotting in Vain

Copyright © 2024 by Lady Kilroy

All rights reserved.

No part of this book may be reproduced in any form or by any electronic or mechanical means, including information storage and retrieval systems, without written permission from the author, except for the use of brief quotations in a book review.

Published by: Lady Kilroy

First Edition Published February 2024

Cover Artist: Amber Thoma

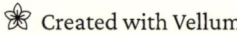 Created with Vellum

PLEASE READ ME FIRST

The content in the book is not suitable for readers under the age of eighteen, and should also be read with caution. Please keep in mind that this is a DARK fantasy book. Some of the content can be very triggering, and may include content such as death, torture, sexual assault, attempted sexual assault, attempted necrophilia, self-harm, substance abuse, & PTSD.

PRONUNCIATION GUIDE

Dhadren (day-dren)
Ghaldir (gall-deer)
Titáine (tit-awn-yuh) or Áine (awn-yuh)
Conláed (con-led)
Søren (sir-en)
Rodgärd (rod-gard)
Visha (vee-shuh)

ROTTING IN VAIN
TAUNTING DEATH SERIES

LADY KILROY

PROLOGUE

Hate filled the eyes of the King.

Alaric, Dhadren King of Ghaldir, overlooked the chaos and bloodshed before him. Seated on his warhorse, Alaric contemplated how he should have done things differently.

He should have killed the king of the elves once he realized who he would become; once he saw the possible future that now lay before him: A future filled with the sounds of screams and clashing steel, along with the smell of blood and shit.

Eadric, The Elven King, remained unaffected across the fields, with an unwavering smirk on his face. He didn't seem to care that despite his efforts, his forces were overwhelmed.

Of course, he brought his latest creations. His half-breed demon fae with their elven braids and unnatural skin that glowed different undertones of blue. Except the one who's skin glowed red, and wore a ridiculous smile as he fought and killed.

They came along with his demon officers. Alaric recognized them immediately. Back from when they terrorized his lands centuries ago. They were taller, and held more advanced weaponry. Alaric smiled. He knew Eadric went all out, and it still wouldn't be enough.

Alaric never expected Eadric, of all people, to resort to this. But losing everything will make you do incredulous things.

Alaric watched as Eadric's sons, amongst the other abominations, fought his people without the matching conviction in their eyes. They didn't ask to be here, nor did they ask to be created for this sole purpose.

That meant nothing to Alaric.

Today, his daughter, his *only* child, turns five, and is currently in the crypt of their home cradled by his queen. If he had to, he would end this right now. Let his power erupt and be done with it, ensuring his family's safety.

But, he would also be taking out their own army.

An army they would need against the High Court of Ancients, who had once been a common enemy of Alaric and Eadric's.

That was no longer.

The red-skinned demon fae killed another one of Alaric's officers, slicing him into fourths with his dual swords.

Alaric shared a look with his General and closest friend, who was seated on his horse beside him. Nodding, the General vanished, appearing in front of the red demon.

In an attempt to eviscerate the threat before they lost

any more of their most skilled warriors, the General unsheathed his dual swords and circled him.

Alaric gripped the reins tighter, now noticing the five giant faeries on horseback, watching the battle like they had nothing to lose, and everything to gain.

The ancients dismounted their horses. One of which was carrying something. Something large, that glimmered in the sunlight. Not a weapon... A stone, and placed it on the ground.

They each stood around it and raised their hands in the air, chanting.

Alaric narrowed his eyes at Eadric, who was now looking back at him with such hateful joy and anticipation.

"What the fuck did you do..." Alaric breathed.

Deep in the crypts, far beneath Castle Kilhorn, a terrified queen Mira holds her child, and prays to any god that will listen. She neared the other mothers, the other children, and together they prayed.

Prayers that would be answered in a way they never would have imagined.

As they chanted the familiar verses for protection, the children began crying.

Pain filled each of their chests.

Mira looked frantically between them; looked back to her daughter who remained quiet and seemingly unharmed.

She couldn't decipher what was causing the pain. Tears

began streaming down her face in fear, fear for them, for the children, and for what also might be coming for her daughter.

A pulse thundered in the room, pounded across their chests, now causing Mira and Alaric's daughter, Titáine, to weep.

Mira could feel the sensation of her heart being yanked out of her chest. She held her daughter while she screamed in her arms. And together, they all watched as the air thickened with magic, and then dissipated.

The only sound in the crypt was their labored breathing and children crying.

No one had died.

The emptiness they felt was an undeniable truth: Their magic had been taken.

All of it.

Mira felt a crack between her temples, and choked down the screams.

She looked at her trembling daughter with new eyes, until the walls shuddered, and everyone fell from the impact of magic exploding.

The explosion came from outside, from far away, where the ancients had tried siphoning the entirety of the Dhadren's magic into an ancient stone that had been charging for many decades. For this exact moment.

And it didn't work.

Alaric struggled to stand after being blown off his horse.

Eadric and his men were retreating, even though Alaric could feel the powerlessness amongst him and his people. Which could only mean that they were simply a means for distraction.

Alaric tried to listen for the swearing that ensued at the top of the hill where the Ancients had gathered; tried to listen to anyone.

Nothing.

He could only hear who and whatever was nearest him, and he started to panic.

That stone exploded from trying to hold their power, and now it had turned into powerful and frantic gusts of wind, knocking people down.

He stood there and waited for it; waited for the return of their power they so foolishly tried to take. You couldn't take the power away from gods and keep it for yourself. That power was meant for however they willed it, not petty fae who became overconfident.

Alaric waited for it, but it never came.

He waited for the moment that power would return; the moment he would allow his power to erupt. The ancients being there changed everything. And he refused for them to come near his family.

Then everyone outside watched as that power took form; a raging tempest twisting into a whirlwind.

They watched as it rescinded into the sky, and those mighty clouds made way towards the castle.

Alaric's chest heaved as he watched what he could not control: the whirlwind descending into the castle, and vanishing.

He felt his chest sink into his stomach. When he turned around, they had disappeared. The ancients; All of them had gone. Where, he could not see; not passed the sky that was now thickening with dark grey clouds.

And without another thought, Alaric ran towards the castle, sprinting through the rain that smelled foul.

The scream that filled the crypt came from Mira, who could do nothing while her daughter's head was thrown back, and a storm of magic forced its way into her body; down her throat.

She knew of the horror this would lead to; that a child of this age could never hold that kind of power. Her tiny body would implode, and Mira would end her long life if that happened.

Gasps collected from within the room as little Titáine's body floated in the air, and she absorbed every ounce of power the gods forced her to carry.

Mira stood there crying hysterically, waiting for it.

But it never came.

The child fell to the ground, fast asleep, but breathing.

It was the only sound in the room as Mira stood there, looking at her in disbelief.

She could detect no magic, but knew it was there.

Doors had been slammed open, and in came Alaric.

He was panting, taking in the atmosphere of the room, noting the looks of disbelief and panic on everyone's faces surrounding his queen.

All eyes were on his daughter's small form.

Alaric took in the look of horror on his wife's face, a look he won't forget until the day he died.

Casting a worried gaze back to his daughter, the truth of what happened flooded him.

The truth that would not only change the course of her life, but of the lives of everyone around her.

Never in his life had Alaric felt such fear, than at that moment, looking down at the sleeping vessel.

CHAPTER ONE

ÁINE, TWENTY YEARS LATER...

"Shit! Shit! Shit! Shit! Shit!" I sprinted through the decay of a once-enchanted forest. I could just make out the exit up ahead, a small break between gnarled trees. Our horses perked their heads up at the sound of us crashing towards them. Warhorses are not known to be skittish, but one look at what was chasing us, and even they became nervous. If Maddox spooked and took off on me, I would.... Honestly, I wouldn't do shit to that spoiled beast.

"Hurry the fuck up, woman!" Captain Liam, a.k.a. royal pain in my ass, shouted while we were being chased by ancient spriggans that he *accidentally* woke up. Their centuries-old screams sound like they desperately need a glass of water. These things looked exactly like fallen tree limbs scrambled together with arms, legs, and the makings of a somehow attractive face. And they were getting too close to our heels with the thunderous stomps of their feet.

Not even five minutes had passed since we entered the forest. Visha, the elder druid, sent us out here with one of her acolytes to search for a rift. She felt the shift of magic in the dome of death that surrounded our island. Many times we have been sent out on these pointless expeditions, and each time she *sensed* magic, it ended in disappointment. Another reason I didn't trust her. Everything about these assignments reeked of distraction.

"You had *one* job!" I shouted back between my panting. "Don't. Touch. Anything. Shit!" I tripped and nearly took a tumble over a dead tree root.

"I didn't fucking touch anything!" he squawked. I gave him a pointed look that captain Keira mirrored. He shook his head in defeat while failing to suppress that shit-eating grin.

It didn't help my attitude that Isolde was supposed to be by my side out here, yet once again, she refused to show up tonight. And now we were running from ancient spriggans because our captain and *master* of stealth woke them up. I snorted at the insanity.

I didn't have to look over my shoulder to make sure Keira and the Druid, apprentice whatever-her-name-is, was keeping up. I could clearly hear her grumbles between panting breaths; some choice words about being stuck with stupid children. And thank our bloody fucking stars, Maddox and the other horses were still there. We broke through the edge of the forest, threw ourselves onto their backs and took off towards home, the Kingdom of Kilhorn.

We rode hard over the barren fields, surrounded by a

suffocating fog that settled from dark clouds that never changed.

And now we needed to return and inform Visha and my father that we fucked up and found nothing. Not a single clue or anything to find a way to freedom.

The dome surrounding our island has held firm for nearly twenty years, and no one could seem to get us out. Not that I held out any hope for it. People hated us for the power we used to hold. Able to raise our middle fingers in the face of bullshit oligarchy. Eventually, we fucked around for too long and found out.

We approached the portcullis, illuminated by flickering torches and surrounded by battlements made of volcanic rock. Beautiful and intimidating to look at, but since there were no volcanoes on this island, the material felt out of place.

The ground cracked and kicked up dust when I dismounted Maddox. Dust that you did not want inside your lungs.

Growing up, my elders would tell me that our curse was simply *that of humans*. That the magic used was of gods who punished their creations for whatever reason they deemed necessary. But from what I'm told of humans and their fables, they didn't live in worlds such as this. So if that was our curse, then why hasn't anyone aged like humans? None of it added up, but I nodded along anyway.

With the horses now back in the stables, the four of us made our way to the throne room, to meet with Visha and my parents. Another pointless check-in to let them know their *senses* were wrong, yet again. My sense of sanity was ready to explode and unleash that anger on someone. Playing with hope was a dangerous thing.

Of course, these were not assignments that we allowed to be known to the general public. In fact, only those who were on a need-to-know basis were told. The last thing we need is our people, who had already begun to shred their morality, to feel the same emotions I felt during these chases. In my lessons, there was one universal truth: that the general public were to be treated as animals. Animals that were waiting for the signal to give in to their baser urges.

They call it baser, but I had a hard time believing that the evilness spreading like a disease was *instinct*.

Our footsteps on the marble floor echoed throughout the halls, alerting the guards to open the doors to the throne room. Liam snorted, like he does nearly every time they do that, and I quickly narrowed my eyes at him before turning back to face my parents.

To my surprise, my mother was sitting on my father's throne while he stood beside it, hand on the backrest. Once upon a time, before our lovely curse, my mother had her own smaller throne that was seated beside my father. They never told me what happened to her throne beyond it being *smashed to bits* during the last battle against the High Court, the Elves, and the Demons. How we weren't obliterated off the map, I hadn't the slightest idea. I felt my eyes rounded when I noticed her sitting there. She looked so powerful for someone who wanted the world to think she was weak and useless.

This woman *refused* to accept his offer to rule at his side, to be the first ruling queen, yet here she was sitting on the throne. Her fingers were rubbing her temple as she took in my look of surprise. "I have a headache. Your father made me."

I rolled my eyes at that last statement, but said nothing as Liam and Keira stepped beside me. The druid that came along with us shouldered passed me, muttering about children having too much power. My father gritted his teeth, but I just snorted under my breath. Let her have her moment to vent after being chased.

"Where is Isolde?" Visha's voice surprised me as she sauntered around a pillar, . Her simple black dress danced around her unnaturally still body. Her matching dark hair framed a youthful face. A face that didn't reflect her true age, with laughing eyes contradicting the blood soaked centuries she had seen.

My jaw clenched. "She was unable to come with us."

My mom snorted obnoxiously from the dais, as if I needed another reminder of her obvious opinion of her. I bit my cheek to keep my mouth shut. Something I've been doing a lot lately, if the constant bleeding in my mouth was any indication.

Ever felt the need to scream and throw shit?

Same.

"Aine," my father called. I turned my expression of feigned boredom in his direction. "You gave her a command, and she didn't show. Make sure it's handled."

I kept my expression neutral and remained silent. Something he taught me, which has become an invaluable skill set. For him, it was mostly out of respect. But for anyone else, keeping silent allowed others to dig their grave further.

"Yes, because the next time it happens, I won't hesitate to send someone else to do the job for you," my mother sneered.

"Mira," My father whispered softly to her, but she didn't take her cold eyes off me. He brushed it off and turned towards us with an impatient expression. "What happened?"

I swallowed, but before I could speak, Liam stepped forward and cut in, royally pissing me off. "We found nothing. But we didn't have enough time to look before the spriggans woke up and chased us out of the forest."

My parents' eyes rounded, and then looked at me like it was my fault.

"It was me," Liam objected. "I was sure I was silent, but I didn't notice the one sleeping two trees over. It noticed me immediately."

The look of surprise on my father's face nearly made me chuckle, until he said, "*You* woke them up? Not her?" pointing at me.

I rolled my eyes and faced the other way towards Keira before I gave myself away.

My mother, however, didn't find any of it funny. "How did you escape them?"

"We ran."

The look on her face reflected my lack of control of my tone. "You ran." It wasn't a question. "From *spriggans*. And made it home safely?"

I wasn't certain what she was accusing me of and hoped

my face reflected that. "How else are we supposed to escape them in this state?"

Her nostrils flared. "And why exactly didn't Isolde join you?"

My teeth were grinding. "The three of us are perfectly capable."

"That's not what I fucking asked you."

My eyes widened. She stepped away from my father's hand he had placed on her shoulder, and stood at the steps of the dais, looking down on me with anger and... fear?

"If I... if your father orders a specific number of people to be there with you, then that's how many go. You should've pulled her out of whatever tavern she decided to attend and made her go with you."

I swallowed down copper flavored saliva. My friends appeared to be counting the specks of dirt on the floor. I clenched my fists behind my back before speaking. "This is getting old. Am I to never step outside the castle without an escort? Like a *child*?"

Her voice lowered. "Don't tempt me."

My father stepped beside her, "If something happens to you,"

My mother cut him off. "You're a *vessel*. If you die, *they* could make your body rise as theirs, even if they have to preserve it. Imagine what could happen if they waltzed into this room, right now, appearing as you."

I was growing exhausted from this conversation. This constant lecture. "I am their *commander*,"

"Then fucking act like it," she snapped, then stormed out of the room, leaving me to stare daggers into the floor while trying to control my breathing.

A familiar sigh sounded from the dais. "Dismissed."

I didn't bother waiting for Liam or Keira as I stormed out of there, now too pissed off to enjoy drinks at the tavern. Too pissed to face Isolde after that disaster she caused. And she'd likely be there.

For someone who begged me to train her all those years ago, she sure as shit didn't seem motivated now.

I reached the main bedroom halls, just further down from the King and Queen's quarters, and didn't slow my steps. I didn't bother knocking on Sloan's door to bitch in her ear. I would've exploded if I did. I decided I'd take a bath that took way too god's damned long to prepare in this hellhole. Maybe if I'm lucky enough, I'd fall asleep in the tub. How peaceful would that be?

I opened my bedroom door and stilled when I walked inside. Because sprawled out on my bed was Isolde, wearing another one of her tight, feminine clothes she'd wear out.

The smirk on her face was infuriating.

The way her hips curved when she turned to lay on her side made me want to throw shit. It made me want to throw her. She let out a low, sultry chuckle as she slid off the bed and sauntered towards me.

Her dark, wavy hair bounced with each step, landing in a different pattern on top of her breasts each time. The littlest bit of olive skin peeking out from beneath her low-cut tunic she had cut short.

She reached out her slender hand, intending to touch me in some manner that I didn't wait long enough to find out.

Too fast for her to catch, my hand snaked up and gripped her jaw, pulling her face closer to mine so she could get a better grasp on how pissed she made me; on how fucked she was. Her lips struggled to form and make words.

"I don't want to hear any fucking excuses," I hissed.

Her throat bobbed, her eyes hooded, and then realization hit me.

With my brows raised, I asked her, "You like it when I'm angry?"

Her tongue slid across her lower lip, and she nodded with the little movement I allowed.

Stepping forward, I didn't let go of her face, forcing her to step back. When her legs were up against the bed, I inched closer, making my body flush with hers.

Her scent mixed with whiskey was intoxicating.

"Well then, *captain*," I ground out sarcastically. "Allow me the pleasure of teaching you a fucking lesson."

CHAPTER TWO

CONLÁED

Twenty long years I have waited.

Hovering above the island of Ghaldir, I continued to follow that scent. Not the lingering, incessant one that I've struggled to ignore, but the magic we've sensed shifting in and out of it for years.

After more than a year, it reappeared. We finally detected a trace of magic being shifted. The moment I sense it, that tension in my neck signaling my father's magic, it disappears.

The poisoned air whirled in black eddies from the cursed dome towards me, seeking any organic component to destroy.

The foul smell makes it hard to stay here without feeling nauseous. Something that took a while for us to get used to.

You'd think that as seasoned warriors, our stomachs would be more resilient. But the curse carried an odor reminiscent of rotting, decaying death. Only the gods knew how the Dhadren managed to survive sitting in it for so long.

It brought a smile to my face just thinking about it. That evil, arrogant bastard finally got what was coming to him. And now he'll have to deal with those he hates coming to his rescue.

I attempted to keep my focus on the joy I felt, instead of the constant state of anxiety that has persisted since I first came here. Since I escaped my own prison.

The only hope we had, after everything we went through to escape the Elven Kingdom of Rodgärd, was that bastard and his daughter. If she's anything like Alaric, one can only guess the opinions she's formed about us. Maybe she became just as hateful.

And I was stuck with her.

With *them*.

And we had to figure out a way of convincing those people to ally with us, running the risk of them slaughtering us.

Despite the doubts plaguing my mind, it was inconsequential.

Ultimately, Alaric's opinion wouldn't matter. He can fight it all he wants, but I won't give *her* a choice.

I clenched my fists before returning to my search.

I couldn't find anything, not an inkling of that tremble in the atmosphere, just that incessant feeling I wanted to rip out and burn.

Fuck.

I vanished, appearing back in the Valley of Dragons, where our rebellion fled to.

It was a sacred and secure place, a pocket of a realm,

meant for dragons to birth and raise their young away from harm. Young ones that took a century to mature. The only ones who could travel in and out of there were those of dragon or demon blood. The perfect fit for the demon fae and myself.

I appeared on the fields in front of our abandoned palace, covered in vines and crumbling stone. It's not in much better shape than Castle Kilhorn, but it works for us.

Waiting for me in the courtyard, filled with wrought-iron tables and chairs, seated Damien. His harsh green eyes were prepared to argue, as if he believes his defense of me as a child gives him authority. As if I hadn't found him as a child, living in the forest, surviving off whatever animal he could find.

He was practically asking to die in those woods. His white-blonde hair draped past his shoulders, and his tan skin made his hair look brighter, making him a walking target. If I hadn't found him, he would have become prey.

It's not like I had any room to talk. With my black hair and pale skin that sometimes glowed blue, thanks to my demon heritage, I wasn't quite blending in.

"Well?" Damien asked with model patience.

I shook my head in answer.

Damien looked away from me with a sneer on his face, violently tapping his foot.

"*What?*"

"Eight fucking years, Con."

"I know how fucking long it's been."

He looked at me that time. If he wanted to start this argument, he had no leg to stand on.

"Maybe if you bothered to help,"

"I do my part," he interrupted.

"You do the bare minimum!"

With a snort, he dismissed it all as a waste of time.

"I saw the idiot running from spriggans today. Perhaps she'll die sooner than later."

"Good. Maybe then you'll finally agree to go to the demon realm."

I gave him a pointed look.

He closed his eyes and took a deep breath, completely transforming his face into that of indifference. "We need to get Liam the fuck out of there. Yesterday."

I smirked at his sudden change of topic. "Then you're coming with me tomorrow."

Damien opened his mouth to argue, but light thunder sounded nearby.

Appearing beside us stood my older brother, Drak, and our healer, Lira, giving Damien the 'hate-fuck me' eyes. There weren't words to describe or understand their dynamic.

Drak towered over us, even though we were taller than most ourselves. "Anything?"

"No," I breathed in defeat.

"Thought so," he started. "Lira found something you need to hear."

I gave her my full attention, in defiance to my upbringing and for the simple fact that she knew her shit.

She curled her hair behind her ear, looking every bit furious at Damien, who was now smirking at her. "I went to Oskela."

All of our eyes widened. "You did *what*?"

No lands outside of the Valley were safe for us. But

Oskela was a place that no demon should step foot in. It was famously called the 'neutral territory', but it was only to hide the fact that every ruler or people of importance on those lands were *deeply* in bed with the High Court.

"One of the texts you had taken from your father's library... pages were missing. And at the front of the book it said that only *one* other copy had been made, and it was in a library in Oskela. So yes. I took a risk and it paid off, because I'm pretty sure that I found out why you can't find the rifts."

She spoke with an assertiveness I had never heard before. If Damien's look of appreciation was any indicator, this was growth for the trembling fawn.

Even though the notion of Alaric having a daughter left a foul taste in my mouth, I respected the princess for her willingness to wear her dress-up armor and fight.

"What did you find?" I asked.

"It confirmed only ancients have the power required to create rifts, as well as patch them up..."

I narrowed my eyes. "Why would they frequently need to open up rifts and seal them back shut? What business would they have on barren lands?"

"Nothing," Drak answered. "That doesn't mean it's the High Court though."

"Those *other* ancients don't care about anything except smoking and becoming one with the fucking forests. It has to be the ancients in the High Court. Likely the fuckers tied to home."

"Or..." Drak started. "It could be internal."

I shook my head. "Alaric is old and powerful, but he's not an ancient."

"That doesn't mean there couldn't be one there already." Damien finally decided to include himself.

Drak nodded and gave me a pointed look. "Exactly. Even your little vessel princess could no longer be,"

"She's not my *anything*."

Drak snorted. "You think the princess died already?"

"No," Damien and I both snapped. We would know if she did.

Lira looked understandably confused.

"So," I redirected. "Who could have enough power to conceal themselves within the veil, patch up the rifts, and go completely undetected?"

The four of us stood there silently, staring at nothing while we pondered who the hell would have that kind of power.

And if Alaric knows, then what kind of genocidal hell was he planning?

I walked around the table and grabbed Damien's arm, then took us to the skies above Ghaldir so we could try to get a sense of that power again.

Damien choked on the air, clearly not used to it from his bare minimum.

He never liked coming here to patrol. He once said the lingering scent gave him nightmares. And then he found out right after, that we were having the same fucking nightmare.

You'd think that smell was the makings of a curse.

One could say that, but they'd be wrong.

It's much worse.

Twenty years I have spent hiding, rotting away while the kings of this world destroy each other. My father may also wear a crown, but as long as he keeps my mother imprisoned, he'll just be another burning king on a funeral pyre. So now I wait... I watch... and I learn... As the princess of Ghaldir, the Ancients of the High Court's precious little vessel, is stalked and hunted.

Only, it won't just be me in those woods.

CHAPTER
THREE

ÁINE, EIGHT YEARS PRIOR...

B lack ocean waves crashed beneath my feet, far below against the rocky cliffs.

Poison fills the air, smelling of rot and flowing beneath clouds as dark as the sea. As dark as the magic wielded to curse this island to blight it to its death. Never have I felt the warmth of sunlight against my ghostly skin.

When I was a small child, people revered the Dhadren Faeries of this land. I guess I should include myself when I talk about them. However, since we remain cursed, I've lived most of my 17 years of life with no magical abilities. None of the superior strength and speed or rapid healing, and nothing to tell me what kind of power I inherited.

A cold and wet nose nudged my arm. Minsi, my hound, gifted to me when I was eight and wouldn't stop sneaking out of the castle. My mother's raised voice filled those days when they found me and brought me home.

You see... I fucking hate cages. And my whole life, this entire island has been nothing but a cage. A cage crumbling from the inside out, thanks to the magic being sucked out of our lands. A cage, a death trap, and a sideshow, apparently.

A sideshow, I say, because for as long as I can remember, I've felt a heavy presence watching over me. It didn't help that occasionally, I would look up and find a shadowy figure beyond the near-black clouds, just standing there in the sky, watching me.

Not that I could see its eyes or anything resembling a body with arms and legs. No, just a figure I knew in my soul wasn't a part of the clouds. And every time I caught sight of it, despite my fear, I refused to look away. I knew I would die one day, but I often wondered if it would be the curse that sent me into the afterlife... or whoever was constantly watching me.

Done with the morbid ocean view, I rose to my feet and turned back. I faced the woods east of the castle and made my way to them. Each step was a crunch against the petrified earth.

Minsi trotted off in front of me, sniffing for gods know what. Gods, I didn't care to fucking ask since they left us here to die, if any of them were still alive. All that praying the druids did. What a fucking joke. If the figure in the sky was any indication, no one would give two shits if the Dhadren fell to their deaths today. Not the nymphs, and especially not the elves.

Minsi made it past the tree line into the forest's graveyard, as I prefer to call it. When these trees were beautiful willows once long ago, they were now even less alive than in the dead of winter. Not a single hue of green, or hint of life, existed on this island anymore. Which made me want to paint my auburn hair black or silver just to blend in.

Never would I be able to hunt stealthily, with my hair being a literal red flag. Not without my overly sized black hooded cloak.

Something beneath my skin was roiling the further we explored the forest, like it was luring me towards the lake. Something that occurred every time we came here, and it made my skin hot no matter the cold and dreary weather. Once again, I followed that feeling. I approached one of the dead willows with low branches, and a raven appeared on one of them, looking me dead in the eyes.

It didn't *caw* at me. It didn't make a sound at all as it stared into my soul with an unnerving stillness. I didn't flinch or give away any sign that I considered it a possible threat, but its eyes unnerved me. Where Ravens typically had black eyes, this one's eyes were silver. That silver continued to hold my gaze, even as I took slow steps forward to move on.

Minsi caught sight of it and started barking. The raven's eyes shifted in Minsi's direction and hadn't flinched. It returned its too-intelligent gaze to mine for only a moment and then flew away. I shook off the fear and continued our walk through the forest.

Leopard print fur sniffed out several trees in our path, repeatedly running back to make sure I was safe.

We finally reached the lake, which was so massive that the trees across the water appeared the size of mere pebbles.

In the lessons taught to me, children would learn to swim in this lake. They would swim with their families, play in the water with their friends... But I had never learned to swim. My father instructed the kingdom not to step foot in the waters without the proper measures to ensure a safe bath.

I stared hard at the water, hating that I couldn't swim. What kind of warrior could I ever hope to be if I couldn't fucking swim?

I continued staring into its black depths as I dared a step forward. What could be in that water that's so deadly? There was nothing that moved beneath the surface. It was as if the water was shielded with a black shell protecting whatever horror lay inside. I dared take another step forward, and then a growl stopped me in my tracks.

It wasn't Minsi. It was far deadlier and with a heavy resonance in its voice.

On top of a hill to the east, overlooking the lake, was a massive beast of a wolf. Black fur, with red glowing from its chest, and silver eyes. It stopped growling when I noticed him.

I had seen this wolf many times in my life, but mainly during the night after I woke up from dreaming. It would appear in my room, which stood on the highest and unclimbable floor of the castle, watching me while I was unable to move.

My body would become paralyzed, no matter how much I willed it to run for safety. But the beast never hurt me. It just made its life goal to scare the shit out of me on a regular basis. Even now, as it stood there watching me silently.

I wondered if I took another step towards the water if it would growl again... It tilted its head as it knew exactly what I was considering and dared me to try it. I sighed.

Fear for this animal had passed me. Not now that it has been a constant in my life for as long as I can remember. It was almost comforting, if one could find comfort in a stalker.

"Come on, Min. Let's go." I turned, and thankfully, she followed. We entered the forest again with the beast at our backs. And then we heard the scream.

My back went rigid. I turned around, but the beast was gone. "Come on," I said urgently. "Let's go." I turned, but she didn't follow. "Minsi," I called to her, but she stared deep into the forest. Stared at something that I, myself, could not see. And then I heard the scream again. A blood-curdling scream that made me tense again. That definitely belonged to a girl.

We high-tailed it towards the source of that sound. When we made it past the clearing, there was a creek. And in that creek was a girl. Like someone had shoved her into the water, her clothes ripped. And older males surrounded her. They surrounded her like wolves around their prey. They laughed menacingly.

On top of the girl was one male with his hand over her mouth to stop her screams. My blood went cold, realizing what they were about to do to her. And what they thought they were going to get away with.

Knowing that I was standing here alone, aside from a dog, and there were four full-grown fae men, the odds were stacked against me, but I couldn't let this happen. What kind of future queen would?

Minsi seemed to understand the situation. Because a growl, vicious and rumbling, emerged from her. I smirked and decided to mimic her. We slowly stalked towards those males, growling with each step. I recognized their faces. They were Carsen's friends. A Dhadren soldier I truly hated.

The one on top of the girl, muffling her screams, stood but remained close to her while the rest of his asshole friends decided to spread out and surround me and my hound. One tried to move towards my blind spot. So, I slowly turned. I trained with the armies daily, just like the boys. If they thought they would take me down easily, they had another thing coming.

Minsi was right behind me, monitoring my other side. One wrong move, and me, Minsi, and that girl in the creek were all dead. Or worse. We were several miles away from the castle. Likely, nobody even heard the girl scream. If I couldn't handle this situation, we were fucked.

One of them threw me a punch, but I ducked. They all laughed, low and threatening under their breath. The other to his left threw me a right hook. I ducked low and then upper cut his chin, sending him flying.

As impressive as it may have been, it was rendered useless when the other two tackled me to the ground and pulled me up by my arms. Each one stood at my side, holding me up against my will, while the angry male I hit stalked towards me. Even his laughter was angry.

"You're going to regret that, you little *cunt*," he sneered.

I wondered if they had any idea who I was or if they even cared. I'd go with the latter, with the state we all lived in. Inhibitions were thrown out the window, including morals. They thought, why should they even bother if we would all die soon, anyway?

I repeated the mantras I taught myself when I became the first female in the training yard.

I will not fear.
I will not panic.
I will not lose control.

"Go fuck yourself," I snarled. And then he punched me in my gut. My back bowed as I tried to breathe through the pain. And to not vomit. Who was I kidding? I hope I vomit all over him. He hit me again. But I didn't throw up, only gagged up a little blood. The situation wasn't looking good for me.

Minsi kept trying to run up to him and bite his legs, but each time she did, he kicked her so hard she went flying. Even so, she got back up each time she fell and came to my aid.

I couldn't take this anymore. Being held against my will, while something I cared for dearly, was getting hurt. This was the worst kind of torture. He hit me again and again. And I started to accept the realization that me and that girl, maybe even Minsi, might not make it out of this forest.

He stopped for only a moment. Long enough for me to pick my head up and notice an unfamiliar male standing behind him.

The ones holding my arms tensed and stared at him, but said nothing. They didn't even warn their friend before he was roundhouse kicked in the face and fell to the ground, unmoving.

Time seemed to have stopped around me, and I had given myself over to my rage, now consuming me. I tackled one of them to the ground, digging my fist in his face repeatedly until he wasn't moving.

A yelp of unimaginable pain echoed, and I froze. And

then there was complete silence. Silence in the forest or in my head, I couldn't tell.

I climbed off the man that I had beaten and stood up slowly. I turned in the direction of that heartbreaking sound and found Minsi lying there, still with a knife in her chest.

And then I looked towards the male beside her, panting in fear as he took in the state of his friends and then to me and my rescuer. The odds were now stacked against him.

And he just killed my fucking dog.

I screamed as I pulled the knife out of Minsi, charged towards her killer, and tackled him to the ground.

Fear had turned into rage, because a strange male had come to our rescue, and if he hadn't, Minsi would still be dead.

If he hadn't come to our rescue, they would have raped both me and that girl, and gods knew what they would have done to our bodies. For a female who fought every day to become stronger, to be completely independent from any male, I was utterly helpless and useless.

That was all I could think about as I screamed in terror and anger. The wet crunching sounds of his face beneath my blade made me want to vomit my guts up. I could feel the blood splatter into my eyes, nose, and mouth, forgetting that we were no longer immune to certain diseases now.

The sound of twigs snapping stole my attention away from the first murder I had ever committed. And it was not pretty. I vomited violently at how gruesome it looked. At what I was capable of doing.

I choked down my sobs as I walked towards Minsi. Towards my friend who had guarded me her whole life, who was never afraid of me. I knelt beside her and petted her for one last time.

"I'll help you bury her," my rescuer whispered.

"We'll burn her," I said with a coldness that made me not even recognize my own voice.

"What was her name?" he asked after a few silent moments.

"Minsi," I breathed. "It meant Leader of Wolves."

"Beautiful," he said softly.

He remained quiet while I knelt there. I should have been more uneasy by this stranger's presence, but I felt a consuming numbness within my blood.

After even my knees became numb, I stood to face the mysterious rescuer of mine, completely forgetting about the girl sitting frozen in shock by the creek. I properly sized him up, looking for any hint of a potential threat in his presence. Though I found many, his face looked like those who had never truly harmed anyone innocent.

"What is your name?" I asked him.

His gaze focused on the ground rather than answering my question. Clearly, not the slyest.

I squared my shoulders. "If you think to lie to me, I will *strongly* advise you to reconsider," I warned him.

His eyes looked panicked as he answered. "I don't... I don't have a name."

That must have been the most ridiculous lie I have ever heard in my god's damned life. It was almost sad. "Whoever you are," I started with a bite in my voice. "I owe you a debt."

His expression slightly frowned, eyes narrowed as he

took me in, likely realizing I didn't speak like a peasant girl. The question was painted so obviously on his face.

I didn't have time for this. "You'll forgive me if I insist that we get this over with?"

He said nothing as he frowned at my tone. His not speaking was utterly annoying. I raised my brow, hoping he would answer me. Or at least say something.

"Okay," he said.

Good enough, I thought to myself as I walked towards the girl.

"What's your name?" I asked her, trying to break out of her stupor. She looked to be my age. I recognized her face.

"Maeve," she said,

"You're safe now. They're dead," I assured her. She looked past me to the bodies, including Minsi's, and gave me a pitiful look.

"Let's go," I demanded a bit harshly. I turned on my heel and walked towards the castle gates. She took the hint and followed. I looked back at the nameless hero. "Take care of the bodies. I'll be back."

Maeve walked beside me but at a step back. She at least knew who I was then. I slowed to be in step with her.

"Where is your home? I'll take you to it," I told her.

"Please don't trouble yourself. I can make it back myself."

"I think today proved you can't," I said, right before I mentally stuck my foot in my mouth. As if I had any room to talk...

We walked in silence for several moments before she led me to her home in the village, safe and sound. Alone, without my four-legged shadow, I pushed through a tugging sensation, telling me to turn around.

I ran into Sloan during her daily runs. Those runs were insane, but without them, she would be. She noted the blood all over me and my face, and her own drained of color.

"Minsi's dead. I need your help," I said coldly and flatly, while also failing the tremble in my bottom lip before I bit it. She nodded and walked with me to grab a bow, an arrow, some fire starters, and then back to the male who had piled the bodies. Aside from Minsi's.

Sloan tensed when she took in the male's appearance. If I hadn't just stabbed someone over and over in the face, I no doubt would've noticed that he was, without a doubt, the most handsome male either of us had likely ever seen.

It took a lot for me to notice them. Growing up with pig-headed Dhadren males will do that to you. They had ruined any chance in hell of me ever inviting one into my bed.

"Help me build the pyre, Sloan," I choked out. She whipped her head at me in quiet resentment. The three of us worked to build the ugliest makeshift pyre I had ever seen. Clearly, none of us had any experience of the sort. I just hoped we didn't burn the forest down.

I said a silent prayer to the goddess of wolves and beasts alike, that Minsi would find peace and plenty of adventures in the afterlife. I released the inflamed arrow and watched as her body burned. Watched the fire dance into the sky until the blood in my veins ran hot. The *thing* in my stomach began to roil again, like it danced in response to the fire.

I felt the skin on my cheeks, and the pads of my fingertips burn. A tiny jolt thumped against my ribcage, making me break into a nervous sweat. I shook it off, fighting to think about literally anything else so I wouldn't explode.

I thought of a world in my future where I finally broke this curse, and I slaughtered every piece of shit like the ones piled behind me. A world where I would help unleash the beasts that women hid inside themselves from everyone. I would start with Maeve, and I wouldn't stop until I've reached every single hidden corner of the world.

CHAPTER
FOUR

ÁINE, PRESENT DAY.

At the *Broken Inn*, the whiskey never runs dry. It wasn't the most superior tavern in the Kingdom, but we didn't care about extravagances, only the music.

No matter who was fighting, the bands never stopped playing. The perfect combination of activities when one wishes to escape the cold.

At a table not too close to the raucous noise, I sat with Sloan, the closest I had to a sibling. Though she couldn't have looked more different from me.

With her wavy blonde hair and deep blue eyes, one couldn't help consider her heritage and how my father took her in as an infant. People speculated that her general appearance looked just like those from the northeastern lands. The only other person here with that specific coloring was Liam.

He stood out from the other males here. He was taller, *much* taller, and had eyes as blue as the ocean. His tawny hair was always styled in a low knot. And I couldn't help but wonder if he did that because of those rumors.

Which was a shame, because he was the only male here that I ever considered going to bed with.

Too bad he made it his life's mission to ensure I, as a female, never led an army into battle. Unfortunately for him, we both became captains on the same day, and now I'm his commander.

Even though we fought together, his eyes still held the memory of when Maeve and I were almost killed.

"What do you think that's about?" Sloan pulled me out of my head.

I followed her gaze and found Liam with his jaw clenched, staring down at Keira. Looking up at him, she stood with colder indifference than I'm used to seeing on her. It looked forced. And with the way Liam stared silent daggers at her, those daggers looked like he had to pull them out of his heart. Poor guy.

Her head turned, and I suddenly found the lines on the wooden table very interesting. It wasn't until I felt Keira's presence and heard the sound of her drink being slammed that I looked up.

My mouth opened and then shut when I sensed who entered the tavern.

Looking towards the doors, alongside Maeve, Isolde stumbled in, wearing one of those dresses she made herself. Because there wasn't a seamstress on the island who would make dresses that tight or revealing.

Not that I would ever complain.

I didn't miss the way Isolde tensed. Neither did I miss the fucking asshole creeping up towards her. Captain Carsen had beckoned me when I came in, which I dismissed. He was a captain that fucked his way through the lower ranks. If rumors were to be true, they weren't always willing.

Losing his balance, he peered down at her as if she were his next prey. It's no surprise that he noticed her. Her combination of tan skin, brown eyes, and long dark brown hair in loose curls was deadly, and remained in my mind more than I'd ever admit. Her curves alone could bring this kingdom to its knees.

She neither cowered nor succeeded in projecting strength and sobriety. He knew it, and his predatory gaze made my blood boil.

"How about a dance?" His eyes promised a night ending in his pleasure, forced or not.

"Thank you, but,"

He stepped too close to her. "Just one dance?"

The gravel in his voice made it impossible to ever mistake it for someone else. The sound of it had my nerves by the balls. Every time I heard it, everything inside me tensed and I wanted to vomit.

"She can take care of herself," Keira chastised me.

I met her gaze too quickly, feeling the restraint smothering me. "I know she fucking can, but she won't."

Keira snorted, narrowing her forest green eyes on me. "And I wonder why that is."

Dismissing Keira's valid point, I shook my head and kept my focus on Isolde.

She had nervously leaned backwards, breaking her mask

of strength. It was all Carsen needed before smiling and taking her fucking wrist.

My drink spilled over when I jumped up. Isolde was looking right at me when I saw the shift in her eyes. Like she knew now that she would be safe. And that irritated the fuck out of me more than it warmed me.

I expected her to resist, but she barely put up a fight.

Fucking gods' damn it all. She was counting the seconds before I would come to her rescue, but I stood my ground.

Panic flickered in her eyes, and all it took was the makings of a protest for me to be there in an instant.

I jumped into his path, blocking him from taking her any further.

Ignoring his death-glare, I reached out my hand to Isolde, silently requesting a dance. I needed to avoid a fight. I knew that, but he could disappoint his own hand before touching her.

"*Princess Titáine*," he slurred. "I don't remember giving you an offer."

His hiccup allowed him more mercy than I wanted to give. My warriors needed a leader, not another drunken imbecile. I looked at him after a deep exhale.

"Carsen, perhaps one of the many other women over there without partners would be glad to reject you. I'm merely sparing you the limbs you might lose going toe-to-toe with Isolde." I tilted my head up at my would-be prey.

His smile didn't reach his eyes. "Perhaps the king should finally put you in the place you fucking belong. I grow tired of tiptoeing around you to appease him, since his respect was actually earned here."

Liam groaned at the bar, undoubtedly hearing everything this stupid fuck was saying, knowing what would happen to him.

I couldn't fight the wicked grin growing on my face, and this piece of shit saw what that meant. When I broke Carsen's stare and looked at Isolde monitoring us, he thought it was in his best interest to swing first.

I lunged and had this fucker on the ground pounding punches into his stupid fucking face. *Good*. Maybe he'll be too concerned with healing instead of harassing the women with his unwanted advances.

The tavern became chaotic with the sounds of violence, showing a fight had broken out.

I chuckled as I kept hitting him, even when his fists finally made contact. Until he hit hard enough for me to fly backwards.

I heard Isolde scream while blocking his blows. And now he was on top of me, making it clear my title didn't matter. I would've appreciated it in normal situations, but he was the only person here who needed to understand his damn place.

My arms trembled after blocking the blows. In a blur of motion, I wrapped one arm around his torso, then the other, securing his arm in the process.

With every ounce of strength in my legs, I flipped him onto his back and pummeled him with my fists. I continued even when his body slowed and his eyes were closing.

He *touched* her.

I heard Isolde calling my name, but I couldn't stop.

Large arms scooped under mine and pulled me off of Carsen. "God's dammit Áine. You're going to get me fucking killed."

I threw myself out of Liam's hold when his grip slackened, but I didn't charge after Carsen. I just stared at his bloodied face, and then at my bloodied knuckles. They looked like they were cutting out of my skin.

A tan, slender hand came into view and grasped one of my palms. I held her gaze as she lifted my hand and then kissed it. When she revealed the blood on her lips, I forgot about the many people around us.

I was about to kiss her right there, uncaring of the onlookers. But then she looked over at Liam still standing beside me, like she was reminding me that what we had was purely physical. A complete fucking lie, but one I deserved from the many times I did the same, trying to push her away.

She deserved more than standing beside someone who was constantly hunted by the most powerful beings in the realm. Even if I lived long enough to become the first ruling queen. So if she wanted to fuck around with Liam, marry him even, I would learn to accept it.

Caught in my peripherals, Maeve dragged a man by his tunic across the bar beside us. Liam grabbed bottles and moved them out of the way.

Priorities.

Looking around, people were still fighting for no reason. Except Sloan. She remained seated and drank from her wine while an unconscious figure lay on the ground at her feet.

I glanced at Carsen to confirm he was still napping, then shifted my attention back to Isolde. Her bright brown eyes had darkened.

Liam was leaning against the mess of a bar, watching us

with a smirk. Isolde forcefully pulled me towards him by grabbing my hand.

They both called for two whiskeys and then whipped their faces at each other. I narrowed my eyes at the threatening awkwardness. The barkeep gave me a knowing look as he handed me a rag to clean the blood off my hands. That look confirmed my suspicions. That look sealed my fate for tonight if these two allowed it.

We all worked into the ground today, drank, and danced like the world wasn't completely fucked. We all knew without bringing it up in casual conversation that our curse wouldn't allow us to live to an old age, even if we weren't killed in battle. We deserve to live life to the fullest while we still can.

Liam wasn't wearing anything different from what he usually wore around me. Tight-fitted clothes to show off his massive build... It wasn't a love match, but he knew how his physique affected others. Even Isolde took notice.

I didn't think she liked males, but her face that peered back at me said otherwise. I grabbed both of the drinks that they got me, downing the first one and sipping the next, peering up at them over the rim of my glass under my lashes.

It was all Liam needed before Isolde and I were being dragged out of the tavern. I ignored the gaping stares of others, never having seen me giving that kind of attention to a male before. Sloan threw me a lazy salute before we were stumbling outside.

None of us said a word when Liam took us to his room. We didn't have to say out loud that this was a distraction.

Something each of us needed for our own reasons, but I wasn't about to back out now.

He made it past the threshold when I grabbed Isolde's hand and yanked her inside.

I barely heard the door close when I fisted my hand into her hair, and then kissed her with ferocity. Ferocity that I needed to surface quickly to mask the nerves. Her hands cupped my cheeks, and the gentleness undid me.

Gripping the backs of her thighs, I picked her up until her legs were wrapped around my waist, and walked her towards the bed instinctually. As if we were in my room…

I broke the kiss and threw her onto the bed.

She crawled backwards, never taking her eyes off mine, wearing too many fucking clothes.

Reaching towards her, I gripped her ankle and pulled back to me, earning a yelp of surprise.

Forgetting Liam was still in the room, I started taking her boots off, then continued removing every article of clothing that covered her skin.

She looked up at me, waiting.

I nodded towards the headboard, and started removing my clothes while watching her naked body inch further away from me. It caught me by surprise when I felt a warm, callused hand brush against my leg.

Looking down, Liam had kneeled to remove my boots.

He had been standing behind us, watching and learning

our dynamic. And rather than fighting me for dominance over her, he chose submission.

I smiled, not having a fucking clue on how to handle this, but I'd figure it out.

I lifted each foot while he removed my boots, and then he looked up at me just like Isolde had. Expecting an answer to an unsaid question. I nodded when he quickly glanced at my pants, and watched as I allowed a male to undo my pants, and desperately pull them off like a starved animal.

Isolde was watching us, pinching and twisting her nipple with one hand, while the other hand covered her pussy. She was rubbing that bundle of nerves I wanted beneath my tongue, between my lips... and she was doing it without my permission.

Liam was behind me, pulling my tunic up when I asked her, "Did I give you permission to do that?"

Her hand froze, and she looked up at me with a worried lip.

I smiled. "No, I don't believe I did."

A quick, breathy chuckle escaped Liam from behind me, now tugging at my shirt again. My eyes remained on Isoldes when I lifted my arms up, letting him pull off my tunic, and then the brassiere.

"Come here." I ordered her.

I heard Liam start to take his clothes off, and stopped him.

"Isolde," I called to her while looking still at Liam. "Come take his clothes off."

I didn't have to look to know she'd obey.

Her skin slid across the bed, and then she walked up to Liam.

Naked and completely unashamed, I stepped away from them, and sat on the edge of the bed, watching them.

"Take off his shirt, first." I ordered.

His physique was no secret, but this wasn't the same as watching him at training.

I wasn't blind. His attraction was undeniable. But it was difficult to see attraction in someone who irritated the shit out of me on a regular basis.

He wasn't irritating me now.

"Now take off his pants."

She undid the laces, then knelt down while serving him as he served me.

His cock looked painfully hard, and his throat bobbed while she and I stared at him. I swallowed, now feeling nervous while looking at his size. "Now take him in your mouth." My voice was thick.

She turned to face me in surprise. Liam never stopped looking at her.

I raised my brow. "Don't you want this?"

Isolde was the one who initiated this whole thing. If she was having doubts, she needed to say so now. Her head turned, and she stared at his cock intensely, licking her lips while nodding.

I looked at Liam. "Tell her how much you want those luscious lips around your cock."

He stared down at her, and slowly started stroking himself. "If Áine doesn't tell me to fuck your mouth right now, I'm going to make myself come while I stare at nothing but those lips."

Holy shit.

I could see her chest rising and falling, faster and faster

as I stood up. Walking over to them, I fisted my hand in her hair, yanking her head back to look up at me. "Is this what you want? Say yes or no."

"Yes." she answered immediately.

I smirked, then pushed her face towards him until she took him in her mouth.

Liam let out a groan of violent need and satisfaction, feeling the magic of her mouth I've grown too attached to.

With my hand in my hair, I controlled the pace, fucking his cock with her mouth. When the sounds of gags turned into choking, I pulled her head back so she could breathe before shoving her forward again.

The sound of Liam's moan was music to my ears, and apparently Isolde's too, if her moaning around his cock was any indication. I let go of her hair and looked at Liam. "Fuck her mouth right now."

Isolde's eyes sparkled, looking up at Liam's face. He smiled deviously while grabbing her hair and doing exactly what I told him to.

Kneeling onto the carpet behind Isolde, I turned and laid on my back. With both hands, I smacked her ass twice, signaling her to raise it up so I could slide underneath her.

I gently sucked her clit between my lips, moaning at her taste. The vibrations from my lips made her moan around Liam's cock, making him growl.

I grabbed her ass, lifting her up enough for me to slip my tongue inside her, getting her ready for what I had planned for them both. Her moaning got abruptly louder, and then I looked up and saw Liam had pulled himself out of her.

Isolde was breathing heavily. "Is something wrong?"

He shook his head, glistening sweat over his tightening skin. "Áine didn't give me permission to come yet."

"*Very* good." I smiled up at him, incredibly pleased. "That deserves a reward."

"Well then maybe he should take your mouth?" She challenged, looking down at my face not an inch from her pussy.

I laughed loudly, mostly to cover up how nervous the thought made me. "Someone is *determined* to be bad. Well then," I smacked her ass twice again, letting me out. "Ask, and you shall receive. Liam, on the bed."

He was there instantly, laying on his back while stroking himself. The visual affected me more than I wanted to admit, not being comfortable with the prospect of wanting cock. But here I was, marveling at the width of his. Isolde's throat softly cleared.

I had been staring at his cock for too long.

And now they were both smirking at me, which was exactly how I lost the power here.

Liam sat up abruptly, kneeling at the edge of the bed in front of me. "And what of your pleasure?"

Isolde's body pressed against my back. Her hands were now exploring me, twisting my nipples, and lightly grazing over my heat. "The princess deserves to be pleased, doesn't she?"

"Did I say you could,"

Liam's finger trailed down my neck, my chest, "Tell us how to please you."

My eyes rounded, and then I gripped his cock in my hand, *hard*. "It pleases me when you do what you're told. Now lay back down so I can use this cock however and wherever we want." I squeezed him harder, and he whimpered before I released him. "Now."

He obeyed with a smirk on his face, and patiently waited while stroking his length.

Isolde's hand grazed up my side, and I grabbed it.

"Go sit on his face."

Liam's eyes sparkled with delight. "Yes please."

She swayed to the side of the bed, and when she knelt onto the bed, he grabbed her by the waist and placed her exactly where I ordered her to be.

The sounds his mouth made while feasting on her... Like he was swallowing down every drop, making my thighs clench together. The guy ate it like he was starving.

I stood there and watched while he grabbed her ass, and had her coming down his throat. I may have been giving the orders, but the two of them obviously had more experience than I had.

His whole body tensed when she came, making his cock swell more if it were possible. And rather than taking anything for myself, I walked around the side of the bed, moving towards Isolde who was in another universe entirely.

With his hands gripped onto her waist, he picked her up effortlessly, and placed her on his lap. I watched as she rocked her body, sliding across his cock before taking it fully. All the way to the hilt, and they both groaned loudly.

It was beautiful, watching her take him so well. I swallowed audibly, worried I couldn't do the same. I enjoyed the sight of them, but then I felt someone, Liam, grab my hand, yanking me towards him.

He grabbed my hips, and picked me up like I weighed

nothing, placing me on his face to devour next. But he had me facing Isolde, who now looked at me intensely. She placed a hand on his abdomen, leaning her body forward to cup my cheek and kiss me, still riding him.

I melted into the kiss, leaning forward, giving Liam the room he needed to insert two fingers. I moaned into Isolde's mouth.

Liam chuckled, "Like that?"

I didn't give him the satisfaction of answering him, but my head flung back in ecstasy when he added a third finger. Isolde reached down and rubbed my clit. And when I looked back down, seeing the two of them working me, I looked back at Isolde.

She was smiling at the site of me starting to come undone, and pulled her hand back. Her rips rocked onto Liam harder, who's tongue had replaced her fingers, still fucking me with three of his own, but she wasn't touching me anymore.

Liam moaned, and the vibrations from his mouth sent me right to the edge, only to fall completely off when Isolde grabbed my nipples and twisted them *hard*.

The pain was delicious. It was something I only allowed her to know about, and hoped Liam didn't notice.

His moaning got louder as Isolde fucked him harder. Large hands painfully gripped my thighs while they both went over the edge after me.

The euphoria behind Isolde's eyes beckoned me. I placed my hand on Liam's abdomen, and sat up, pulling her into a kiss.

She could act cold all she wanted. I didn't care. What I wanted, I fucking got.

She sat up, easing off Liam who was somehow still hard, and deepened the kiss. That's when I grabbed her shoulders and shoved her off him and onto the other side of the bed.

She gasped in surprise, looking back and forth between Liam and me. I went to crawl off him and dive into her heaven, curious about how the two of them tasted together.

Fucking delicious, that's what it tasted like.

I slid my arms under her legs, making my tongue go deeper inside her. That's when my ass was being lifted by strong hands. Liam's body heat enveloped my back.

Hands were at each side of my head, and he whispered into my ear. "Tell me now if you don't want my cock, otherwise I'm fucking you while I watch you feast on her."

I swallowed, meeting Isolde's eyes.

She smirked, like this was her payback for how I toyed with her earlier.

Fuck that.

I backed my ass into him, sealing my fate.

Isolde didn't stop looking at me, nor did that smirk lessen when she spoke. "Liam."

He stilled his movements.

Isolde's smirk turned into a wicked grin. "She likes it rough."

My eyes rounded, but before I could argue that I wasn't sure I wanted my *first* dick to be rough, he filled me completely and in one thrust.

I screamed into her pussy, burying myself in it.

"*Fuck,* that's tight." Liam's voice was strained. It could've been my paranoia, but I thought I heard realization in his voice, and wondered if he knew.

I refused to tell him. I've been fucking for years, but I knew he would take this too seriously.

The groan I made promised violence, but then... It started to feel *really* fucking good. His thrusts were brutal, and I could hear a low growl building in his chest.

I moaned against Isolde's heat, sucking and nibbling away at her while getting thoroughly fucked by Liam. His hand reached down and rubbed my clit, making it increasingly difficult to focus on Isolde.

I thrust three fingers into her, refusing to relent despite the paralyzing painful pleasure I felt. And then Isolde moved on me, on my fingers.

I looked up at her brown eyes that softened, at what she hid beneath the mask, and she whispered, "Come for us, baby."

CHAPTER FIVE

ISOLDE

I deserve love. I deserve warmth. I deserve to have some semblance of power over her. How I deserve it, only time will tell after the misery she has put me through.

Her dominance and protection burned her name in my heart, destroying me in the wake of her touch. Knowing damn well that each piece of my soul will crawl to her every time.

Which is exactly why I told Liam to be rough with her. It's a little reward, getting to watch the woman I love as she continues to lie to herself, and to me. Proving that I will never be what she wants. Someone with a cock.

The control she always maintained shattered bit by bit with each thrust. It wasn't five minutes after Liam came inside her that he passed out. Pregnancy wasn't something we worried about anymore, thanks to the lovely curse killing off fertility completely. Evidently you needed magic to create more fae.

While she was trying to pull herself together, I slipped into the halls, leaving her alone in his room.

I was down the stairs, headed toward the castle doors when her voice echoed my name.

I stopped, but I didn't turn around, not until her footsteps came closer. I rolled my eyes, and put on a show of fluster. "What did I forget this time?"

Her eyes flattened like she knew what I was doing, what I've *been* doing. Not that she was any better... She didn't trust me, and I didn't blame her. I never gave her a reason to.

My intentions were as blurred as hers. And if she wanted to condemn me for it, then I'd have fun along the way.

Her gaze moved to the floor in front of my feet, and her hands were fidgety. "May I walk you home?"

I lowered my chin, giving her a pointed look. She was never nervous, and neither did she ever ask. Every night I walked home, if it was from the tavern or from her room, she'd always go with me to make sure I made it home safe. "I get a say in it this time?"

The nervousness vanished, followed by irritation, and arrogance. "Let's go then."

"You're not even wearing a coat," I argued.

She sauntered past me. "Then I guess we'd better hurry the fuck up."

I groaned, following after her. "You're being ridiculous."

"As are you if you think you're walking home alone."

I stared at her back, noting the lack of shivering. Wasn't

she freezing? Why do I bother questioning her anymore? She's so stubbornly obtuse that if she wanted to freeze, then so be it. I'd let her.

She pushed the castle doors open, allowing me to go first, like males do. Or rather, what they were 'supposed' to do. If that were true, then Áine would be the only real male here.

I walked ahead, my boots crunched on the black snow. Black, because that was the color of the ocean water within the curse's borders. The cold air that greeted me wasn't crisp like it should've been. It was sharp and painful, making it more difficult to breathe as the years went on.

Everything here was rotten.

Everything smelled like shit. Some more so than others, and some days worse than others, but it was all the same.

We walked past the main gates, cracked and crumbling down, more so every day. The guards didn't pay us any attention, fully accustomed to her and I being up around this time of night. And she worried about the council finding out about us... Like not one of these fuckers was in their pocket.

You couldn't trust anyone.

Not here.

I've told her that several times, and though she agreed, she didn't fully act like it. She acted like a princess who never truly had a worry in the world. And I was stupid enough to keep wasting my time with her.

We reached mine and Maeve's village, where the placid quiet had only the sounds of crackling torches. I nearly walked into Áine when she stopped abruptly, a few houses down from mine. It was a quiet home with one floor, passed down to me when my parents died from the curse. They lived for a very long time, but never got acclimated to the air here like the lucky ones did.

She never walked me all the way to the door, which unnerved me. It was either her paranoia that the wrong person would find out about us, or because she didn't want to come in, because then she may never leave.

I knew it was likely the first one, but a girl could stay delusional if she wanted, right?

"Thank you," I said, and met those golden eyes. She looked down at me with an expression vastly different than the one she had when she ran after me.

Everything about her demeanor was cold, and obviously forced.

Fine. Two could play that game. Just like two had *been* playing this game. Maybe for too long.

I looked at her mouth, longing for it like an idiot. Like a greedy fool who acted like that mouth wasn't all over me ten minutes ago.

I glanced back up, and her expression remained unaffected.

"Goodnight, Captain," she said, and then walked past me, leaving a faint trail of her scent I wanted to bask in. That scent of eucalyptus in winter.

I forced a deep breath in, and quickly out before walking toward my home. *My* home.

I unlocked the million locks Áine had installed, and entered the unbothered cottage. Next time I see her, I'll explain to her how much time someone would have to take before unlocking all of these fucking locks.

After latching the last one, I turned to take in the uninterrupted state of my home. Like the table that still had three chairs and three place settings, the dust that kept piling on them, and the locked door to what once was their bedroom.

They were things I depended on when I needed to remind myself what I was doing here, which lately was constantly.

My only true connection here was Maeve.

We had grown up together in this village, and it was she who practically forced me to go to training with her.

It was shortly after my mother had passed, only a few years after my father. And I was sick of everything, sick of breathing this fucking air that killed them, and ready to find a way out of it.

It was that day that I met the princess, and my whole life was thrown on its ass.

Her auburn hair and golden eyes contrasted against an expression that screamed a feral ferocity. It reminded me of Alaric, and it didn't. She was so much more. That, and I wasn't typically attracted to males. Definitely not until I saw Liam.

He was so confusing... With his following after Áine, following after Keira, I started to assume he was just a womanizer and wouldn't feel conflicted about taking the two of us to bed. He was one of the few who knew about us, so it was safe for me to not pretend around him.

Only minutes had passed since I locked all the doors, and someone started knocking. I stared down the door like it was sentient and could understand I was about to murder it.

"Who is it?"

"Maeve," she crooned.

I flung my head back, cursing the gods before unlocking all the fucking locks again.

Maeve was laughing halfway through it, or laughing at me and my violent swearing.

I opened the door, not bothering to look to see that it was Maeve when I walked back inside.

"Did she add another one?" Maeve teased.

"You'd think."

I leaned up against the wall across from the door, crossing my arms. "Why are you here so late?"

Maeve leaned up against the unlocked door, and looked at me knowingly. "I saw her heartfelt goodbye. Figured I'd wait for her to leave first before coming to see you. I couldn't sleep."

Not surprising. The concept of sleep was terrifying, since many before had died in their sleep. It was like the curse physically strangled them without leaving any evidence. I refused to sleep until I physically couldn't stay awake any longer, averaging around 3 hours a night.

She tilted her head. "When are you going to tell her?"

I felt my lips curl at the thought. "Never. I don't trust that bitch with any part of my soul."

She snorted in response, like my resolve was ridiculous to her. Maeve only held Áine on a pedestal because she saved her life eight years ago, before Maeve spent less and less time with me to go train. She didn't see the Áine I saw —the ruthless one with many faces she shuffled through like a fucking deck of cards.

Áine doesn't and could never love me. After all, I'm nothing but her fucking property. Hence all the gods damned locks on the door. If she had it her way, I'd be living inside the castle at her beck and call.

"You know," Maeve started in a serious tone. "And I mean this with the utmost sincerity and care, but you *reek* of sex."

I huffed a laugh. "She sure had fun with him." And that thought alone made me want to burn this entire cottage down and leave Kilhorn.

"Isolde."

"No, it's fine. He's... strange and different from the others here. Perhaps he'd be good for her."

She shifted her stance. "When he first came here..." My gaze bolted to her eyes. She never talked about that day. The day she came home beaten up, and said over and over that she should be there to help them get rid of the bodies. "When Áine tried to save me and got herself held up by three of them," her throat bobbed. "Liam appeared out of nowhere."

I remained quiet, desperate to finally hear more details to this story no one ever talked about.

"There were no sounds of running. Nothing. He just... *appeared*. Right behind the guy socking Áine in the gut over and over."

I swallowed down the rage, and reminded myself that they're all dead in an attempt to calm myself down.

It didn't work, but I let her continue the story.

She shook her head. "Anyway,"

No, not anyway.

"He appeared out of thin air, with no memories, not even a recollection of his name. I watched the panic and confusion grow in his eyes. He wasn't looking at Áine beating the shit out of a male twice her size, but at his hands like he didn't recognize them. It was Alaric that gave him his name, a position and place in the castle, and it was all because Áine took him in."

I listened to her speak in awe of her, and it reminded me of my first day training with the princess. The day Maeve took me with her, and hardly with my consent.

Maeve's head tilted, like she was figuring out what I was thinking about. "Was that when you fell in love with her?"

"I don't love—"

"Because that was the first day I ever saw Áine get distracted," she interrupted.

I blinked, staring at the floor.

"Get some sleep."

With that, Maeve left.

I let out the breath I was holding, then went to lock all the fucking locks.

I was woken up the next morning from banging on my door. The confusion made me nervous. We didn't have training today, and I slept for hardly an hour.

I opened the door to find Maeve and two guards behind her, all of which looked irritated as hell.

"All captains are being summoned to court."

I groaned, walking back inside to change. "Five minutes."

When I stepped outside and walked beside her, behind the guards, I whispered, "What's going on?"

"It appears that someone isn't happy with what happened last night."

I looked at her with furrowed brows. "With Carsen?"

She nodded.

"Seems like a petty thing for the council to give a shit about." Even for them.

"It's the council. They hate Áine. What more can anyone expect?"

We met with Keira inside the gates. Her dark hair whipping around her pale skin only added to the mystery behind those sinister eyes, much like Sloan, except she was more like the silent *I'll rip out your spine and eat you* type.

We all walked in silence until we stepped through the entrance to the throne room. It was still dark outside, which meant no natural light was provided in this dark throne room. The council actually bothered wasting candle wax for this, because they couldn't wait until an appropriate time.

Visha stood beside the council, leaning against a pillar like she'd rather be anywhere else. Like brewing more potions or listening to the wind.

Whatever *that* meant.

Alaric sat on the throne, patiently waiting while nodding at us as we came in. Liam was standing beside his throne, like they were in the middle of a silent conversation. Carsen, nowhere in sight.

Then in walked Áine and Sloan, walking side by side with mirrored expressions of cold indifference. A terrifying duo that exuded violence.

They were sisters in every way that mattered, which Sloan took full advantage of around the council. They feared

Sloan, but mocked and sneered at Áine, as if she weren't equally a threat.

Idiots.

Though, her current appearance didn't help matters. She came in with her comfortable *house clothes,* she liked to call them, even though she never lived anywhere aside from a castle.

She looked exactly like one would expect after the night we had, except she held that cold, emotionless expression around the council.

Her hands looked terrible.

She cleaned them at least twice but there is blood still crusted over her knuckles. It's not a good sign, especially in our world. The council sneered at her appearance, even though they had the same expressions when she looked her best, too.

Well... Second best, since the title of best was reserved for when she was naked and riding me.

"The council has called this meeting to discuss the events of last night," Alaric stated, pulling me from my thoughts.

Áine remained still, but looked over and noticed who was missing in our group. "Alright," she rasped.

Alaric begrudgingly held his hand out to the council, signaling they had the floor, even though he met none of their eyes.

It was Delroy who stepped forward. It was always this nervous fucker dressed in the finest clothes that spoke first. It was usually Velia who followed him with her fangs sharpened.

Delroy was stammering while he struggled to get out

the reason for us being here. Áine slowly turned her head toward him with impatience. He was hundreds of years old and had plenty of time to learn to speak in front of people. But somehow, he never improved.

Finally getting to the point, he muttered, "The council has found it to be highly problematic for the heir and commander to assault one of her captains."

Áine's eyes met the floor in front of my feet, undoubtedly worried they might be talking about me. She instantly moved her gaze to the floor in front of her, like she had to check herself and make sure she didn't give anything away.

Velia swayed forward, tilting her head while looking at Áine with a condescending sneer. "What were you thinking Áine?" she asked saccharinely, like Áine was a fucking child.

Áine held her warrior's stance with her hands behind her back, despite the scowl that grew on her face. Velia hated Áine, which Áine reciprocated tenfold. "He deserved it."

Heavy footsteps sounded from behind Velia, who snarled. "What could that young lad possibly have done to deserve getting his face bashed in and leaking blood?"

The tension skyrocketed, and Áine wasn't the only one who bristled at Osiris's voice. Alaric tilted his head while looking at him, like he had been pondering his death for a long time.

Áine remained quiet, like she was deciding whether or not to tell everyone the entire truth, that he wasn't taking no for an answer. She didn't want to risk them, most of all, finding out about our... *familiarity*. Which sounded way more accurate than a relationship.

They didn't need to know that she did it to protect me, her property.

Would anyone else have done it? It doesn't matter. Because no one else did. It was always her. Even if I instigated the confrontations, which I could admit that I did often to gauge her true feelings and intentions.

She held her head high. "He was harassing another female, got too handsy, even after she made it clear she wanted nothing to do with him."

"What female?" Velia pried, like she already knew the answer.

Fuck.

"What does it matter?"

Velia snorted then glanced at me before looking back at Áine. "Was this female wearing anything particularly revealing?"

Fuck!

Osiris scoffed, "Carsen would never do such a thing. And if he was being forward, then I believe wholeheartedly that the girl was likely asking for it."

"So where does the true fault lie, Áine? The respected captain, or the girl who dresses like a whore, likely as a trap set up by you."

I bit my cheek just like Áine taught me, refusing to reveal anything on my face and prayed it worked. Not that it mattered, I now realized, because Áine's face was redder than her hair.

She clenched her fists behind her back so hard, the wounds reopened, dripping blood down her hand. "It was an alcohol-induced misunderstanding," she growled. "It won't happen again."

Velia chuckled, eyes sparkling victoriously.

"If it does," Osiris threatened, "you can be certain we will be right back here, ready to ensure the proper consequences of a member of royalty abusing their power."

"Council is dismissed," Alaric announced.

They all looked at him in confusion.

He narrowed his harsh eyes on them. "Dismissed!"

The law stated that they would not have to speak to the princess in fear of losing their lives, however Alaric wouldn't let them push that boundary.

Something he likely thought about for a long time.

As the council left the room, Alaric announced, "Everyone is dismissed aside from Áine and Liam."

I gave Áine a worried look as I passed her, which she brushed off and ignored.

Typical.

My presence meant nothing to her. It meant nothing to anyone here. I was a captain with no unit.

I can feel my heart growing colder each day. I only hope Áine is prepared to see what I'm capable of... When I finally decide to murder the wilted flower, and rise into someone who will make her regret it.

CHAPTER SIX

ÁINE

A faint knock sounded on my bedroom door, or maybe someone was banging on it?

"Come in," my voice cracked. My hands were searing in pain. It didn't help that I didn't bother to put any healing ointment on them or cover the wounds properly. I may have gone too far with Carsen's emasculation last night...

"I'm sorry to wake you so early, Princess..."

Holy shit, it was dark as night outside. I never got up before dawn on my day of rest. Not that dawn here was really *dawn*. Not without a sun hardly ever in sight.

"Pearl..." I groaned. "Is there something wrong?"

"Your father summons you."

You've got to be fucking kidding me... I tried to keep my tone as neutral as possible after the evening I'd had, being woken up before *dawn*.

"Why? *Where?*" Fuck, my hands hurt.

"The throne room. There were no other details provided. I'm sorry, Princess."

"Please don't ever apologize. And *please* stop calling me princess.."

"I'm sorry," she mumbled.

I looked at her flatly. "You've served this family for centuries. You apologize to *no one*."

She looked like she was about to say something else, then she froze. She shook her head, and then smiled nervously while hustling out of my room. If I couldn't get her and the others to stop calling me princess instead of my *name*, I'd get them to stop apologizing.

After dressing in my coziest clothes for my day of rest, I made my way to see what my father decided to lecture me on today. Because if I were being honest, there could've been many reasons for my summons.

I decided that when I became queen, I would be the one who made serious changes. And that couldn't come without making enemies along the way.

The walls within our castle were made from beautiful obsidian that has seen better days. The shift in the Earth from the decay created lengthening cracks throughout the castle. Cracks that they would just fill with melted gold. It made for a lovely image, if not one of strength. But each year, when more gold was filled, I could only feel fear and anger.

My father was never one to give up. Never one that would be called a coward. In fact, I've been told many stories of his reckless bravery and defiance. But I never understood how twenty years could pass, and nothing could be done about our situation.

I understood that twenty years was nothing for most people. My father had lived a thousand years already. But at this rate, I would never reach the young age of fifty.

The druids, or healers, as many call them, never seem to understand the urgency of it. Easy for them to say. They are more ancient than my father, and rarely did they include me in any of the meetings where they discussed fixing our circumstances.

I clenched and released my fists as I walked through the halls, expelling angry energy before the verbal lashing I was about to receive.

Much to my chagrin, servants would turn a corner, notice me, and immediately turn around.

"Fucking ridiculous," I muttered under my breath. As if they had anything to fear from me. Outside these walls maybe, but within them? I was practically a lazy house cat in house clothes. Even if my face didn't look like it, I couldn't help it anymore.

I spent years training my face to intimidate others, to look remotely close to Sloan's, to hold the appearance of fearing nothing and no one.

I met with Sloan at the entrance to the throne room, and nodded to her before we crossed the threshold. We walked side by side across the marble floor, toward the dais, where my father was sitting on his throne. The future throne that I didn't want.

His face mirrored mine when one of my soldiers was out of line. And the entire council was here, testing my fucking patience that's only had a couple hours of sleep. I could see where this was headed already.

While the throne room was being emptied of aristocratic *cunts*, who only wanted to control me and hurt Isolde, I had to focus on my breathing.

The doors closed, and then I looked at my father.

He leaned back on his throne. "They expect a prompt apology."

"I refuse."

He didn't say *he* expected it.

He raised his chin like he expected it, and maybe even hoped I'd say that. "I gather you had fun last night." His tone was full of authority. Gone was the bullshit political agendas, and here was the true lecture.

But last night *was* fun, and it was written all over Liam's face. How the hell does he look so perfectly put together this early after last night? Did he ever sleep?

His devilish smirk was putting memories from last night back into my mind. His callused hands gripping my thighs, pumping his cock into me while Isolde rode my face. Not exactly a memory that bastard should be putting into my mind while getting a scolding from my father.

The court had every right to hate me. I took their picture-perfect view of how a princess should be, burned it, then fucked two of the most beautiful people in the kingdom on its ashes.

I didn't say anything back to my father. He dragged me out of bed at the crack of dawn. A girl needs her beauty sleep after beating the shit out of handsy men. He narrowed his eyes at my knuckles.

"Captain Carsen is to spend the rest of the week healing in bed, though I'm sure I don't need to assume *how*... based on the sorry state of your hands." Keeping a straight face was definitely going to be a challenge.

"Reports from his healers state that when they replaced his bandages, he cried out strings of profanities while in tears, that the 'stuck-up fucking ginger' was going to pay. I imagine they were directed at you?" A challenge indeed, since Liam started coughing violently to stop the laughter from escaping.

"Some of the council members that have grown *close* to him... are demanding your apology and groveling." I kept my mouth shut while he continued, something I wouldn't do for anyone else. "Good, and I hope they beg for it. However, you will do no such thing."

Liam whipped his face toward him. Did he agree with the council, then? *Figures.*

"Instead, the captain and his unit will be absorbed into your ranks, rather than remain independently as they've had, and for too long." It was my turn to gape. His frown told me I wasn't concealing my feelings on the matter very well. "You don't approve?"

"All this to appease the council? Why do we even bother?" His head rose with a kingly arrogance that screamed I wouldn't like his answer. But then I noted how he was telling me this *away* from the council.

"Because having a council means having power. It is the stability of the land. In every land there is a council where some members might've even once been peasants, which gives the people hope that they matter, and that the hierarchy knows they matter. Hope, Áine, is the kind of power that we need in this land suffocated by the high court."

"And why should I give a shit about the High Court?" I didn't want to consider them more than I already had to, being their precious vessel.

He stood slowly. "Because one day when our curse breaks, and war ensues, we'll need to tell the world what happens when the Dhadren are caged like animals."

I raised my chin, absorbing the words that beckoned the call to begin that journey.

"There are times when power means brute strength, but that is only a fraction of it. Some things you will learn in due time. If you slaughter all of your council because you don't agree with them, well then, that makes you no better than those who caged us."

I nodded. "Then why the merge?"

"Because you will be the one to oversee him and his men. *You* will be the one making sure that the bullshit they've gotten away with for too long is removed at the source. Including those who will commit treason over it, and I am counting on them to do so. Just as I'm counting on you passing the sentence if need be."

He paused, waiting for me to argue, ready for a fight that I wouldn't give. Does the thought of working with that asshole infuriate me? Of course. But the opportunity to end him? Abso-fucking-lutely not.

The snarl growing on my father's face, however, unnerved me.

"*You* wanted this future for yourself, Áine. *You* wanted to lead, and I've allowed it. I've even dismissed the constant drinking, fighting, and fucking of anything in your path, which is the shit of nightmares for a king, for a *father*."

I swallowed audibly. He had a point, even if I now had to play babysitter.

"Time to grow up. You've proven yourself in battle. Now, it's time to prove your strength in leadership. How you move forward with this group will set an example of what people will expect of you one day when you're sitting on this throne. If you are to be the first ruling queen, your future after I'm gone depends on it."

Liam immediately looked to the ground, frowning. I kept my eyes from rolling to the back of my head. He was strong, sexy, and utterly fucking disappointing.

Of course, the thought of a female ruling made him uncomfortable. Last night's regret was making an early appearance.

"Yes, father."

His brows raised. "That's it? Yes, father? No tantrums?"

I sighed. "It is a fair sentence. Albeit something that seems like a decision that was already in the works, but I won't argue. I will do as you say. But I won't pretend to be solemn when one or twenty of them get what's coming. The council won't be happy about this at all."

"Oh, I'm counting on it."

His smirk won the battle this time, and I couldn't fight my smile creeping up as well.

Unlike the quiet statue standing there, my father always understood me. My companions are not going to be happy about this. But maybe they'll find some excitement in throwing Carsen and his men on their asses during training. Perhaps these men weren't all bad, just stuck with shit leadership they didn't ask for.

"I have nothing but confidence that you will train these men into those of honor, and those worthy of being amongst our armies."

"May I be excused? My bath and breakfast are now cold."

He snorted. "Go. Don't forget to pay the tavern for the damages."

I smirked as I spun on my heel to leave the throne room, still in my house clothes.

"Oh, and Áine?" I half-turned around to look back at him.

"Try not to let Sloan have too much fun nailing their balls to the wall?"

I allowed my smile to reach my eyes this time. "No promises."

I was panting by the time I made it to my room, too exhausted and struggling after the night I had, and with so little sleep.

When I opened the door, I shouldn't have been surprised to find Sloan and Keira lounging on my bed, giving me shit-eating grins.

"What do you assholes want?"

They snickered in response, and I nearly fell trying to take off my boots that didn't match my house clothes.

"To give you shit," Keira started. "What else?"

I rolled my eyes, shoving her over so I could crawl past them and under the covers. I pulled the blanket over my head, hoping they'd take the hint and leave.

They didn't.

Covers were being yanked back down, making me cold again.

"Will you fuckers at least let me sleep."

"No. What did Alaric say?" Sloan asked.

I didn't sit back up or open my eyes. "To not let you have too much fun nailing their balls to the wall."

"Whose balls?" I heard the excitement she *almost* succeeded at masking.

"Carsen's. Him and his unit are being absorbed into my ranks."

"*WHAT?*" Sloan snapped. "What is the purpose of that kind of punishment?"

I turned on to my back, to give some semblance that I'm present in the conversation. Even though I was ready to fall asleep at any moment. "I don't think it's punishment.

Something's up." I furrowed my brows, staring at nothing across the room.

"So he told you?" Keira asked.

My door opened, and in came Maeve and Isolde with worried looks on their faces. Did princesses ever get privacy?

"Told me what?"

Keira paled.

"No," I started, shaking my head. "Cat's out of the bag now. Spill it."

She exhaled. "Carsen has been schmoozing over the court for a while now. Liam and I keep watch over it, but when he joins their meetings, they tense up. We hear Carsen talking in his room at odd hours in the night, but there is never another voice in the room. We never see anyone go in, and there's never a woman leaving down the halls. Either he's fucking them and eating them, or he's somehow meeting with those he doesn't want anyone knowing about." She and I shared a knowing look, like both of us were silently suggesting magic.

It was the most words I'd ever heard her speak at one time. Silence was what made her so good at what she does. But it also kept her alive while she grew up in the castle across the island. That castle belonged to the Cult of Assassins.

The evil bastards who raised Keira didn't deserve to have such a badass name.

She never talked about her life there, about how she escaped, none of it. But after the information I gathered, after the fights that turned into small battles, I wanted to vomit anytime I thought about it. There was a reason we didn't hear her speak the entire first year after we found her.

"Perhaps you should give us the green light to kill him and all of his men in their sleep," Maeve casually suggested.

"We're not murderers," Keira argued. "They need to hand us that option on a platter." Maeve rolled her eyes.

I turned to Isolde, who stared at the floor and remained quiet.

She looked up to meet my gaze and flinched. "I'm new to these discussions and barely have the same rank as most of you," she stammered. I didn't miss Keira rolling her eyes.

Keira then gave a pointed look at Maeve. "You are suggesting we act on a level beneath us. Isolde," I also didn't miss the contempt behind Keira's eyes when she looked at Isolde and snarled. "It doesn't take an idiot to realize that."

Isolde bristled, but kept her composure. Tension between the two of them skyrocketed. I took a mental note to figure that out later.

I sighed. "I'm assuming there's a plan in place, then?"

Keira quieted her voice. "Liam and I have been spying for weeks now. Your father has been egging them on in meetings, watching and waiting for the reaction to give anything away. But nothing. All fingers are pointing at Carsen, but we know he's not working alone."

"He's not smart enough," Sloan added. "So we set a trap? Or are there ones in place we can't know about?"

"Both," Keira smirked, and then looked at me with mischievous eyes. "But I have an idea."

As much as I loved playing cat and mouse with my enemies, sometimes I wish it were as simple as just killing them. Keira was a mastermind, Sloan was intimidating, and I was a blade.

Maeve was finally smiling, and Isolde nodded to Keira. Hopefully, this will help bridge the gap between them. Everyone looked to me for confirmation.

I smiled. "Tell me."

"At least they didn't hinder your wild night." Sloan taunted as she lounged at the foot of my bed, nodding toward my wrapped hands. The others had left once we heard footsteps sounding down the hall.

Sloan teased, but I couldn't find any humor in it. "I don't understand why Isolde grabbed him. She knew I was only fawning over her."

"You think she likes him?" She gave me a knowing look.

"I didn't think she liked men that much. They had fun, but she practically spent the entire night all over me." It was only a tiny lie.

"Well, then you should probably figure out what it is you're doing with them."

I rolled my eyes. "We fucked. It's not that big of a deal."

She made a *hmph* noise under her breath. "They probably feel the same then."

"They do," I said firmly, even if I didn't fully believe it. "They have to."

She just shook her head, standing to leave. "You may be princess in title, but that's it."

"Fuck off," I said as a way of goodbye, and cocooned myself under the covers.

The next morning, I stood facing my entire unit.
And Carsen's.
They were all in a readied position with their hands behind their backs and remained facing straight ahead and silent.

Except Carsen's.

I took in the sneers, but held my gaze strong despite the roiling in my stomach.

We came outside the castle gates, taking advantage of the space outside instead of inside, where I knew I would choke this fucker to death.

"Begin," I ordered, and then nodded at Isolde. As a newly appointed captain, she didn't have a unit yet. She would stay close to the other officers to learn from them and prepare herself.

Did she spend most of that time near me? Yes, but I wouldn't let Sloan's words affect me. As if I'd believe Isolde wants more than one thing.

Because she refused promotion, Captain Sloan would lead her group, running laps around the castle walls. Maeve would be working with the archers, focusing on aiming while riding, while I kept Isolde close, not trusting Carsen within five feet of her.

The women under my command trusted me to provide a safe place for their inner beasts to grow. I wouldn't allow these fuckers to try to destroy that, and the gods above couldn't save those who did from Sloan. Her eyes promised blood.

The bulk of the female warriors attempted to force the same look, but we saw the fear in them. They may be fierce, but these men had a leader with a reputation that would make any woman nervous.

Three hours into training, Isolde and I were sparring. I felt Carsen's predatory eyes on us. My face must have mirrored hers of disgust since she nodded and then picked up the pace. It was dangerous, training like that, but Isolde could handle it. And we needed to if we wanted our plan to work.

The area became quiet of voices. The sounds of swords clashing were reduced to only ours, and I could feel eyes on us as our intensity picked up.

Isolde's ferocity broke into the most intense smile I had ever seen on her.

I blocked her sword and stepped back, wiping my brow. "Dual."

Her eyes narrowed, but then she looked around at the people watching us, not training. We dropped our shields and grabbed a second sword. I tried to ignore the vulgar comments of Carsen and his men. Tried and failed as I gave them a cruel smile that didn't reach my eyes.

Isolde lunged as she swung her blades in tandem. I ducked and spun in a full circle to swing from above.

She blocked both swords with hers, gritting her teeth through the strength needed to hold back not one but *two* blades. I wouldn't hold back, and she knew it.

She gave a low spin so my blades would slide to the ground away from her. I smiled, unable to help the pride blooming within me.

"I want to play," Sloan casually stepped toward us, and the men watching turned to gape at her. The perfect distraction.

"Ok, but you'll play with me. You're the only one I can train the glaive with."

"You could train the others more, and you'd have more partners," she argued.

"*Yes*, but you're the only one who has the years of skill as I do."

Isolde nodded and walked toward Liam and Keira, who were just now walking back from the forest of dead trees. Keira and Liam were titled as captains, but they only worked together on special assignments my father assigned.

Liam stood beside Keira at all times, and flanked her everywhere she went. If he wasn't monitoring my every move, he was not-so-discreetly looming over her. But currently, he wasn't taking his eyes off Carsen, who has been murdering me with his eyes for days.

Sloan went to grab her glaive while I warmed up, spinning mine around my body. I tried to fight the smile threatening my face, since I wanted to keep my look of indifference with the current party present. Tried and failed.

During this dance, I felt nothing but pure joy. This was the dancer's high they spoke of in ballrooms. This was the peaceful grace they felt when spinning on their feet, twirling their bodies.

I spun and spun, twirling the glaive around my body with nearly inhuman speed that I'm supposed to have.

Sloan stood a few feet away from me, twirling hers in one hand above her head, staring at me dead in the eye. No spinning and dancing. Just a pure, threatening promise of knocking me on my ass.

Good.

I went into position and felt the wind around us pick up, and then come to an abrupt stop. Sloan looked up, and I followed her gaze, looking to the sky above the forest near us. It was hard to see anything above the dark clouds in the sky, but we both saw it.

I knew it had to have been someone like us. Someone who could stand in the sky like that. Someone who hadn't been cursed to die on this island. I grew familiar with that presence, feeling the pull to keep watching it and never look away.

I heard her chuckle under her breath before she was in front of me instantly, and I cackled. We were like two demons relishing the dance of battle, twirling our glaives, and slashing them through the air in ways swords couldn't.

In one moment, I spun while I released one hand off the staff, allowing the bladed end to snap to Sloan's right. I did this the fastest I could. So if it hit, I ensured it was the blade's flat side. Which was deemed an unnecessary thought when she blocked it.

She knocked it out of my fucking hand, smiling. I mirrored it, which unnerved her. She ran for me, so I ran for her. Without any weapons, I reached both hands out, grabbed the glaive she held, and threw my lower body into the air to flip over her.

I landed behind her and charged toward my glaive thrown across the field. She was quick on my heels before I finally reached it. Lifting just barely in time to block her blow.

I struggled against her strength, unable to stand while holding the block. She chuckled, and I couldn't help but mimic her. We were smiling when she released her attack and reached out her hand. When I stood back up, I saw two court members watching us from the castle battlement.

Velia and Delroy. As soon as I had looked up, Delroy turned around. Not Velia. She looked at me with her nose crinkling in that old, familiar way. I smiled in response.

"Alright everyone, let's eat." Sounds of relief ensued, followed by the wind picking back up. I looked back to the sky above the forest. There was nothing there anymore, but I could still feel the sensation of being watched. Maybe he was just watching and waiting for his future meal to finally drop dead.

CHAPTER SEVEN

DAMIEN

"*Sshhhhhkk.*"

My blade glided against the whetstone for the fourth time this week.

If I don't find another hobby to occupy my thoughts when sleep becomes impossible, I'm going to end up with a heaping pile of bladeless hilts.

After the incessant dreams that wake me in the middle of the night, I can no longer go back to sleep without my soothing ritual. I have memorized every path within the dream's forest for the last two decades.

The scent of steel and crisp winter air, even in the summer, suffocates me in my sleep. They drive me into madness when I can't find her. When I can't find the source of those snarling growls.

Knocking back the remainder of my bourbon, I set the

crystal down and reached for the oiled cloth I used to polish each blade.

A pointless task, since this particular collection was reserved for gathering information.

That was my duty, yet none of these blades had felt the warmth of blood in ages.

I had finished only one before the door to the study opened.

I merely glanced up at Conláed to acknowledge his presence. Having the same dreams as I, he sometimes would find me. As if my presence of all others could possibly be comforting.

Mine.

As his officer and interrogator, I provided nothing aside from helping train the others, keeping their abilities from squandering.

I wasn't the pillar of strength that was Drak's monstrous form, not the natural leader like Conláed, nor was I the rock of this little family like Liam.

"Anything stand out?" I asked him, still polishing my blade.

"No. But it's getting worse."

"It's *been* getting worse."

"But I can feel it."

I flicked the tip of my blade, leaving a tiny cut that healed immediately.

He watched and waited for my response, but I didn't have one.

"Do you not?"

I set the knife onto the table, reached for the next one, and smirked. "Are you scared?"

His brows furrowed. "Yes. Are you really going to sit there and tell me you're not while you polish those knives? You already did that one."

I dropped it onto the table. "Do I look like your fucking wet nurse? You want me to sing you a lullaby until you fall back asleep?"

He stared blankly at me, refusing to show that my words affected him at all. "You look like shit."

I pinched the bridge of my nose. "I know."

He grabbed the crystal decanter and poured himself a glass. "We're running out of time, Damien. Any day now we're going to be face to face with the enemy, and you need to be ready for it."

I snorted. "Worry about yourself. I'm not the one with boiling hatred over someone I've never met."

"I don't have to fucking meet her to know that only evil survives in that castle. She's not going to be any different."

"Even so, you're not going to hurt her."

His nostrils flared. "I'll do what I wish with her, and if that means I have to kill her—"

He couldn't even finish that sentence, and instead, knocked the entire glass back and left the room.

An hour had passed before the morning arrived, gleaming into the windows of the study, waking me from my nap in my chair. My body vanished from the small room, and I reappeared in my bathing room. I ignored the reflection in my mirror that told me my eyes had gotten darker.

Cleaned up, hair braided, and fully dressed in my training gear, I went to the kitchen. The heavenly smell of Drak's cooking saturated the air of the palace.

This was our palace that the rebellion fled to, seeking refuge. Still covered in vines and crumbling stone on the outside, but beautiful in an eerie way. It was the only building in the entire valley, and we had no idea who resided in it prior. The beds were big enough, and the walls kept us warm in the winter, so it would have to do.

That, and the valley kept us safe from Eadric, the king who took me in, thanks to Con. That delicate cry-baby wouldn't have lasted a day away from the castle if it weren't for me. And now we follow him into the most dangerous path our kind could face. We left the home where we were created for a purpose, and now we needed to survive while the rest of the world despised us.

I sighed, grabbing a plate, and then found Alastair and Søren sitting at our table in the dining room.

Our too-large table that was clearly meant for grand dinners or a family with too many children.

They said nothing as I sat down at Con's left. The right spot was reserved for Liam.

The room was silent, unlike the silence that thickens the moment I enter most rooms. Søren was always quiet, similarly to the silent storm that was Drak. Even Alastair's voice quieted upon my arrival.

Alastair was an annoying cunt who knew I thought of him as an annoying cunt. If he did this out of fear or to prove me wrong, I appreciated it regardless.

Con cleared his throat after he finished his breakfast. "I

invited you two to join us, because you need to know that the magic around Ghaldir is thickening. We all need to be ready."

We looked at the table, like our thoughts were the same. We'd come so far, sacrificing everything to get to this point, all so we could go play nice with those fucking people.

At least I could look forward to all the fun I was going to have torturing the idiot.

Con seemed to have read that on my face. "You're going to have to keep your torturing knives in their roll-up bag."

As soon as my mouth opened, he spoke over me.

"I still require you to do what you do best, but without drawing blood. Do you want Alaric to destroy us? Because that's exactly what's going to happen."

"Not if I go down there right now."

He looked at me with exasperation.

"And how the hell am I supposed to do what I do best without any of my fucking tools?"

Drak snorted, "This will be a new challenge for you. That is to be certain."

"Maybe you could use your cock," Alastair teased.

I raised my brow, looking at Conláed.

I could see the vein pulsing on his temple. "No."

A huff of laughter escaped my throat, and I vanished, leaving a half-eaten plate of food behind. It was difficult to grow an appetite in the mornings.

Coming here definitely didn't help.

I covered my nose and mouth, trying not to choke on the air as I peered through the dome. I strained my eyes trying to seek her out, and there she was.

In fighting gear.

I rarely came here, but the few times I had, it was always in the evening or at night.

She was wearing fighting gear, a long battle braid, and it was a shade of auburn she only could've inherited from Alaric.

The red figure in tight leather clothes spun around her opponent, wrapping her braid around her neck and twirling her spear. No, not just any spear.

I laughed, admiring the princess playing with a glaive. Did Conláed know?

Of course he knew. And I bet it made him just as pissy as ever. An easy feat as of late.

I smiled each time the princess got knocked down.

Every time she falls and wipes the blood off her face, she laughs. What a delicious little prize Conláed hated the thought of winning. Of course, he wouldn't have a choice. I wouldn't let him. I would make sure he was prepared with powerful chains, ones that were strong enough to restrain the little vessel.

Because when he does, I'll be the one to make her bleed.

My breathing stopped when she looked up at me. Could she see me?

A breeze started to pick up, and I caught the scent of that magic. First, the magic of fate, and the other of malice.

The latter was becoming so thick I could taste it.

I immediately appeared in the training fields, finding Con who stopped sparring the moment I arrived. He appeared in front of me, eyes rounded and impatient. "What?"

"It's time."

CHAPTER EIGHT

ÁINE

Winter was preparing to pass the torch to spring.

It was too quiet, too peaceful. I didn't believe that Carsen was the only enemy, even though I should have been relieved by the idea.

I strolled down the halls of our bedroom chambers, prepared for a much-needed bath and sleep. Liam had his door cracked open. He likely waited for me to go to bed before he felt comfortable enough to close it and go to bed himself.

You'd think the male was in love with me, but Liam only ever looked at me like an errant child he lost track of. All irritated relief when he caught sight of me. That's what everyone wants, right?

I entered my bathing room and found several buckets of steaming water outside the tub.

I loved taking baths growing up. I enjoyed playing in the bubbles, dodging handmaidens, and resisting tutors' attempts to make me a subservient lady. Disregard the fact that the servants had prepared water in buckets. The water had to be boiled and filtered twice before it was considered safe for bathing.

I held my oils and soap in one hand while trying to pour water from buckets into the tub above the soap to create bubbles. Relaxing shouldn't be this much work.

A knock sounded at my door.

Are you kidding me? How long did having an inner battle with himself take before he decided to bother me? I knew I could be nicer to him, but he didn't make it easy. Opening the door, I kept my composure and held my breath.

Carsen looked past me, sniffing the air that smelled of scented oils. He gave a smirk that made me want to vomit all over him.

"Long day, was it?" he crooned while tilting his head like the predator he thought he was.

I found him attractive when we first met years ago. That changed when he opened his foul mouth and revealed himself as the absolute worst.

From the moment I opened the door, I kept my arms crossed and didn't say a word, refusing to blink, daring him to make a move.

"I think we should start over," he said as he raised his chin. "My men practically begged me to come here tonight.

They want your officers to sheath the daggers and try to play nice."

I might actually vomit on him. And it wouldn't entirely be in my control, depending on what bullshit he decided to say next.

"Maybe if your *men* kept their hands to themselves, my officers wouldn't feel the need to dig their elbows into their fucking throats."

He chuckled at that. "They're just boys trying to flirt as boys do."

"They're grown ass fucking males. There will be no sympathy given to their bullshit," I argued.

"Hmm. Or perhaps they need new skills in leadership to command them," he threatened.

The silence was palpable before I smiled. "You know Carsen, I think you're right. I think we should start over. How about next time you come to my bedroom doorstep with the stupidity you're trying to portray as bravado, I dig my elbow into your throat?"

His nostrils flared.

"Sleep well captain, we've got a long day tomorrow and my bath is getting cold." I slammed the door in his face and walked toward the tub, feeling triumphant and powerful.

That lasted about five seconds before my door was being kicked in, hitting the floor. I turned around, cracking my neck, fully prepared to put him out of my misery.

He was halfway to me when Liam swiftly wrapped his arm around his neck. Carsen's eyes grew wide while trying to pry Liam's arm off, then he slumped. It looked like he was about to die. Liam dropped him, ensuring he only passed out. What a pity.

"Do you have to taunt assholes like that every time? What if I wasn't here!" he shouted at me.

"Then I would've taken care of him myself! Or have you forgotten I'm a highly trained killer? Stop talking to me like I'm a fucking child!" Yelling like that didn't help my case at all. I sounded like a child, but it didn't help that he always made me feel like one.

He prowled toward me, fuming at my words and the situation. He stopped in front of me, this tower of a man. His chest rose and fell with frustration, staring daggers into my soul. I was denied my kill. He can heave until the walls come down for all I care.

"I'm taking a bath. I trust you can handle him? Or fucking leave him and I'll deal with it, but I'm taking a bath now."

"Áine," he snapped.

I looked over my shoulder, waited the five seconds of my attention he earned, and then turned back toward the tub. He stood there, saying nothing. Typical babysitting statue of a male, he was always yelling at me as if I was the one who made Carsen the monster he is. As if I was the one attacking Maeve by the creek those years ago.

I was near the tub when I heard him dragging Carsen into the hall and then lifting my door back up. As I raised my hair from the water, I could hear doors closing and scraping on the floor. Considering I'm the future queen, I should have gotten up to see if there was anything I could do to help. But I was filthy, and he yelled at me.

The males of this land needed to learn one thing: I am not the damsel. I am the weapon their parents warned them not to touch.

I opened my eyes and found myself above a sea of trees, blooming in their splendor like they once had long ago. I twisted my body that floated in the air, stretched my arms out, and then above me, inhaling the peace of it all, soaking in the beautiful moonlight I only experienced in these dreams. In these dreams, I learned that true beauty lies in the darkness, where the monsters come out and feed their starving souls.

That's all I was here: A soul of a beast, starving for what was powerful enough to make me see this.

There were quick movements through the brush, snapping twigs beneath their feet. Fear danced wildly in my heart as they growled, scanning the darkness through the trees, trying to locate the source.

As I floated, the air was being sucked out of me, causing me to choke. I grasped my throat as I felt the panic of dying. Panic was the enemy, the *killer*, I reminded myself. Not the beasts in the dark forest. The beasts that called to me...

The growling grew. Snarling like the stalking beast in the woods. I wasn't breathing. They were waiting for me.

I looked down and saw two sets of eyes glowing beneath the trees. One a light shade of blue and another of a precious green, beyond the trees that were getting closer and closer while I slowly fell toward them.

Passing through the canopy, I felt the heat at my back. I turned my body to look and found that the trees had caught fire. All of them, the moment I entered the forest. Smoke being shaken in waves.

The growling continued, loud and whimpering. The sound of pain and starvation. I was about to be eaten. But, even if I fought them and won, this forest would take me soon after. I wouldn't make it out of here alive.

As I got closer to the growls, closer to death, I tried to turn back and face them, but was prevented by something. Something held me back from facing the impending outcome that awaited me.

I heard the snarls close to my ear until I felt hands all over my body, four dragging me down. The snarls stopped abruptly, and then lips pressed to my ear let out a sensual and masculine chuckle.

I awoke to my balcony doors being slammed open.

I awoke, but I couldn't move anything but my eyelids. Paralyzed to the bed, I couldn't even move my fingertips. This happened periodically since I was a child. I couldn't run or hide when the growling ensued from outside. I knew what was coming.

The beast from the forest crept in from the balcony, which lay many stories up and was impossible to climb.

He entered my room with his head dipped low. Those silver eyes... unrelenting and menacing, never leaving the spot where I lay trapped.

I watched as it stood motionless in the center of my room, my breathing quickening. I thought of the horror stories told growing up and wondered if he had been biding his time before he inevitably ate me.

Someone started banging on my door.

Still paralyzed, I gave pleading eyes to the beast, who

didn't seem to concern himself with whoever stood outside my door. More banging ensued.

"Áine!" It was Liam. And he was about to awaken the entire damned castle.

I whipped my head toward the door, then back to the beast, surprised I could move. He was gone. Vanished.

I struggled to stand, shaking off the lingering effects of my body being paralyzed, and stumbled toward the incessant noise. I opened the door, and it instantly fell to the ground. So only fixed-ish, then.

Liam stormed into my room and toward my balcony glass doors.

"You picked a fight with a monster and decided it was a good idea to leave the fucking balcony doors open?"

I couldn't say anything back as I frowned, narrowing my eyes at the doors like the lie would just magically appear.

"Why are you in my room, Liam?"

"I heard something."

"And you didn't stop to think that maybe it was just me?" I couldn't hold back the irritation. It wasn't even daylight yet, and he had clearly been right outside my room this whole god's damned time.

"So, you opened it then?" His eyes pointed with challenge.

"I must have and don't remember. If someone opened it, I don't think we'd be here chatting right now, since I would probably be bleeding out or something." The wrong thing to tell him, I realized, when he stormed into the hall, returning moments later with a cot, and was now unlacing his boots.

He was serious, then.

"Is this how it's going to be? Every time there is a threat, you lay on the ground like a watchdog?"

"I don't give a shit how you want to spin it. You're not dying tonight because you refuse to shut the fuck up when death taunts you. Your father will have my head for not keeping my word to protect you."

Looking past my irritation, I could see a decent male just trying to keep his word. That didn't change a fucking thing, though, as I was trying and failing to keep my temper in check from him invading my space. He noted it and looked up at me, raising his brows, daring me to try to kick him out.

I let out an irritated and un-ladylike groan before jumping back into bed, shoving my feet back under the covers. At least the doorway was open in case anyone wanted to make assumptions. I turned away as I heard him try to get comfortable for the night.

"Liam?"

"Yes?"

"Thank you."

He sighed and then rolled over.

CHAPTER NINE

ÁINE

I awoke to an empty room with the door appearing to be fixed. Which hopefully meant no more watchdog. The thought brought me a short-lived semblance of peace, until there were rushed footsteps moving in the halls.

I grabbed my ankle-length, black satin robe and peeked into the hall. Liam was barking orders. I heard another door open and saw Sloan across the hall, peeking out from her room and then at me. I nodded my head toward the inside of my room.

She didn't wait for a clear path. She just walked straight from her door to mine. Not bothering to step around the others blazing through, but making them stop before trampling over her.

This woman was the complete image of a queen. Flowing wavy blonde hair, long dark lashes complimenting deep blue eyes, and a warrior's build. Every single person in this kingdom balked at her presence, and I couldn't blame them.

Whether it was something in her genes or a personality trait, her eyes told the world she was the monster they should fear. I closed the door when she moved past me and turned with my eyes wide with questions.

"Apparently, someone paid an uninvited visit last night," she taunted, angling her head like a predator. Which visit was she talking about? There were three, after all.

"He's locked up, isn't he?" I couldn't help my irritation lingering from last night, now taking it out on my pants that I was struggling to shove on.

Sloan raised her eyebrows in question, to which she already knew the answer. I left the door open for a reason. My eyes rolled in frustration. Or maybe she was checking to see if I needed to talk, and I was being immature.

"You know you don't make it easy on Liam with your recklessness, but he might not want to pull shit like last night if you were more opposed to it," she accused. Glad to know everyone agrees this bullshit is my fault. Maybe even me.

"I was a total bitch to him, Sloan. He took it as a challenge and brought a fucking cot in here. Perhaps if I get on my knees next time and suck his cock, he'll leave."

She pursed her lips in response.

"What am I supposed to say here, Sloan? If you have any helpful suggestions, I'm all ears," I spat, then heard feet scuffling before I saw Liam leaning against the doorway, frowning. When did he open the door?

"I was just leaving," Sloan said.

"Don't bother, I have shit to do. I'll see you both later."

I started to leave them until Liam blocked my path. I slowly looked up to meet his eyes that held mirrored venom.

"Carsen is gone. Vanished. No trace of him," he said sharply. He probably heard my conversation with Sloan. Then I absorbed what he just said.

Sloan spoke the words for me, "How the fuck is that even possible? Who let him out?"

"There was no forced entry, and all keys were accounted for. The guard just looked over and he was gone. Not even a sound," Liam added.

We stood there silently, taking in what that could mean.

"Even if someone helped him—" I whispered.

"The guard would've heard. Even if he was lying and fell asleep. Again, there was no forced entry. Not even footsteps."

Sloan interjected, "Then get Keira, all the others,"

"She's already on it," Liam interrupted. "If we can gather even the slightest intel today, we leave tonight."

"And my father?" I asked.

"He is insistent on going as well, not wanting to risk Carsen around you. I couldn't talk him out of it."

"I'm sure your little report of last night didn't help matters," I sneered.

He sighed and then looked toward my balcony in defeat. I just shook my head at him.

"Where is he then?" I asked while staring passed him, ready to get the fuck out of this conversation.

"Visha's."

With that, I left.

I cut through the courtyard until I was greeted by garden plots that have long since died. I took a deep breath of the chill air, only to feel my body struggling to take more, to take what oxygen this land had left to give my constantly aching body. Another gift. Without hardly any water, without oxygen, we were in a constant state of pain and dehydration.

Visha's cottage was a mockery of what her apothecary once was long ago. I ran away from lessons as a child to hide there once. Shelves were lined with glass containers that hadn't moved in ages. But that was only what I could see near the entrance to the underground hideaway.

It was pitch black and looked like it was meant to be a tomb. The further I walked into it, the more my bones would shake in terror. It could've been normal child fears, but I will never forget that core memory of feeling a presence there that could've been evil.

Since there was no magic to keep the room lit or enough candles to make sense of wasting them all, they moved to a small stone cottage across the courtyard. Keeping the druids easily accessible to the public and close enough to the castle's entrance should we need them.

Religious and manipulative monarchs they might've always been, but their healing skills were unmatched, even without magic.

I heard voices hushed as I knocked twice before slowly opening the door. I raised my brows high as I walked in, questioning the sudden secrecy upon my arrival. To my surprise, my mother was here with my father, seeming to be somewhat involved in whatever discussion they deemed I couldn't hear.

Visha stood still like a statue, keeping her dark forest-green eyes on my father.

"What is it?" I asked the uncomfortably tense room.

Visha and my mother were now looking at my father, leaving him to answer for them. I fought the urge to roll my eyes. My father looked at me.

"We were discussing Carsen's sudden and untraceable escape," he answered. I had an idea, but didn't dare speak it out loud. Hope was a dangerous thing here, especially if lost amongst the people. *Especially* when others had already lost their sense of self and gave themselves to monstrous temptations. Uncaring of the consequences since we were all dying anyway...

"It couldn't have been anything but magic," he continued. "Visha can still sense it looming in the air, and its trail heading for the forest to the south of the island."

My eyes widened, but I didn't say anything. This was the first time any of us had felt magic aside from the feeling she had weeks ago from the forest filled with spriggans. I fought the hope in my chest, screaming that this was it.

"How," I demanded, ready to move.

"There's a considerable size rift coming from the south," Visha started. "It hasn't closed up, and I can feel it growing. It smells like elven magic."

"When do we leave?" I asked immediately, and caught the grimace on my mothers face, there and gone in a flash, before storming out of Visha's.

My father didn't chase after her, but he stared at the closed door for several seconds before speaking again.

I shook my head in irritation. Sometimes her feebleness made me want to scream. "And what happens when we find it? *If* we find it?"

He gave a knowing look towards Visha. "They'll be coming with us. Only they can manipulate the magic if it's rich enough for her to wield it."

My blood was roaring in my ears. "How can I help you?"

Visha smirked as her wavy, dark brown hair fell over her shoulders. "By making sure I don't get murdered while I try to save our asses." She was ancient yet still youthfully beautiful and bold. You'd think we would be fast friends, but she has made it clear that she has zero interest in spending time with me more than necessary. I nodded, nonetheless.

"I'll make sure preparations are made in between meals. Now when do we leave?"

My father finally answered, "Tonight."

I was placing my glaive onto the snap hooks welded to the back of my chest plate, fighting the shivers while we all were about to mount our horses.

My father had been furiously looking back and forth between me and the army, and then Liam, who wasn't doing anything different. They were going to get themselves killed if they didn't have any faith in me.

I was trying to tighten my bandolier under my glaive

when Keira came to help me, with Liam right behind her. He was never too far.

"Keep your eyes and ears open. Absolutely no straying from the pack, Áine," Liam demanded.

I wanted to punch him for talking to me like that in front of everyone, but this wasn't the time. Everyone was unnerved by the situation.

This land hasn't had a trace of magic in twenty years. When we investigated Carsen's cell, my father incessantly sniffed the air. As if he was holding onto hope that his senses would work.

"Áine," my mother's voice sounded from behind me, clipped and on edge.

I turned to face her in her dress and crown, while she took in my armor, and the steel strapped all over me that weighed almost as much as me.

The eyes that met mine were harsh, but I could see that they were filled with worry she couldn't voice. I nodded at her, understanding her silent plea, and spun on the heel of my boot.

I was mounting Maddox when my father cupped my mother's cheek, and they looked at each other like they were having a conversation no one else could hear. Something only few in this world could do when they found their mate.

I *hated* that word. If not equally, than more-so than the words *husband,* or *marriage.*

They were all words that had the same meaning: You were no longer your own person. And if you were female, it signified the castration of free-will. Even if my parents were happy, and my father treated my mother well, that was a rare event, so I'm told.

To our left, Sloan was getting her unit in formation. A group of the strongest warriors amongst us. They had the kind of strength that one punch would make you puke your guts up.

To the right, Maeve was waiting patiently with roughly fifty other archers. She became captain at a very young age, for the reason that not only was she loud and overbearing as hell, she never missed.

I didn't have to look to know that Isolde was right behind me, pretending she was paying me no attention. I rolled my eyes and kept looking forward.

Keira and Liam, our top trackers, mounted their horses and went ahead of us with Visha to scope out potential trails and traps. I had the honor of being at my father's right. That, or he refused to allow me any further away from him. Visha would rear back with her apprentices far enough behind our army, just in case the worst happened.

We silently waited for the signal.

I loved and hated these moments. The tension rising, the restless noises from the horses... The stillness that our minds became to prepare for death's dance.

My mother hated that I loved this, but my entire being was made for battle. The world thought I would be this obedient thing to one day be married off to another prince or lord.

All to better the kingdom.

My vision for improving the kingdom was drastically different from theirs. I would mount princes' cocks on spikes if they believed in enforcing my servitude based on having tits. My tits were meant to be encased in black armor adorned with gold.

We heard the whistle and moved in quick formation. "Come on, Maddox," My warhorse was solid black with armor matching mine and was the biggest spoiled brat in Ghaldir.

We caught up with Keira and Liam, who fell into step beside us, and rode on for an hour until we heard the unmistakable sound of hissing.

Keira's breathing was heavy, and her horse became jumpy in response to her nervousness, which only meant one thing.

"Shit," Isolde breathed.

Ahead of us, the Cult of Assassins broke through the clearing, clad in their hooded black robes. In army formation, they wore sigils of dead gods, symbolizing their absurd cult.

They wore leather armor matching Keira's old ones. The ones she was wearing when she escaped that hell and found us. And far in the back, seated lazily on a horse amongst people I didn't recognize, was Carsen.

It was a trap.

CHAPTER TEN

ÁINE

Next to the pig with shit-colored hair, was a woman with markings all over her face and body. She wore a robe, and I could see her eyes glowing from here.

And in between the two, was an officer, based on his apparel. His height was terrifying, and I wondered if he was one of the Demon Fae my tutors told me about; the race of fae that was half demon.

My father refused to speak of them. The only information I *did* receive told me they were extremely powerful, and that they never should have been created.

Though it was a terrifying thought since we had an army of fae without magic, he appeared to be the only one here.

My father and Liam were swearing under their breath and then started shouting orders. I fastened my helmet and visor, slid my hand behind my back to pop the glaive from its snap-hooks, and nodded at my father. Grasping the reins in one hand, I twirled my glaive in the other alongside Maddox.

The most important part of the beginning of battle is intimidation. So, I laughed.

A screeching, cackling laugh. Loudly.

Sloan echoed, and then the rest of my girls followed. An echoing, chaotic cackle for the anticipating joy of battle. The men with us gaped in horror, only to look ahead and see that the enemy's enthusiasm had lowered.

Good.

My father grinned brightly before giving the order. My mother would be mortified if she saw us now.

Slamming our heels into our anticipating beasts, they jumped forward as if hungry for blood like their riders. Maeve gave her archers the command to nock after moving to the far east of the field.

Sloan and her team, exceptionally skilled with agility and strength, moved west at almost inhuman speed, preparing to slam into them hard from the side.

These were assassins. They were adept at stealth murder, not battle formation. Most of us were trained for both.

Unlike any royal family before, my father and I held the front lines. His face was cold, but I could sense his fear.

As my father, he didn't want me here. As a commander of his army, I had no choice. Even if I did, I wouldn't want to be anywhere else. Armies weren't led by their kings, much less princesses, but here we were.

The hissing grew louder, and my heartbeat became a storm. Liam approached my right. As if I'd expected anything else. I looked straight ahead into the shadows of death and screamed my battle cry, and we slammed into the front lines.

The crunching beneath the hooves was sickening. This was my least favorite part. This wasn't the beauty of battle.

I swung my glaive through the one that had thought to disable Maddox. However, I didn't catch the shadow on the other side in time before it rammed a mace into Maddox's head. It hit the plate on his cheek, but from the whinnying of pain, it must have also hit some flesh.

He swerved to the side, almost ejecting me. I squeezed my thighs and held on as tightly as I could, but was slammed into the mud.

My father screamed as one assassin came up behind me.

I grabbed a knife from my bandolier and threw it at him, landing it in his eye socket.

My father and Liam were ahead of me, ensuring we had a moment to straighten back up. They had already dismounted and were on foot.

I ran towards the line, glaive in hand that had a much cleaner blade than theirs.

Maeve had their third round of arrows blazing forward.

I caught Sloan's glaive from the corner of my eye. She didn't twirl hers as fast or as gracefully as I did, but her strength was out of this world, taking down multiple at a time.

I went into a running start, smiling when I saw Isolde come into my line of fire, ducking down, holding her shield over her head. I pushed myself faster, feeling the adrenaline spike, my heartbeat pumping against my chest, and I jumped.

I landed one foot on her shield before launching myself forward. She added power behind it that I didn't know she had. I was soaring above my father and Liam, screaming my battle cry as I landed my glaive straight through the body of one who had frozen in fear, from head to groin.

I felt the blood splatter across my face and grinned as I began death's dance.

I kept a distance between myself and my people since my glaive was too dangerous to anyone close enough. One dared to lunge forward before his head fell to the ground with little effort. I spun to my right, heaving up and disemboweling another.

Liam's dual blades cut one of these hooded fuckers into thirds behind my last victim. He grimaced when he saw me, still not happy that I was here, surrounded by enemies.

Enemies that were all about to die.

I looked ahead at the two charging me at once. I spun to the right, holding my glaive horizontally. I let go of my left hand once I almost completely twirled around, snapping the glaive through both bodies, just like I did while sparring with Sloan, cutting them in half.

I heard Keira yell to my left, ramming her sword through the one that sought my father's head. I nodded in gratitude before my attention snapped back to my right.

Four of them had crept up and were now circling me. I heard Liam swear, but he was occupied. I wasn't afraid. We trained for situations precisely like this one. I could switch to my swords. That would be easier. But opportunities like this didn't come often.

I began spinning my body while twirling my glaive in a figure-eight motion, building a shield.

It took two swings to take down two in one eight-motion. Another eight took down the third until the fourth one came behind me, thinking I didn't see him.

The last one. I twirled my glaive with my right hand, the non-bladed end meeting the front of my boot, to kick it up in front of me, snapping the bladed end in a downward motion behind me, landing in their skull. I pulled it out of him, marching forward, not bothering to see his current state.

I was no longer Princess Titáine in those moments.

I was death, unleashed.

CHAPTER
ELEVEN

CONLÁED

I didn't realize I was holding my breath when I saw what the princess did to that idiot, thinking he'd sneak up behind her.

This girl was on the front lines, not wielding, but *dancing*.

She had an entire armory attached to her body, but they only weighed her down. Her dancing told the world that the only weapon she'd ever need was that glaive.

I looked beside me, floating in the sky near the rift, to find Damien looking at me with a shit-eating grin on his face.

So what if she had talent? It wouldn't take away from who she is.

All of them were raised to believe *one* way. Did I know that there are always exceptions? Of course I did. I'm not an ignorant ass. But I knew better than to think a child of that piece of shit had anything good about her.

They had been at this for a good while now, and the horizon was starting to show a lighter shade. I considered what we were about to do.

The three of us watched as they pushed through the lines, obliterating the enemy forces. I could barely see them through the poison-riddled dome, wondering if she sensed us watching her again. It was obvious who the victor would be, even without our help.

Too bad that victory would only last for a short while, because coming from the east towards the rift, was an elven army, with many demon fae soldiers like ourselves.

I nodded at Drak and Damien. "Let's go."

The sensation when we neared the rift was awful. Keeping it in our sights, a tear in the veil had glowed, beckoning us to enter and feed it the magic it wants. Too bad the demon blood inside us would destroy it, which is exactly what we counted on.

"On my call, leave the rest to me and grab the army."

Damien was looking at me like I was the biggest idiot, and he'd be right. "You understand how dangerous that is? You likely won't die but—"

"But we don't have a choice, and we've been over this."

Drak was staring at me with his cold, quiet, expression

that didn't need words. They're both right, and I'm an idiot. But an idiot that would do anything for our cause, which is why I made the decisions.

As the younger brother, that role should've fallen to Drak. However, he never had any intention of leading or ruling. He only entertained the lessons to appease our father enough to distract him from our plans.

While he did that, I made the decisions, then led the rebellion.

I saw the flash of light from deep within the forest. The male they hunted, reeking of my father's magic, was twisting his blade to flash a beam of light in her direction enough that she took notice.

That asshole went into the forest with Captain Ulrich from the elven army, a demon fae soldier who I knew was expendable. Alongside them was a witch named Giselda. She was hundreds of years old, and sworn to serve the King until she died.

Which would be very soon.

The princess surveyed the battle, noted their advantage and took off after Carsen, not realizing a much stronger army was coming and could end them all *very* quickly in their current state.

That wasn't going to happen today. I wouldn't let her have a choice.

We approached the rift, and apprehension flooded our faces.

I shook my head. "We can't back out now. Let's do it."

Damien chuckled like the unhinged maniac he is, and touched the veil.

The curse within the veil acted as a magnet to magic, tethering itself to it, and absorbing it to strengthen it.

The three of us roared in pain as the veil began to drain our magic, and the rift started to close.

I heard them. Looking behind me, the elven army was approaching and fast.

"GO!"

They both hesitated for a moment, understanding the pain once they vanished, but they did it. And I screamed.

The putrid smoke forced itself within me, and ripped my fucking soul apart. I couldn't even imagine what the princess was about to feel once I found her, but I wondered if it would be anything like this.

If she could handle it while still in a putrefied state, in comparison to what she was supposed to be... No, that was impossible. She would be knocked out and injured for days.

I could feel my conscious slipping, right before that army neared and ours arrived, blocking their path, and my body encased itself with my flames. It defied the veil, exactly as we'd hoped.

Commanders Alastair and Søren led the armies, slamming our forces into the ones we'd trained and fought with, and Damien and Drak returned to my side instantly.

Their bodies turned to flame like mine, but even after they touched the veil, the pain inside me didn't lessen.

I only hoped this didn't make me unable to fight, and wondered if Alaric could see us, if he knew what was happening and would remember that before decimating us.

I gasped when the power flooded out of me. Fire violently spread across the veil, moving itself around the entirety of Ghaldir.

Fear scratched in my chest, and Damien vanished instantly, as if he felt the same thing.

I roared, echoed by Drak, releasing the flames with everything we had.

CHAPTER
TWELVE

ÁINE

The cramps in my legs pulsated, threatening to slow me down. It would've worked if our enthusiasm wasn't skyrocketing.

If the sadistic glee on Liam and Keira's bloodied faces were indication enough, we had the advantage. I smiled at the picture they painted, and wondered what our paintings would look like after this. What I wouldn't give, to watch this veil around us burn.

Carsen's face had grown nervous. His horse was jumpy and all over the place. I heard him shout, and the three of them abandoned their army and fled into the forest.

I swore violently, cutting down another assassin who thought to sneak up on me. My father's face zeroed in on Carsen. Our eyes met, and he had a look of furious understanding. We couldn't let him get away. He didn't nod in agreement before swinging his sword towards another. In fact, his eyes were frantically rounded and ready to stop me, but I took that as an opportunity and ran.

I ignored Isolde's voice screaming my name, tried to wet my throat with saliva that wasn't there anymore, and kept running.

It's not like I wasn't used to the dehydration, not that it would kill me, but it hurt like fuck.

Maddox was running in my peripherals, and met me at the tree line. The blood that ran down the side of his face twisted my gut, but he didn't let it stop him. A tough and loyal brat, at least.

I lept and mounted in urgency, and we took off into the forest.

Did I know this plan was stupid? Of course. This wasn't even a plan. I just knew that if we let him get away, if we couldn't find the rift and break the veil, we were dead eventually anyway.

Carsen was weak, and easily manipulated. It was the other two I was worried about.

Too many unknowns, and I had just been battling for over an hour.

Fuck.

This was stupid.

I pulled on the reins when I caught three horses tied to a tree, and no one nearby.

I dismounted Maddox, and stood still for several moments, listening for any disruptive sound in the woods.

Nothing.

But a light flickered, shining brightly from far away.

My eyes squinted, attempting to focus through the stinging of blood and sweat dripping down my forehead.

Wiping it away was practically useless when my forearm wasn't any different.

My sight cleared, and there he was; in between two trees and by himself.

An obvious illusion, but at least I wouldn't go unknowing.

I dove into the chase and entered the depths of the forest, pushing further and further away from my family. I had to have faith in them. They could handle themselves if they stuck together. Which coincidentally went against everything I was currently doing.

I lost many soldiers tonight tracking down this bastard and his source of treachery. Soldiers I spent many years training. I needed to keep running to finish the job I should've done long ago.

Carsen was fast, but I was faster. Much faster, actually… That, and he kept looking back at me without any fear on his face. My heart stopped at the sounds of twigs snapping from multiple different directions right before an arrow shot through my forearm.

Fuck!

I grunted through the pain, and held Carsen's stare while ripping out the arrow.

Glancing around me, I counted roughly thirty of his men. Behind Carsen, a bored looking demon fae that towered over all of us, was leaning against a tree. The woman with the markings coating her body, I now realized was a witch.

She had crystals decorating her arms, waist, and anywhere one could place jewelry that laid atop the many tattoos I wanted to admire. And the piercings. If only.

Carsen had turned around, slowly walking back towards me, keeping his distance. I was completely surrounded by him and his men, alone.

I kept my hands close to the small blades on my thigh scabbards.

"I see you're still pouting over me humiliating you in front of Isolde," I sneered, not allowing him to see any of my fear. I may have the skill set, but the men surrounding me trained in the same exact fields as I had. And there were too many of them.

Even if I managed to take all of them, he had a witch and a demon fae behind him and was impatiently waiting. As if they hated his company just as much as anyone would.

Carsen's grin went sinister. "You don't need to worry yourself with Isolde, dear princess. By the end of the day, she'll be chained to my bed, celebrating our victory with me and my soldiers."

Those surrounding me grunted in agreement with him before laughing.

My grip around my emotions was tightening so hard I thought it'd snap.

I will not fear.

I will not panic.

I will not lose control.

I repeated this to myself in my head over and over as the rage and fear consumed me until I was interrupted by the ground briefly trembling. I repeated the mantras again. Not all of us were walking out of here alive, but I sure as shit wouldn't allow Carsen to be one of them.

I slowly crouched, anticipating their attack, but they were waiting for mine. They knew me. They knew how I fought. I would have to utilize the element of surprise by any means necessary. I would think of Keira and her attack style, which usually killed the most at once and as swiftly as possible.

They didn't have time to think before I unleashed the six blades I grabbed between my fingers, each making their mark.

Carsen stood back, crossing his arms and barking at his men. "Do *not* kill her! The power will do that anyway."

My head snapped up at that. This motherfucker needed the witch to release the power my body held.

I snarled at him before quickly releasing my last set of six, landing each blow before withdrawing my dual swords. *Twelve down, eighteen to go.*

The safest option would be to utilize a shield, but there were too many. My swords needed to slay faster than it would take to block and strike again. It was stupid, but would end with swifter kills.

I flipped my swords in my hands, expelling nervous energy while they were charging towards me. They weren't ten feet away before I began twirling my blades around me, starting the next dance.

I wished I was using my glaive, wanting what might be my last dance to be my favorite, but it was heavier. I've already expended too much energy, and dual blades *were*, in fact, the more efficient option here.

They weren't five feet away from me before the ground started shaking again, viciously, knocking several off their feet, the rest frozen in fear.

Carsen narrowed his eyes at me as if I was causing it. What a complete fucking idiot.

My chest *burned* with an ache, like it was telling me I was close to passing out. I looked around and saw the illuminance of my surroundings was turning into a warm hue. Even if the sun was rising soon, it shouldn't be this bright... It shouldn't be *warm*...

They looked up before I did, assessing the real threat here.

Above the graveyard forest of dead willows, surging waves of fire and flame exploded through one of the dark clouds. All of us froze in our tracks, and I considered if I should even bother fleeing, if the end was here to take us all, anyway.

I never believed in any of that. But if something here was powerful enough to set the entire gods' damned sky to flames, I may as well lower my swords now and accept my fate.

Swords were grasped in shaking hands as the flaming sky took the stage. Carsen, the witch, and the demon fae officer were nowhere to be seen.

Darkness from within the clouds expelled to the ground, blown mercilessly throughout the forest, like it feared what lay in the sky.

It caused a fog to settle that hindered my already bloodied vision, but when my eyes caught sight of what was in the sky I stilled.

There were three beings of fire, *burning* down the veil, and they were screaming.

I was gripping my chest when one of them vanished, and all hell broke loose.

The ground shook violently. I felt it before I heard it, thick tree roots slithering out like snakes, knocking me and several others on our asses. Followed by a sinister laugh that made my heart pound.

Most of Carsen's men were running away, which was rendered useless since the branches were either impaling them through their torsos, knocking them down, or being set on fire by... roses? And then I saw him.

The forest was filling with more branches, searching for their next victim to impale, but curiously avoiding me. And on them... bloomed large roses that exploded.

Like beautiful little bombs, they melted the skin off my enemies... before turning black with embers still glowing from within.

And coming from behind those branches, stalking towards us, was a towering soldier with long, white-blonde hair that was braided back, wearing an officer's uniform with no sigils, and the most beautiful face I had ever seen.

In the blink of an eye, he vanished, and then reappeared in front of the last two of Carsen's men. Smiling wildly, he punched his hands into each of their chests, lifting them off the ground effortlessly.

He threw them to the ground, while still holding their hearts in his hands. Hands that I could now see had long and sharp black talons, before the hearts turned to ashes that fell between his fingers.

He was still smirking when he turned to face me. Terrifying, but I refused to let it show, so I chose anger.

"You couldn't have left one for us to question later?"

He snorted. "Apologies, princess. Next time I save your ass, I'll be sure to remember." That accent... Those eyes... those unnerving green eyes surveyed me slowly. The arrogant gleam in them heated me in more ways than one, but I was sticking with the rational one. My nostrils flared, and I struggled to find the words, the *questions*.

My mouth opened and closed when more appeared behind him. All wearing the same style of uniform, similar to the other officer with Carsen, but their sigils had all been ripped off.

The one approaching his right flank... he was beautiful too. With dark skin you rarely saw in Ghaldir, and bright blue eyes that made him look like a treasure. But that beautiful face sneered at me before heading south. Where the battle and my family were.

I swallowed, straining my sore throat. "Are you here to kill us?" my voice was so raspy, i didn't recognize it.

The one with the green eyes, still staring at me curiously, raised his chin, "Run to your family, little one."

My eyes rounded, and I opened my mouth to say something, to ask *anything* rather than do as he said. While my legs froze in place, the *thing* roiling in my stomach thundered. I couldn't move. Was this panic?

His lips pulled back to reveal his teeth, now serrated and terrifying, and he emitted a low growl while surveying my body. "I *said*," he met my eyes with a twinkle in his, and vanished before appearing right in front of me. "*Run.*"

I didn't need to get told a third time.

I spun on my heel, and ran back towards my family as fast as I could. I tried to channel Sloan's speed, Keira's stealth, but none of it worked.

The panic built when I heard his footsteps behind me.

He was taunting me.

A predator playing with its prey.

But I wouldn't go down without a fight. One that he looked like he would enjoy immensely before devouring me.

Several moments passed and the sounds of his steps disappeared.

I dared a look behind me, and the white haired demon was gone. Though I knew there weren't any trees directly in my path, I was slammed backward by a surface harder than a tree, and felt more like marble.

After falling on my ass with a grunt, I made the stupid decision of looking up, and regretted it immediately. Why couldn't I have just passed out? Is it too late to play dead?

If it were even possible, a male just as beautiful as the last was staring down at me with... disgust?

I narrowed my eyes as I stood up, refusing to back down even though he was only a few feet from me, holding his hands behind his back in a warrior's stance I knew too well.

With the opportunity to take him in, I nearly stopped breathing. His raven-black hair was braided back in a style like the ancient warriors from across the seas. Eyes of the clearest crystal blue. *Celestine.* His uniform was just like the others, with the sigils removed, doing nothing to cover up the fact that his body was pure muscle. His *very* tall body that had at least three feet on me.

And though he was arguably the most beautiful person I'd ever set eyes on, the hatred in his eyes was pure and unwavering. Like he was looking at the ugliest thing he'd ever seen in his life.

I snorted, looking him up and down. I already ran from someone today, and I wouldn't back down this time. My family was waiting for me, and he was in my way.

A smirk grew on his face as he looked me over, making me bristle.

I dared a step around him, and he once again stepped into my path, not letting me by.

I bared my teeth at him, taking another step, which he followed, daring me to run to my inevitable death if I tried.

Fear and anger coursed its way through me. "Kill me or don't kill me asshole!" I screamed at him like it was my battle cry. The roiling *thing* in my stomach was crying, like a rage threatening to take over.

"You feel that?" He asked, and I didn't know which he was talking about. The pain in my arm, the roiling rage in my stomach, or the fact that I suddenly stopped feeling the need to run away from him. *What the fuck?*

It must be in their magic since I had to be threatened multiple times before running from the previous one.

Nothing about their presence was friendly, and if anything, they were here to slaughter us all.

I guess I was right not to get excited when the veil broke.

Disaster *always* follows in the footsteps of hope.

With that fucking smirk still on his face, he sauntered towards me.

I didn't move.

This must be what panic truly felt like, to give up hope and paralyze yourself until the inevitable happened.

Each time I tried to find the will to run, my body screamed at me to stay, that he wasn't going to hurt me. Was this magic?

He interrupted my thoughts. "It's still inside you."

I raised my brow, revealing nothing. If he knew I was a vessel, that could be why he was here.

"You need to purge it if you want to survive," he said while looking me over again, pissing me the fuck off.

"By survive, you mean against the world, or you?"

He smiled then, and it wasn't friendly. "Both."

My mouth opened and closed when he took the last few steps to be right in front of me. He smelled of pine that I didn't hate, which I ignored.

He stared down at me like I was a mere bug, and I was ready to hit him for it. Nevermind the fact that I would have to jump to reach his face.

He snarled. "We don't have time to waste." He didn't let me question it before his large arm wrapped around my waist. We moved at a speed I couldn't track or decipher *how* he was moving or if he was just flying.

I bit down the yelp, but couldn't hold back the gasp.

He brought me into the sky, that I could now see. The horizon I'd only seen drawings of, it was right in front of me. And across the fields, I saw my army nearing the end to their victory.

He whispered in my ear, making me jump. "Look further away." And he pointed, leaning down at my level so I could see it. My eyes rounded in fear.

An army was headed this way. An army from outside the curse, which meant they all had their powers. And even though our cage had been broken, my body hadn't released the power.

There were hundreds of them, enough to slaughter us all within an hour. I couldn't make out their faces, their sigils, anything recognizable. But I knew malice when I saw it. I felt it when this asshole looked at me.

I shivered when his finger pulled my hair behind my ear, and I felt his face lean down to whisper. "In just a few minutes, all of your people are going to die."

"Is this your doing? Is this your way of torture before you kill me?"

He chuckled loudly. "No, you little battle *princess*." I didn't like the way he enunciated princess. "This is my way of ensuring your obedience."

I growled, slowly turning my head to face him.

He was smiling. "I could always order my men to return home, instead of helping you."

"And how in the *fucking* hell do you plan on helping me?" I nearly spat at him. I wanted to punch that fucking smirk off his perfect face.

"I can get that pesky little power out of you."

"*How?*" I snapped.

He just kept fucking smiling. "Agree to a bargain with me, and you'll find out."

I only stared at him. Bargains weren't something you fucked around with. They were permanent, and bound by magic that would kill you if dishonored. I didn't know which would hurt worse, what he planned to do with me right now, or...

"Oh, don't think it won't hurt, but I'm certain you could handle it."

I didn't like the way he said that. "Who are you? *What* are you?"

His smile faltered. "If it's my name you want, it's

Conláed. As far as what I am, do you always ask questions you already know the answer to?"

My throat bobbed, and I looked to see where my family was. The assassins were nearly eradicated, and they no doubt would come looking for me soon. If Isolde hasn't already.

I shook off the ridiculous thought.

My voice lowered in defeat. "What do I need to do?"

He hummed in thought. "Nothing major, just agree to obey me for as long as I need you to, and I'll do the rest."

I whipped my head towards him. So he wasn't joking, then. "You've got to be out of your fucking mind."

He sneered and grabbed my jaw, forcing me to look back at my family. "You have two options. You agree to my terms, and be ready for whatever I need from you, *whenever* I need you, or we watch as your family gets slaughtered."

I choked down the sob of defeat threatening to explode.

I could do this. As a princess, as a vessel, perhaps this was my destiny after all.

I nodded.

"You need to say it for the binding magic to work."

"I agree to your bargain. To be there for whatever you need from me, and whenever. Just please tell me what I need to do," I choked out.

He chuckled softly, and with his hand still gripped on my face, he pulled me towards him. We were floating in the air, and somehow I didn't need his support from falling. My body turned to face him on its own, which *had* to be a part of this fucking magic.

"You don't have to do anything." Flame flickered in his

eyes when he said that. Actual fire, which I could also see behind his teeth like he was a fucking dragon.

That smirk turned into a vicious sneer before his arm slid around my waist again, pulling my body flush with his. My throat bobbed, which those terrifying eyes tracked. With his large hand still gripping painfully on my jaw, he slammed his mouth against mine.

I felt fire in my mouth.

Actual fire.

A flame that didn't burn as it made its way down my throat and throughout my body. When the fireworks in my core ignited, so did the surreal pain. It spread to the pads of my fingertips, the hair on my scalp, and deep into my bones. Deep where the roiling resided within me.

He wasn't relenting, and I couldn't fight him off if I tried or wanted to. The pain was welcoming with the ferocity of his not-kiss until it became unbearable.

My head shot back as I screamed towards the clear sky I didn't recognize. I felt him pull away when my arms shot out to my sides and my chest heaved.

I was paralyzed with pain. It felt like a physical force was shooting down my limbs, blazing through my skin. Something inside me was growling like it would rise and shove its way out of my chest. Which is exactly what it felt like. Something shoving out of my chest. I taunted death's door and got what I deserved. Liam was right, and that thought alone pissed me off.

I opened my eyes and thought I might faint. Fire was shooting out of me and into the sky. Into the heavens if one could believe such a thing existed. I couldn't look down to assess anymore.

This attack on my body was ultimately out of my control. I just hoped I wasn't murdering innocent lives with it. My skin wasn't burning like it should've, but it was still so painful. I know there are worse ways of dying, but this was fucking awful.

I dared to look down as far as my eyes would allow, and almost passed out.

Fire had poured out of me, exploding and separating in the sky, before cascading down in the direction of where my family was, and behind me towards Kilhorn.

The last of it poured out, and I watched it travel in clouds of flame and shadow towards my people. My family.

The smell was atrocious. Looking down for the source, my eyes widened in fear. Because not only was I hovering in the air above the lake when I didn't know how to swim, but the water was boiling, and I could see crystalized rock glowing from the bottom.

Then my body seized up. Shaking profusely while every muscle cramped together. I felt like I was near caving in on myself, about to pass out from the pain.

A pulse where the roiling used to be, exploded, and the trees around me flew backwards as I fell towards the water.

I heard a monotony of explosions far into the distance, and hoped that was the sound of victory.

I was nearly asleep when I felt someone catch me, carrying me, and I passed out immediately when I was laid onto the hot ground in winter.

CHAPTER THIRTEEN

LIAM, EIGHT YEARS PRIOR

I appeared right behind the male committing the assault. Punching this young girl in the stomach repeatedly while his men held her back.

Minutes prior, she had approached them with her hound after finding them attacking another girl. I roundhouse kicked him to the side of his face, knocking him unconscious. As he fell, the two holding her let go, tripping backward over their feet.

She should've also been afraid. She should've screamed and run away to safety with her friend and hound. Instead, she just looked at me with an impatient expression. Like she thought it had taken me fucking long enough.

Her face as she slowly turned around to face these guys, turning her back to me like I wasn't a threat, was one of a predator. I swore under my breath when I saw her scream while tackling one to the ground.

She didn't even hesitate to consider what these men were capable of. What I might...

What *I* might be... *Holy shit.*

My breathing labored, and I could hear my own heartbeat. I fought the need to vomit violently, realizing I didn't have a fucking clue where I was before this. My brain had become nothing but fog. This was *not* the time to panic. Not when this... *child*, who should be protected, has gone entirely feral on these monsters. I let go of my death grip on my chest and forced myself back to the present.

One attacker had a thirst for blood in his eyes when the dog came back and leaped for him. I didn't act fast enough when that man pulled a dagger and rammed it into that young hound's chest.

When the silence followed the heart-wrenching yelp, I looked back at the feral girl whose copper hair was reddened deeper with blood. She stood, leaving her victim fast asleep behind her.

I couldn't remember why I was here or where I was just moments before. I foolishly let that panic take control at the worst possible moment and let her hound get killed. I felt an irrational need to protect her. I didn't understand it, but my stomach was thrown in disarray at the thought of leaving her defenseless. What is this feeling? What the fuck was happening to me? Why can't I even remember my own god's damned name?

Her scream woke me from my stupor, and my breath caught when I looked at what was before me. She was on top of the male, responsible for her dog's demise, with a blade in her hand. Her face became masked in his blood. She continued her raging scream filled with grief, followed by wet, crunching sounds that were undoubtedly torn flesh and blood.

I watched her blood-soaked face go from rage to complete despair as she slammed the knife into the man's face. I stilled when I saw her golden eyes flicker. There wasn't a sun out here, only dark, unmoving clouds.

I wanted to stop her. I wanted to pull her off the piece of shit and tell her everything would be okay. But I had no right. I didn't even know who the fuck I was, which meant that this child needed to get as far away from me as possible.

I turned to look at the poor hound lying lifeless on the ground. My feet shifted through the grass, and she stood up, gasping for air through the cracked sobs, and then vomited. She slowly crept towards who must have been so dear to her. For the two of them to go from heroes to fighting to keep each other alive, and then to this...

The girl who was attacked first was still laying in the creek, frozen in fear, rendering herself completely fucking useless. Couldn't even be bothered to get up and help her rescuer.

I waited for the hysterics to arrive, but they didn't. The girl whose face was covered in blood just knelt there... staring at the lifeless animal. I had to help. The need was stabbing and burning my insides like a hot poker.

"I'll help you bury her."

"We'll burn her," she said harshly.

I was silent for a moment, but nodded to myself in agreement. "What was its name?"

"Minsi," Her voice was utterly void of life. "It meant Leader of Wolves."

"Beautiful."

We sat there for several uncomfortable moments. I didn't feel sorrow for the animal, but guilt for the part my panic played. If only I'd been paying attention instead of rapidly losing my mind, *that has yet to come back...*

I'll think about that later.

She stood and faced me. She was beautiful in a way you admired a large cat before it ate your face off. The auburn color of her hair was intensified by the blood on it. She angled her head and looked me over, sizing me up to see if I would be her next victim. Something told me I'd rather be buried alive, safely in the ground.

She raised her blood-dripping chin as she spoke. "What is your name?"

My eyes dropped before I could look back at her eyes. She had an authoritative voice for someone so young. One that made you answer even if you didn't want to, but I didn't have one to give.

"If you think to lie to me, I will *strongly* advise you to reconsider." Her hunger for blood had clearly not wavered.

"I don't... I don't have a name," I lied anyway. That didn't sound any better than the truth she wouldn't believe, anyway.

If she knew I was lying, which I'd say she did by her unamused expression, she let it go.

"Whoever you are, I owe you a debt," she announced like there was an audience. *Who is this girl?* I must've thought the question out loud since she gave me a half-smile that didn't reach her eyes.

"I don't have a name," she stated sardonically.

I fought the smirk threatening my face.

She went on, "You'll forgive me if I insist that we get this over with?" I felt my brows furrow in confusion at her coldness. This must be a ruse or a mask she had time to practice. She raised her brows at the words I pushed down.

"Okay."

She took the girl she saved, Maeve was her name, and left me alone to deal with the bodies. Really, I just piled them and prayed no one saw and murdered me, assuming I killed innocents. None of them likely knew me, and this current picture wasn't pretty.

After what felt like hours later, I saw her walking back with another girl around her age. She had blonde hair and a terrifyingly familiar gaze. I wondered if it was because of my presence or if their faces always looked like this.

"Help me build the pyre, Sloan." Her friend Sloan turned to gape at her with resentment. Either for putting her to work or letting me know her name, I couldn't tell which. Considering the intensity of it, probably both.

I silently helped them build a pyre, if that's what you'd call this last-minute mess of twigs and leaves.

I stayed out of the way in silent support as the blood-crusted beast of a girl dipped her knocked arrow into the fire. She whispered something I couldn't understand and launched her arrow. I watched as she stood there as still as death. Watching her pyre burn smoke into the air that was already difficult to breathe. Sloan was behind her, looking like she was giving everything she had to force a mask of coldness.

Several moments later, both girls faced me with looks of promised interrogation.

"You will come with us," they said in unison.

"Okay," I hastily replied. What else should I say or do here when my brain is completely fried? Plus, there was no way I was letting this girl out of my sight. I told myself it was fear of what else she might do with her rage or if she'd have another victim. But there was something profound in my soul with a hot poker threatening me.

She looked me up and down like she contemplated if I was either insane or stupid, then turned on her heel towards the castle. Sloan held her hand out for me to follow, so I did. Then I realized she only let me go before her in case I made any move toward her feral friend. They landed on stupid, then.

Walking through the castle, I noted the beautiful obsidian walls cracking from within, the cracks that were filled with gold, the sickly look on the people's faces, and the suffocatingly thin air around us as if it were running out of oxygen.

Everywhere we walked, across the courtyard, through the halls within the castle, everyone bowed in her presence or avoided her entirely. Sloan was smirking at me, undoubtedly due to my confused expression. This girl was *someone*... Someone walking through the people with her head high despite her current state of appearance.

I thought a silent prayer to whoever the fuck I may have believed in, that I wasn't about to get slaughtered by her or her parents. Or fed to the rest of her dogs...

Men opened two large doors as she approached, and we entered a large room.

Several gathered people wearing fine clothes turned to gape at her. Some looks were not so friendly. There were a few gathered on the dais next to the throne.

On the throne sat a king with short, wavy, auburn hair.
Well, shit.

His eyes widened as he slowly stood, taking in me and the blood on her face, and looked ready to lunge forward to ensure she was okay.

Yep, definitely her father.

He grabbed her shoulders when she reached the dais, looking for injuries. Everyone murmured as he threw her to him in an embrace, letting the blood and mud ruin his regalia.

"I'm okay," she choked out, then he pushed her back in front of him. His hands were still grasped on her shoulders as he took in the state of her appearance.

"Leave us," he ordered the throne room.

I made my way to follow when I heard him clear his throat. "Not *you*."

I turned slowly and found Sloan smirking at me.

He demanded she explain. She hadn't left out a single detail, not even when the men held her arms while getting punched repeatedly. This man's eyes were of pure fury and fear. I knew I did nothing wrong, but I still didn't want to be here while the king heard his daughter was assaulted and that I was there.

"He saved me," she snarled to the ground.

Um, you're welcome?

Sloan snorted. They must be close. Sisters, maybe.

The King turned his head and strode towards me with purpose. He stopped not three feet away, staring down at me with a familiar expression. He seemed to be staring into my soul, knowing exactly who I was and everything about me.

"Please don't misunderstand her as ungrateful. The Princess never even let me tie her bootlaces as a small child." I suppressed a smile at that, but remained silent as he continued.

"I owe you a debt. You saved my daughter, my heir, and my only child. What is your name?"

Fuck.

"He doesn't have one," the princess interjected as she crept towards us. The King frowned at me, considering.

"You don't have a name?" he asked, waiting for the absurdity I was about to explain that he saw coming. I sighed.

"Something is... wrong... with me. I'm not sure when it happened, but my memories are completely gone," I replied, while staring at the floor in shame.

I heard another set of footsteps walking this way, surely to gawk at the freak show.

It was Sloan's voice. "Many people are sick these days. Some are suffering from mental traumas as well. It's not totally implausible that he could be suffering the same."

"He doesn't look sick." He appeared like he already knew the answers. "Look at me," he demanded with an edge.

I obeyed. He stared for a few moments, then lifted his chin, preparing to make some declaration. The bloodied beast had to have learned it from somewhere, after all.

"Do you have the slightest idea of where your... *family*... might be? Where you might live?"

I dared a glance to the ground before slowly shaking my head once.

"Marcus!" he called out before a large man in armor came in. "Have them prepare an empty room for the young man, and baths for both of them. As wonderful as it would be to see the court's faces when they see their future queen bathed in the blood of her enemies," I could hear the smile in the King's voice. "I'd rather not smell brain matter during dinner."

"Yes, your grace." And the sound of armor clanking together left the room. I felt like a rabbit in a wolf's den.

He turned towards his daughter, who was smirking at my discomfort. "Áine,"

Áine...

My stomach sank. Lightning shot through my body like hearing her name was an Amen.

So be it.

This wasn't a romantic feeling. This felt like a newfound duty. Maybe I wasn't ever a boy, just something made this morning, sent here with a purpose.

This lunatic of a girl was sure to get into more danger. And if this king would allow it, I would be Áine's protection. If I hadn't been there before she was inevitably raped and murdered, I would likely be living outside in the woods with the possibility of a similar end.

I panicked at the worst possible moment, and this girl lost her little bodyguard. One that was undoubtedly gifted to her by her father to keep her safe when she defiantly wandered wherever the hell she wanted. Their arguing interrupted my revelation, pulling me out of my head.

"Please allow me to stay here." My voice cracked as I failed to not sound desperate.

Áine narrowed her eyes at me with a look I could only

take as irritation. The King's expression hadn't wavered. Like he had expected that question to fall from my mouth.

"I'm not going to have collectors in the middle of the night demanding your head, am I?" he mused.

"If they do, grant it. I am nobody," I assured him.

There was a painfully long silence after that, too long.

"Liam," he called, but no one came.

"It means protector."

My narrowed eyes went wide.

"You will live here, Liam, where I can keep an eye on you. You will train to be a soldier, where you *will* earn your keep and protect my daughter with your life." He was serious... And he was smiling.

I fought the threatening tears of gratitude for not having to sleep outside. Of not being a *nobody*.

"Thank you, your grace." One tear escaped, and the King's smile nearly became warm.

I had no idea where I was from or who sent me here, but this felt like fate. Áine may not appreciate me watching over her and protecting her. She might even hate me for it.

But when I heard my new name, I no longer cared about anything before today. I had a purpose, and she'd have to get over it.

So be it.

CHAPTER
FOURTEEN

ISOLDE, PRESENT DAY

What else should I have expected of her?

I swore vehemently at her, cutting down assassin after assassin. Protecting the king to ensure she didn't lose her father, knowing firsthand how that felt.

Why did I bother to do everything in my power for her happiness? I'm an idiot, that's why. She has become everything to me, and I hated it.

Though each night when I'm desperate to hold her, I'm fleeing before that thought costs me my heart. Before I stayed, before I asked, and then the bitch ripped my heart out.

I screamed, taking my frustrations out on the now dead soldier. Alaric narrowed his eyes at me for a moment, but something flashed in my peripherals.

Everyone froze when we saw it, even the assassins.

A hole in the veil, *burning*.

My eyes widened at the sight, at the screaming coming from the shadows above it, the source of the fire.

As if the veil had a heartbeat, it pulsed power downward, blowing smoke toward us. I choked on it, trying to cover my eyes while also trying to see what was happening.

I gasped when that hole burst open wide, and fire spread across the entirety of the poisonous dome.

Tears were running down my face in hope. Hope that we made it, that we finally have a future worth living for, worth seeking out.

Hissing ensued from in front of us while we all stared at the fire.

When I looked down, my eyes rounded in fear. Though I felt no power growing within me, none of that magic we were supposed to have, the assassins had grown in height. Shadows emerged from within their robes.

Their confidence grew, even though they were outnumbered a hundred to one.

And then the earth shuddered. A low tremor that rumbled until it quaked beneath our feet.

I crouched to remain balanced, lest one of these shadow bastards decided to come after me. Could I even defend myself?

I didn't have a choice, because one was charging for me.

I stayed in a crouching position, maintaining my balance while he effortlessly ran over it.

I decided to use it to my advantage, even though this move would likely kill me.

With both swords, I staggered my right foot forward. I

flipped my sword hilts, so the blades pointed behind me. And when the rumble threatened to knock me to the ground, I slid my left foot around.

With my back now to my enemy, I drove both swords up.

My breath staggered out of me when they made purchase, and he slumped to the ground.

I'm never doing that again.

Looking up, there was only sky. No veil.

Tears ran down my face, and it wasn't just from the smoke surrounding us like shadows.

At least I would've seen it before I died.

I rotated my swords back, ready to attack another, and heard an explosion from behind us.

Alaric and I both turned in that direction where Áine had taken off, when we were knocked down from the aftershock.

Struggling to my feet, hands still on the ground for support, fire once again filled the sky. It came soaring through the sky, and then down towards us in ribbons.

"No," Alaric breathed. A panicked look overcame his face.

"What is th—" I was cut off when fire shot down Alaric's throat, and held him up off the ground.

I turned, and watched as fire shot into me like lightning. The pain...

It burned me, all the way down. Burned, but didn't destroy.

It conquered my body, making me a slave to it.

Perhaps this was it. There are certainly worse ways to die than having your body burned by ancient magic.

I closed my eyes, accepting whatever fate this led me to, but then I collapsed to the ground.

My arms and legs felt like they were being pulled apart. And in between the groans of pain, I gasped when I saw Alaric in the sky.

And then I heard it.

The multitude of voices from far away, the chants and the songs of battle.

I didn't get the chance to see what was coming for us when Alaric erupted. Fire exploded from his body in waves, headed towards whatever threat was coming.

I shouldn't have, but I ran into the forest.

If our power came back, which I knew it did based on the speed of my sprints, then that meant something happened to Áine.

I fell down multiple times, and swore when Alaric ran past me.

It was one thing for me to abandon them. I didn't matter.

I couldn't go back.

I got back up and kept running. Kept following that tug on my instincts, focusing all of my senses on searching for her, and there she was.

I found her beside the lake that was now clear, and a circle of embers and ashes surrounded her. She had somehow looked taller, with pointy ears and sharper features.

I stepped towards her, reaching down to pull her up and take her home.

Whatever you need from me.

I stilled.

I heard her voice, like a muffled sentence that was too loud, but not loud enough for others to hear.

My body started to shake with fear, and I stepped back. That better not have been in my fucking head...

Twigs snapped, and I looked towards Alaric now walking up, staring me down with confusion, like he didn't understand how I could've found her first.

I didn't either.

I accept the bargain.

I didn't want to.

CHAPTER
FIFTEEN

DAMIEN

High up above the tree canopy, I watched Con as he gently placed her on the dirt, and disappeared.

I waited a moment longer, listening to her heartbeat to make sure it didn't slow down. With the amount of blood smothering her, she looked like she died several times already, and he still kissed her.

He'll spin it and say it wasn't a kiss, which maybe technically it wasn't, but I knew already that he didn't have to make any physical contact for it to work. Stubborn bastard.

The girl I frequently saw the Princess with in secret, had run up to her, which meant Alaric wasn't too far away.

Which meant I needed to get far away and fast.

I would've disappeared at that moment, if not for the girl's body trembling in fear.

Their scents were mixed, which was to be expected, but I wondered…

That girl looked at the Princess like she loved her.

I gritted my teeth and shook off the itch, like a burning sensation in my gut. I could give a fuck less who the little shit fucked in her spare time. She'd better enjoy it while she can.

I sensed Alaric's power nearing and vanished, appearing back at the palace in the valley.

Con sat slumped over in the study holding an empty glass.

I chuckled. "Drak brought the soldiers back to the village, right before you had your little fun."

"I don't know what you're talking about."

He answered that so immediately that I laughed. "You could've just transferred your power through the air, rather than looking like you wanted to fuck her in the sky."

He raised his head, looking exhausted. "I wouldn't have done that under *normal* circumstances. It was a moment of weakness."

I raised my chin, feeling the need to poke the bear, because why not? "She may already be spoken for,"

Almost too quietly to catch, he growled, *"no,* she isn't."

"Because I was patrolling the night she went to bed with that girl and Liam."

Too slowly, that information resonated with him before he faced me, looking like was going to murder someone.

I laughed and disappeared to my treehouse. The one I crafted for all of us to retreat to, but was mine to play in. He could brood all he wanted, but I preferred a different way of relieving my frustrations.

Currently in the main living area, I grabbed a quartz decanter from the bar cart, and poured me a knuckle's worth of bourbon under the fae lights. They floated in each room, slowly bobbing around to give a relaxing effect.

The walls, the floors, all of this was made by my magical control over the branches and roots of the earth. A talent I was teased for as a child, and then later feared for what I could do with them.

A feminine gasp sounded from the other room while I took a drink, and then swirled its contents before knocking the rest back. Not to get drunk. Never before what I was about to do.

With casual steps, I strolled to the room, passed by Lira who was now suspended in the air by my branches, and flipped my trunk open. I surveyed my options, tossing a few onto the foot of the bed.

I paused when I saw she picked a few for herself. She went into my trunk without my permission.

I clicked my tongue twice before putting the *nice* toy with its soft tresses back into the trunk, and grabbed the one she hated instead. After today, the beast within me felt a renewed lust for blood.

I turned to face her then. Her eyes were rounded with fear for what I swapped.

"Oh I see. You thought your little disobedience would get you the punishment you liked?"

Her throat bobbed, but she didn't look at me. She only stared at the object she hated, the act she never listed as a hard limit, but she wouldn't. Not when the reward was one she loved above all else.

A smile split across my face, one that I knew terrified her.

My teeth must have caught her attention, now serrated, and she trembled deliciously. Goosebumps spread across her creamy skin covered in runes, now glowing a hue of blue from the effect this had on her.

My first step towards her made her tense. When I reached behind her for the end of her braid, she flinched.

I spoke while removing the hair band. "How about we play a game? You obviously like playing games, don't you?" She kept quiet, following the rules of the current game in hopes I'd go easy on her.

We'll see.

I ran my fingers over the silky braid that threatened to undo themselves. Her hair normally was smooth and straight. It would only take a handful of sudden movements before the braid was completely undone.

"You make it through a five-bar gate without undoing your braid," I ran a finger across the side of her face, more threatening than affectionate. "And I'll reward you with the *nice* toy."

Her bottom lip trembled, like she had decided already that she couldn't do it.

I chuckled, turning to grab the cane. "Say the word, and I'll free you." Knowing full well she wouldn't.

She didn't say a word when I faced her. I held her gaze

looking for any sign this would end terribly for her, but then I saw the slightest curve of her mouth. The slightest smirk to let me know she was ready for it.

"*Good girl.*"

CHAPTER
SIXTEEN

ÁINE

I awoke to muffled familiar voices, unable to open my eyes.

My mothers voice became loud and clear. Now I didn't want to open them.

My father's voice crooned. "We know you're faking it."

I sighed, or that's what I meant to do. What I actually did was raggedly spew coughs and groans that struggled to push out air.

My voice was hoarse. "What the fuck..."

Visha tilted her head in that creepy analytical way. "Your body is cleaning out the toxins. Everyone's already thrown—"

She was interrupted by me vomiting on the floor beside the bed. Or rather into a waste basket I didn't expect to be there.

"Thrown up... at least once," She finished.

I heaved, in and out, struggling to catch my breath.

"Amazing how clean air can be difficult to breathe when you haven't in such a long time."

I looked at Visha, inspecting me like an experiment. She didn't look any different.

"As a druid, my magic is of the earth. I likely won't have the magic I used to until the land has been replenished fully, which could be some time. So in the meantime," she straightened, glancing at my parents. My mother had silent tears and eyes filled with panic, which worried me. "I don't have the powers to heal you properly. You'll need to rest and allow your fae body to heal itself. I have ointments and some tinctures but, I'm scared to use any of them on you."

I looked up at her in confusion. "Why?"

"*Why?*" I heard my mother's voice crack. "You should be asking how in the hell you're alive?"

The words were harsh, but the eyes were panicked. What did she know that I didn't?

I rubbed my chest with my palm, trying to loosen the tightening I felt since waking up.

My father stepped closer. "What's wrong with her?"

I rolled my eyes. "I'm capable of answering a question. And I don't know. There's pressure here. Not quite painful but definitely not pleasant." And it continued to get tighter and tighter…

Visha looked dumbfounded, but my parents exchanged a look I didn't understand. I was getting sick of their secrets.

I jolted at the sound of the door to Visha's healing cottage being kicked open.

My throat bobbed when Isolde stormed in with tears on her face that was contorted with rage. She was still in her fighting leathers, and looking so fucking stunning I wanted to die. How did she know I was awake?

"I DON'T KNOW WHAT IN THE HELL YOU WERE THINKING TAKING OFF LIKE A FUCKING MARTYR LIKE THAT, BUT YOU SCARED THE FUCKING HELL OUT OF ME ÁINE!"

She was now standing at the edge of the bed, screaming at me. I nodded in agreement with her reaction, sort of, but then glanced over to my parents.

Isolde turned towards them and gasped in surprise.

Their brows were raised, likely at her audacity to speak with me like that. Or they were confused about why she would care that much. Wouldn't a captain normally freak out over their commander doing stupid shit?

Her cheeks were stained red with embarrassment. She turned on her heel and bolted out of the room.

I tried to force myself up to go after her, but I struggled and was too slow. Visha pushed me back down. "THAT can wait. You are in no condition to move around right now."

I didn't like the way she said *that*, and I especially didn't like the implications that seemed to be written on my parents face.

I said nothing in response to their expressions. No matter how I answered, it would be a lie, or a truth they really didn't want to hear.

I swallowed down saliva, desperate for my throat to not be so painfully dry. "Carsen got away."

"*How?*" My father's voice was cold.

"I'm not sure. But when I was fighting them in the woods, when the veil burned, he disappeared. Abandoning his men too."

My father shook his head in disbelief. "Carsen, the hybrid *thing*, and the witch ran away? From you?"

I blinked slowly, preparing myself mentally for this conversation. "No. Not from me."

My father nodded, like he already knew the answer, but how could he? "Who?"

"I don't know."

His eyes narrowed. "What did they look like?"

They. "Tall. Unnaturally tall." And terrifying... "They wore armor that bore no sigils, but looked elven. Like the sigils may have been scraped off."

My mother sighed and turned her back to me to face the wall.

"There were many of them, but I only got one name," I looked at my father before I spoke. "Conláed."

My mother swore under her breath, and my father's eyes flickered with fire. Fire that burned mostly blue.

"How do you know him?"

"What did he want?" He ignored my question.

Not that I wanted to answer him, but the words refused to come out.

"WHAT DID HE WANT?"

"To talk!" I lied.

He snorted, like he knew it too.

"He didn't say when, but that he'd be coming back soon. I'm sure it's to speak with you. About what, I have no idea."

I had an idea, but I wasn't mentally prepared for that conversation yet.

"But we need to go get Carsen. We have power now, and the cult's numbers must be little. We need to go now, give Keira the justice she deserves, and be done with it."

"You are not going anywhere," Visha instructed. "Not until at least tomorrow."

I sighed, and then wondered why in the hell my mother was so silent. She kept looking at me like she couldn't believe what she was looking at. What else was she expecting?

My father put his hand on her shoulder before ordering, "Rest up, and we'll go tomorrow."

My mother shook out of his grasp and stormed out of the room. We both looked at the door in confusion.

He slowly turned, facing me. "We need to go and ensure stability in the land while the others prepare for war." Words likely meant for my mother.

"Others? Who else?"

He looked at me gravely. "Everyone."

CHAPTER
SEVENTEEN

CONLÁED

The smell of blood and sweat filled the dining room, our unofficial space to hold meetings.

Immediately after freeing the Dhadren, I met here with my other commanders and Lira. Her nose was initially buried beneath her tunic, clearly not used to the smells of battle. Perhaps soon she would get used to it, at least enough to show the fuckers in this room, my most trusted companions, that females had a place at these meetings.

I grasped my wrist behind my back. A warrior's stance it may have been, but what they didn't realize was that I was gripping my wrist so hard to remain upright with my shoulders square. The pain hadn't gone away, and likely wouldn't for a while.

Most wouldn't have lived to tell the tale of suffering at the grasp of an ancient's power. I wouldn't have lived if I wasn't also a demon, but that didn't mean it didn't come with consequences. I only hoped it would be a short-term hindrance.

Damien leaned against the far wall with his arms crossed, smirking like he knew. Alastair trudged into the room, practically throwing his helm onto the table. Soren sat beside him, but not before smacking him upside the back of his head for his rudeness.

I cleared my throat. "Please, everyone sit down."

I waited until each of their eyes were focused on their chairs before sitting down, struggling to keep the grimace of pain off my face.

Damien and Drak didn't miss it, but thankfully said nothing.

I leaned back in my seat at the head of the table, opposite Drak, whom everyone expected to lead, including myself. But alas, here we were. He'd better be ready if a certain throne becomes available, because there was no way in hell that I was ever sitting on it.

"This is a different kind of war, gentlemen, lady," I nodded at Lira who sat beside Damien, ignoring him. It was likely an assurance that she didn't sit by Alastair. "Everywhere we go, we are surrounded by enemies, just for being what we are. What we are about to do, what we've *been* doing, working towards these past two decades, it all comes down to this."

Lira spoke first. "Is she not also, are *they* not also hated for being what they are?"

I raised my brow at the sudden topic change, wondering where in the hell she was going with this.

It was Søren who answered her. "They earned that

hatred. We have done nothing except having been created."

"Debatable, but she is only twenty-five years old. Why is *she* the supposed enemy?"

Damien smirked, raising his brows to everyone here while he kept quiet and listened. A tense silence loomed over them from her words, like they disagreed but didn't have a solid argument for it.

And because I didn't want any of the males in here to give any reason for Lira to no longer attend these meetings, "You have a point, but it doesn't change the fact that I just forced her to make a bargain. She will see us as her damnation, which will ensure her hatred towards us. The fact that we are her people's salvation will keep war away, but it doesn't change how our relationship started."

Drak's too-deep voice reverberated throughout the room. "But it had to be done."

"Yes, it did," I agreed.

She mumbled quietly. "I still don't understand why you had to go about it this way."

"Because there isn't a single thing I won't do to ensure our people are safe, and that we get the rest of our people out of that shithole we grew up in. That is a promise I made to you all long ago, and if being the bad guy is what I have to be to do it, then so be it." *Amen,* the word for it from Damien's native lands clanged through my head.

Lira sighed in defeat. "Fine. Then what will you have me do?"

Damien finally spoke up. "Right now? Nothing. You are here to learn."

She sneered at him, earning a smirk and his attention

turned away from her. I internally shook my head at them. Whatever works, I guess.

Alastair crossed his arms. "Our men need to rest before any other ventures, Con. Even if they only sparred with each other to keep the appearance of an elven army coming, they're exhausted. The veil erupting affected all of us. And we barely escaped in time before Alaric almost decimated us."

"Stop being a lazy piece of shit," Søren chastised, earning a smile and shoulders shaking from Lira.

Alastair eyed Søren incredulously. "Don't sit there and pretend with your *big boy energy*," he mocked with a very immature facial expression, "that you're not fucking drained right now."

Søren angled his head at Alastair, his short black hair fell across his tan skin, looking more related to me than Drak did. He looked like he was going to embarrass him with his next words, but decided it wasn't worth the energy.

Alastair fumed, and then looked at me expectantly.

"The princess will need at least a day to rest regardless. Take advantage of it until tomorrow. I will pay her a visit tonight to ensure she's recovering and ready when we need her."

Damien raised his brow. "And if her lover is there when you visit?" He was taunting me, but I snarled in response. I said nothing to his bullshit that didn't warrant a response. He chuckled under his breath.

Drak raised his chin. "You've been able to mask your scent and trace in the past, but what about now with her powers awakened? Do you think Alaric will find out now?"

Søren asked, "Find out what?"

Alastair lowered his chin. "You know... that—"

"That she's my fucking mate?" I cut him off, unintentionally with enough disdain in my voice to be anything but curious to others. "It's possible. But if he *does* sense that, he would know better than to kill me and that tether, risking her sanity. A piece of shit he may be, but his wife and daughter seem to be the only thing he cares about."

"And you?" Drak pressed.

I met his eyes for a moment before answering. "I will keep her safe to ensure my *own* sanity isn't at risk if she dies. Also, with her being a vessel, we have no idea what her death would lead to, or which ancient would take over her life force. As long as she is protected, Alaric will see a reason to remain on our side. That is, if we can convince him and his fucking council in the first place."

Søren mumbled. "Some of the worst fucking people I've ever met in my life..."

Everyone grunted in agreement.

"And what of Liam?" Damien asked.

I nodded. "We need to extract him without the others knowing. Unfortunately, it was he who was our expert in that."

Drak snorted. "That's even if he'll come willingly."

Pain shot up my spine, making it almost impossible not to cringe. "Get some rest, everyone," I said abruptly to them before vanishing to my room.

I practically fell onto my chair, gripping my chest while keeping my breath steady.

I growled at the arrival of Damien, now leaning against my door.

"How much pain are you in?" he asked with a sadistic smile.

"Enough," I answered honestly.

He snorted. "You think she's in any better shape?"

"No. I doubt she'll be conscious for a while."

"I'm going to check in on her tonight."

I looked at him in surprise, then brushed it off. "Do what you want."

He smiled again. "I'll remember you said that when I visit her room."

"You will do *no* such thing," I ordered.

He strolled further into my room, stopping at the window to look out at the valley. "That's the thing Con, you can't actually demand that of me, can you?"

I fought the growl building. "In all this time, I have never pulled rank with you."

"And you won't start now," he said coldly, not bothering to look me in the eyes. "You think you're the only one fighting it? Get over yourself."

He vanished before I could say anything, and I swore loudly before slumping into the chair and falling fast asleep.

CHAPTER
EIGHTEEN

ÁINE

An hour after my father and Visha left me alone, after staring at my bed covers the whole time, I jumped at the sound of the door being opened.

Maeve and Sloan walked in. Followed by Keira and Liam, who still... My eyes narrowed. Keira was taller than Liam. He didn't change.

"What's going on?"

Maeve and Sloan sat on the bed beside me. Sloan leaned back against the headboard like she would rather nap than be a part of the conversation.

Liam cleared his throat. "We're not exactly sure. So if you'd keep the tiny male jokes to yourself, I've gotten enough hell for it since we got back."

I didn't doubt it. Keira rested her hand on his shoulder, which he shook off. We both exchanged a knowing look, biting our cheeks to hide the amusement. Males and their fragile egos...

I cleared my throat, and gave Keira a serious look. "We head for their castle tomorrow." I saw the emotion flicker in her eyes, and then gone in an instant. I smirked. "Does it feel good?"

She answered like a cold soldier. "I'll be satisfied when the job is done."

I nodded, not having an answer to that.

"Care to tell us what happened?" Maeve asked, and maybe I was defensive, but it sounded awfully accusatory. Sloan was still off in her own mind, pretending to ignore us entirely.

I cleared my throat, and then found smoothing the blanket more interesting before speaking. "What part would you like to know?"

Liam's voice was harsh. "The part where you took off by yourself and somehow made it out without being slaughtered, or maybe the part where you fucking exploded in the sky."

I fisted the blankets, not wanting to tell them or anyone what I agreed to. How I'm now at the end of a fucking leash to a stranger. "An army I didn't recognize appeared in the forest and killed all of Carsen's men, right after he disappeared."

I could feel their eyes staring a hole into my head. "And then another one of their soldiers gave me a birds-eye view of the approaching elven army that would've torn you all apart. So he helped me before that could happen."

"Out of the goodness of his heart?" Maeve looked like she was ready to yell, per usual. I appreciated having another who understood me in that manner, but then there were times like these when I wished she would just shut the fuck up.

I slowly blinked, letting loose a breath I'd been holding, "That's not something I wish to discuss right now."

Suddenly, a *very* pissed off Maeve stood, towering over me menacingly.

"You going to beat up someone wounded?"

Maeve was looking at me harshly, and whispered, "She took off after you, you know." My throat bobbed. "She was the one who found you."

I didn't need her to clarify. "Where is she?"

She shrugged. "That's not something I wish to discuss right now."

I rolled my eyes and refused to meet hers anymore. Liam was staring at me in confusion. Like my mother had. That shock in her eyes...

I refused to look in the direction of Maeve storming out, forcing myself not to flinch when she slammed the door behind her.

Liam's voice broke the tense silence. "What did he want from you?"

I shook my head. "Nothing truly important. I'm pretty sure it was them who burned down the veil. If anything, we have a new ally."

Rage flickered in his eyes. "If it's not important then why aren't you telling anyone?"

I hardened my expression, looking at them both. "Dismissed."

Liam's eyes widened, and looked ready to throttle me. Pulling rank wasn't something I did with them, but they couldn't know. I didn't break eye contact during his bullshit stare-down contest. It was Keira who grabbed his arm, and led him out of the room.

Feet shifted, and I looked over to see Sloan was getting comfortable in the bed, swinging her feet crossed at the ankle from side to side. I shook my head at her. At least someone was done interrogating me.

I sighed in relief.

"Oh, don't think you're safe yet."

"Mother..." I clenched my fists and glanced at the ceiling, praying to whatever gods may still be out there. "Everything fucking hurts. Can I just please get some rest?"

She snorted. "*No.*" I looked over at her, and she was examining her nails like she'd been waiting for this conversation. "You're going to tell me now that everyone is gone."

I rested my head back, on the headboard. "I don't want to talk about it, Sloan. I still have yet to decipher how fucked I am."

The silence was deafeningly loud.

"You did something stupid, didn't you?" she whispered, barely audible. And I worried who might be listening from outside the room.

So I whispered back while staring at the ceiling, "Yep."

CHAPTER NINETEEN

ISOLDE

I hadn't broken a sweat since I started running from Visha's cottage. Being near Áine was dangerous, but her family knowing about us was worse.

I'd known her mother and father were mated, and even if it was only Alaric's power that was that of legends, only someone equal in power could become his mate, and the queen hated me.

I ran past the people in the castle, away from that pull, towards the menacing aura surrounding Visha's old cellar.

Inside would be the most ancient tomes, deemed unsafe to be placed in the grand library for anyone to read. Surely one of them had knowledge on how to be free of it, because I needed to leave. I felt the need to do so more than ever now. To run as far away from her as possible.

I nearly knocked the doors off their hinges upon opening them, and gasped in horror when I stepped inside.

Each of the hundred or more candles in the cellar lit up with flame.

Footsteps sounded behind me, followed by the sound of dress skirts brushing against the stone floor of the cellar.

Visha stepped around me, and then turned to face me curiously.

"Did you do that?" I whispered to her.

"I don't have any magic yet, so no," she answered, and then proceeded to look at me like she was discovering a new creature. "Do you know what your parents were? What kind of magic they held?"

I shook my head. "No. I was young when they died."

"Who were your parents?" she asked.

"Ivaylo and Sigrid Mavros."

Visha hummed, pondering. "I have no idea who they are, Isolde Mavros."

"You wouldn't. We were poor."

"Poor they may have been, but they created a captain, one who now lights candles when she enters a room."

I said nothing, channeling Áine to see if she'd get to the point.

"I will look into your family, to see if I can find some answers for you."

I nodded in gratitude, ready to leave.

"Don't you want to know why I'm doing this for you?"

I shrugged. "So I don't burn all of your candles?" I didn't want to know.

She smiled. "Your soul smells like roses and red wine."

I felt my throat bob on its own accord. "That makes sense."

"Does it?" She was inching uncomfortably close to me.

After the awkward silence threatened to drag on, I turned around and went to leave.

"You came here for a reason," she said. It wasn't a question.

I stopped walking, but I didn't turn around. "I need information."

"Aah. Too bad the information you seek doesn't exist."

I whipped around, looking at her questioningly. "No magic, you say?"

She smiled. "Come see me again soon."

I turned on my heel and left, and I wouldn't stop no matter what creepy thing she said next.

She called out after me. "I'll find you if I find any information on your family."

As I kept walking, I heard the unmistakable sound of a beast snarling, and I ran.

CHAPTER
TWENTY

ÁINE

I t was several hours later that Visha's door was once again kicked in, and I thanked the gods because I was losing my mind in here.

I took it back when Maeve walked in, not wanting to fight with her anymore. She came by herself, so I braced myself for impact.

"HEY!" she shouted at me.

My face blanked in surprise and confusion. She was standing maybe ten feet away from me but found the need to shout.

"I'm sorry for being an ass!" she shouted again, like this was her first time apologizing, or speaking.

I huffed a laugh. "You have nothing to be sorry for."

She nodded. "Good." and stalked over to the side of my bed. "Because we need to go." and then proceeded to grab my boots.

"Where? And Why? You know what, I don't care. Get me out of here."

She smiled. "I thought you'd say that. Now come on! You don't want to miss this."

I shuffled on my pants and then boots, tripping more times than I wanted to admit before she came over and held me up for support.

"Hurry!" She whisper-yelled.

A giggle escaped me when I put on my cloak, and she echoed.

"Shh! Visha will be back soon." She stood still, staring at nothing.

"What are you doing?"

"Listening."

Oh! I forgot we could do that, and a giggle escaped me again. There were no familiar voices, or the sound of Visha incoming, so we opened the door and snuck into the courtyard.

I gasped loudly when we made it outside. The sun was beaming above us in a blue sky. I had to shade my eyes, still not acclimated to this level of brightness.

She smacked me when I started giggling again, halfway through the gardens. "We want to actually make it there, if you'd shut the fuck up."

"Where is there?"

"It's a surprise."

"I'll literally know in a few minutes. Just tell me."

"Do you even know what surprise means?"

"Do you? Because I'm not even wearing a blindfold."

She turned towards me like she was debating it.

"Hey. I got hurt but I can still kick your ass."

She smiled and shook her head, and then grabbed my arm. "We're going to run, ok? Can you run?"

I shrugged. "Like RUN run, or normal run?"

She sighed. "Your NEW normal run. Try it."

We were so close to the main gate, but there were several others who would take notice and send word.

I tried, and fell on my face halfway there, for every citizen and guard to see. Maeve had run up to my side, lifting me by my arm and I limped beside her out of the gate.

"Open it!" I shouted with the confidence of a commander being crouched over like my back had given out.

The guard by the gate shook his head like I was an idiot and opened it for us.

We stepped out into the fields surrounding Kilhorn, and I stilled.

The ground had growing patches of green, and the forest was no longer a graveyard of trees.

Maeve pulled on my arm. "Come on, this isn't it. Are you really going to limp the whole way?"

"Fuck off," I failed to bite out with the frozen look of shock I could feel on my face.

Several minutes passed before we got close and she told me to close my eyes. I could feel a breeze get stronger and stronger the further we walked, and I grew excited knowing we were headed to the cliffs.

"Open your eyes Áine!" Maeve shouted.

I opened my eyes to an ocean that was blue! Motherfucking BLUE! Not black as death, not filled with poison, but blue! When the waves crashed, it was white, not grey. And the sun was beginning to set over the water, creating a warm atmosphere that felt like a hug, despite it being the end of winter.

I bit my cheek hard, but it didn't stop the tears that fell. How could I have missed something this much when I don't remember ever meeting it?

I barely even noticed that near the edge of the cliff, Liam, Keira, and Sloan had been building a fire and were drinking around it. Well, Liam and Keira were building it. Sloan was laying back with her wine and watching the ocean waves.

"Where's Isolde?" I asked them.

Maeve's mouth flattened. "She's not coming."

I nodded through the disappointment.

She put her hand on my shoulder and urged me forwards. "Come on. We're going to drink, burn shit, and watch the first sunset."

Sloan and Keira were perfectly content in quietly observing, per usual. It was Liam who handed me a glass of amber liquid. "Cheers Áine, to our... to all of our futures."

I clinked my glass with his and brushed off his choice of words I didn't particularly like. Keira gave him a dirty look over her shoulder before looking back to the ocean.

I inhaled deeply, catching the salty scent of what the ocean is supposed to smell like.

Noises sounded from the castle, and we all stopped and turned towards it.

People were starting to flood out of the gates at a leisurely pace.

I tried focusing my listening, and heard the unmistakable sounds of excitement and cheering.

"Are they *all* coming out here?" Sloan complained, never having been a people person.

A wind gusted by me suddenly, and then my parents appeared beside us out of nowhere.

"Holy shit!" I clutched my chest. "How did you do that?"

"How are *you* out of bed?" my mother demanded.

"I stood up and walked out of bed. Walked all the way here even. Drink?" Would you call it antagonizing? Sure. Maybe. But why couldn't she just have fun?

She stepped forward and stole my glass before shouldering past me.

My mouth rounded in surprise. "Rude!" I shouted at her retreating form.

My father went to follow her. "Glad you're up and about. But try not to pick a fight on such a special occasion," he pleaded.

"Fine." I was still smiling anyway. Everywhere I looked, there was beauty. And best of all, our people were smiling as well.

Hope may have been a dangerous thing in the past, but we made it. It really happened. I freed our people, just like I promised.

Whenever I need you.

Conláed's words replayed in my head. I only hoped that it wouldn't be anytime soon.

CHAPTER
TWENTY-ONE

DAMIEN

I came out here to check on Liam. What I didn't expect was to see him surrounded by a handful of fae female soldiers, and they were all wasted.

I caught them running from the cliffs, away from the gathering of hundreds of Dhadren watching their first sunset in twenty years. I say running loosely, because the little princess ate the dirt several times, laughing and pulling everyone down when they tried to pull her up.

I couldn't understand a single word any of them said in between the wheezing.

I noted the girl from before wasn't with them.

"You're embarrassing yourself!" Liam barked at her, only making her laugh harder. *"If I beat you there, I get to wear your commander's pin for training tomorrow."*

Her smile dramatically transitioned to disbelief. One of them, blonde and scary looking, yanked her to her feet and shoved her forward. Liam took off after her, even though he knew he'd lose.

With a loud smack, she tripped and fell on her face again. I nearly shouted at her for not protecting her face, and then bit onto my fist to stop the laughter. Her friends, however, were dying from it.

Liam won.

With no powers, and the speed of a mortal, the tortoise beat the very drunk hare.

She cried out a lick of profanities while her friends dragged her by her feet.

Con appeared right beside me, watching them. "Not a care in the world..." he shook his head. "Never have they known suffering."

I narrowed my eyes at him. "I think she's *been* suffering most of her life."

"Not enough," he answered coldly, still staring at her. "Which one is the girl?"

"She's not with them."

He watched them a moment before breaking the silence. "Doesn't it bother you?"

"Of course it bothers me. I just know how to handle it."

He sighed.

"You're more than welcome to join, you know."

He side-eyed me, but I just shrugged.

"She rather misses Liam, I think. Or she just hates being stuck with me."

Con snorted. "Lira's wasting her time with any of us."

"Perhaps."

"What the fuck are they even doing?"

Indeed. We watched as they staggered through the

woods, unintelligently shouting at each other like they lost their hearing. It was dark out now, and we didn't know how much she had been drinking today.

"She doesn't seem hurt at all," Con said while watching her lively attitude.

"She is. Between the alcohol and what happened, she can barely stand upright. She's pretending." I smiled at him. "Just like your impressive performance earlier."

He punched me in the arm, but I only laughed.

"Áine told them she wanted to show them my roses that they didn't believe she saw. I think she's just drunkenly following the pull."

"Do you know what your power is yet, Áine?" someone asked her.

She whipped her body around to face whoever asked that. *"Shall we find out?"* She asked before stumbling over from whirling around too fast.

"NO!" Liam shouted at her. *"You're fucking hammered and if your power is anything like your father's, you'll kill us all!"*

Áine rolled her eyes at him, making me dig my nails into my arms.

They were too drunk to even notice the will-o-wisps bobbing around, headed towards the lake. But why the lake, I wonder?

Con tilted his head. "Interesting."

Later that night, I lay in bed after drinking enough bourbon to knock out a small drake, waiting for sleep to arrive.

When it did, I awoke in the same forest I always had, and chased after that scent. Like I always had, and would again and again.

CHAPTER
TWENTY-TWO

ÁINE

T his time, I didn't gracefully fall through the tree canopy towards familiar growls. I awoke inside my dream, falling on my ass and surrounded by a forest completely on fire.

There were no growls, only the smell of smoke, pine, and guaiac wood.

I stood and turned in a circle, unsure of how this could be happening after how drunk I got before passing out. I walked normally down a path through the trees, hearing nothing aside from the flames and burning branches falling.

A twig snapped behind me.

I spun around, but no one was there.

Keeping my body still, I listened for any other movement, but it was hard to hear anything over the forest fire.

An entire tree fell behind me, *right* behind me, making me yelp in surprise.

Something about this dream was different, *off*. There was no beautiful night sky followed by the beginnings of a fire, one that could easily be controlled I thought.

Now, it was chaos.

I heard more of those familiar chuckles, and ran.

I was caught by surprise at how fast I was running. Trees were passing me by in a blur, and I couldn't fight the smile growing. Despite the insanity surrounding me, this felt freeing.

That blissful feeling lasted about a minute before I heard footsteps further behind me. Not just one, but two sets of footsteps, each one flanking me from a different direction.

I slammed my heels harder into the earth, fighting to control my breathing.

Another burning tree fell in front of me, but I easily leapt over it, catching myself by surprise. Although I failed to notice the branch coming from the far right, tripping me so I fell on my face.

Those chuckles turned into full blown laughter, and nearing *way* too close for comfort.

I swore under my breath when I looked behind me and saw them. The two males from the forest. Conláed, and the other green-eyed demon who looked like he was going to skin me alive before Conláed ate me.

I scrambled to my feet, swearing vehemently in panic, and ran.

The smell of pine grew stronger before I was slammed into a tree, face first.

I gasped awake upon the impact.

Sitting up in my bed, I struggled to steady my breathing,

which I choked on when I looked towards my balcony doors.

The beast stood at the doorway, staring at me, but I noticed I wasn't paralyzed to the bed this time.

Shadows swirled in and out of the doorway. He nodded his head towards the door, and walked out onto the balcony. He disappeared. Was I supposed to *follow* him?

The shadows that kept going in and out of the doorway were hinting at it.

I put on my boots and hooded cloak, still in my house clothes, and stepped onto the balcony. I gasped. The shadows swirled around the bars of the railing, and on top of it, bright little balls of light bobbed around me.

I lifted my arms, looked around myself and watched them. They were... *cute.*

I smiled until I saw the shadows and balls of light descend onto another rooftop, signaling for me to follow. It was late, and I shouldn't be as lucid as I was after how much I drank earlier.

I shook my head in disbelief of myself, and climbed onto the railing before jumping onto the other roof. I followed them in the night, where everyone was asleep, until we reached the castle walls, nowhere in sight of the guards.

And then I realized we were climbing over a small coved corner in the wall. The same one I climbed over as a child before my mother got me Minsi and made me swear to never climb it again. But now, I wasn't a defiant eight year old with no power.

I jumped over the ledge, landing on my feet, surprising myself.

"Ok," I whispered to myself. "That was badass."

The lights bobbed around me, and I thought they looked like they were dancing.

"Where are we going?" I asked them, and the shadows slithered on the ground beneath the lights, that now formed into a line leading into the forest. I shrugged before following them.

After thirty minutes of following them through the forest, admiring the stars in the night sky, I asked them. "Is it far?"

They answered by bobbing up and down, and I had *no* idea if that was supposed to be a yes or no. I decided it was a yes and started running.

Several seconds went by of trees whirring past me, and I realized I felt no pain. Was I fully healed? I smiled, and then ran faster.

The shadows racing ahead of me were dancing underneath the balls of light, but I was too fast for them. My new challenge would be to keep up with the shadows.

I halted, nearly falling on my face when I saw the familiar branches.

Looking around me, we were now in the same place I met those males, the army with no sigils.

Which means that the shadows were leading me southeast. The beast was nowhere in sight.

I followed them at a brisk pace until we reached a patch

of burnt grass on the ground. It created a circle, and was right beside the lake.

I stopped breathing at the sight of the *moon*. The one I've only seen in my dreams. It reflected off the water and was... it was the most beautiful sight I'd ever seen. I had no idea Ghaldir could be anywhere near this beautiful. Even the ocean view during sunset didn't hold a candle to the sparkle of stars and the moon reflecting over the massive lake.

As I admired the view, several balls of light bobbed past me, bouncing up and down in front of me. The shadows moved beneath them, like they were their own stars and night sky.

Once again, they moved until they were a straight line, leading me to the... lake?

I couldn't swim, *yet*. Why would they want me to enter the lake?

"Uh, I can't swim you guys." And internally rolled my eyes at myself. I was talking to shadows and light.

The lights bobbed above the water now, like it was a party they invited me to. Shadows swirled towards my feet, and whirled around and up my body.

I reached my hand out in front of me, and a tendril of shadow weaved around my fingers like a serpent. I looked deep into the shadow, trying to gauge what kind of magic this was, or if it was some kind of creature.

Too quick, almost unnoticeable, silver eyes opened and closed within the shadow.

I yanked my hand down in fear, and there he was. The beast was across the lake, perched on a cliff overlooking it, staring right at me.

Not taking my eyes off it, I took a step towards the lake. The same lake he growled at me to make sure I never went in.

He didn't flinch, only waited like he was ready to observe. I threw my hands up and dropped them at my sides in exasperation.

"What in the fucking hell am I doing here?"

In answer, he lowered his snout to the water and back up to me.

"I can't swim!" I whisper-yelled, not wanting to draw attention to myself. How was I supposed to be certain this thing would protect me, say if someone like Carsen popped up?

The beast didn't move, deeming my previous statement unworthy of a response.

I sighed loudly, and took my boots off before stepping both feet into the water.

"There. Are you happy?"

It didn't move, but the balls of light bobbed around me faster, expectantly, and kept trying to lead me further into the water.

"Are you trying to kill me? I said I can't swim!"

They ignored me. Was this some kind of spell leading me to my death?

I took another step and then halted, remembering that I am a vessel. One wrong move, and my death could lead to a catastrophe amongst my people.

Footsteps sounded, and I whirled to my right to find Isolde.

She looked like she ran the whole way here in a panic.

"Isolde," I breathed.

From here, I could now see that her brown eyes had specks of gold in them. She looked to the lake in question. When I followed her gaze, I noticed the beast, the lights, even the shadows had disappeared.

The only thing providing any sort of light was the moon and the stars. And her beneath them... I couldn't breathe.

There was a tugging pull in my chest, relieved with each step I made towards her, but then she started backing up.

Why did she lure me out here?

My eyes shot open, because those words in my head were of her voice, clanging loudly in my mind even though her mouth hadn't moved.

"I didn't lure you out here, Isolde. The shadows," I was cut off by her running away.

"Isolde!" I shouted, but she didn't stop. Neither did I, because I couldn't. I couldn't even remember how I started moving in the first place, but I was now chasing her.

Perhaps it was because my parents were powerful, but I was much faster than Isolde, and caught up to her quickly. My brain had no thoughts when I grabbed her arm, and then we appeared in my room.

I gasped loudly. "What the fuck... What did I just do?"

"You have the nerve to tell me that after forcing me here?" she whisper-yelled. We were now in the castle, and it was the middle of the night.

She reached for the doorknob, but again, without thinking, I had her back up against my door. "Why do you keep chasing after me?"

The question came out cold, harsh even. She answered by kissing me, wrapping her arms around my neck, and I couldn't fight it even if I wanted to.

She always had this effect on me.

No matter where we were, or what we were doing, her presence had total authority over me.

My hand slid up her back, sliding through her hair before pulling her into a deeper kiss. Her mouth opened up to me greedily.

My other hand slid beneath the front of her pants, and I ran my fingers through her soaking heat.

I smiled, barely breaking the kiss before I whispered against her lips, "Always ready for me, aren't you?"

She groaned in irritation before forcefully kissing me again.

I slid my hands out of her pants, and used that wet hand to grip her by the throat, backing her up against the bed. I felt her throat bob beneath my hand, and smirked, before pushing her backward and onto the bed.

She was lifting her tunic while I yanked her pants down. Boots were kicked off, she ripped my comfy house shirt off of me instead of pulling it off.

I snarled while holding her down by her throat, while my other hand plunged three fingers inside her. She cried out in pain and pleasure, even though she was so wet already that they slid in easily.

My thumb was pressed against her clit, rubbing it while I penetrated her with my fingers. "You think you can destroy my things and get away with it?"

She smiled, and I squeezed her throat harder. Her pussy was starting to spasm around me before I pulled my fingers out of her.

Her eyes widened in confusion.

I smirked. "Earn it."

She swallowed, and I loosened the grip on her throat. "Tell me how."

My brows rose. "I shouldn't have to."

I saw the slight curve on the edge of her mouth, and she began sliding down the bed.

I rose up on my knees, allowing her passage to scoot right where I wanted her.

Never, did I have to tell her what to do. Everything she did was exactly how I liked it.

Her lips pressed together hard after sucking my clit between them. One of her hands slid onto my asscheek, and dug her nails into them at the same time that her other fingers slid inside me.

Her fingers *slowly* slid in and out, curving in and rubbing against the perfect spot, *too* slowly. I was ready to tell her harder before I felt her nails on my ass break the skin.

I moaned so loudly, barely noticing the bed trembling beneath us, or her chuckling against me.

I grabbed her hair, waiting for her eyes to meet mine in understanding, and then she nodded, sliding her fingers out of me.

She licked me ravenously while I rode her face. With each buck of my hips, I was closer and closer to the edge. I danced along it, and glanced at her eyes peering up at me. They looked... angry, but starving.

I frowned before I noticed I stopped moving, but not fast

enough before she shoved her fingers inside me, fucking me ruthlessly while licking me right where I needed her.

Beneath me.

That's where she belonged.

I came so fucking hard I felt tears down my cheeks.

I slid backwards, and grabbed her face with both hands, kissing her deeply.

I breathed against her lips, panting between each word, "That's a good fucking girl."

They were words you told a hound while training them, but if you said them to her, it made her absolutely feral.

I smiled at the smug look on her face, and slid my hands under her knees, lifting them up until her pussy was in the air.

So fucking perfect she was. Every crevice, every curve… it was *mine* to devour.

With my hands on the back of her thighs, holding them down near her chest, I obliged.

Each stroke of my tongue had me growing hungrier and hungrier, desperate for more. I slid my tongue deep inside her pussy as far as it could go, relishing in her taste, refusing to waste a single drop.

I moved up, gently sucking on her bundle of nerves, and with my thumb inside her, and my middle finger pushing into her ass, her entire body shook.

Her moan was deep, emitting a feral sound only intense pleasure can create.

"That's it," I guided her, pressing on those three spots until half of my face was wet.

I lifted my head up, pressing my hands harder on the

back of her thighs, readying to ride her. "And whom does this pussy belong to?"

Her eyes widened in anger.

My brows rose. "Answer the question, Isolde."

Her face contorted into fury before she shoved me off her. Now out of the bed, she shoved her pants on, huffing and puffing.

"What's wrong?"

She turned to look at me.

Me.

I heard her voice in my head again, and nearly vomited in shock.

My fucking pussy, Áine? Belongs to me.

And she slammed the door behind her, leaving me in a stupor.

What nerve did I hit? And how is she doing that!

"Finally," said a male voice with a breath of impatience.

CHAPTER
TWENTY-THREE

ISOLDE

Fuck.
Fuck. Fuck. Fuck. Fuck. FUCK!
This *can't* be happening.
My fists were banging on Visha's door.

I had no idea what time it was, but I *had* to speak with her. She seemed like the only one that I could talk to about this situation. I didn't trust her in the slightest, but if anyone knew *anything* about this, and how to get out of it, it's her.

I refused to live my immortal life, that now had a future, to be dictated by her. I love her, but then there are times where I want to question it. That question *always* leads to me in her bed.

Visha opened the door. Her dark hair fell in waves around her pale skin, and her robe revealed ample breasts peeking out. I swallowed, and forced my eyes on hers, that were now angry.

"I need your help."

"At this hour?"

"Yes!" I accidentally shouted.

Her brows rose in disbelief. "What could've possibly happened to lead you to my door in the middle of the night, just before dusk, and smelling like pussy?"

I looked down in shame. "I need to know what I am." A sob threatened to break through me. "I need to know she's not my mate."

"She's not your mate."

I furrowed my brows. "How are you sure?"

"I'm not," She snorted. "But if it gets you off my doorstep so I can sleep? Sure. You're not her mate."

I snarled. "Please help me."

She snorted again. "Find me at a reasonable hour. Then, we'll talk." And then she slammed the door in my face.

CHAPTER
TWENTY-FOUR

ÁINE

I whipped my head towards that sound. Conláed was leaning against the wall opposite the room of my bed. His arms were crossed against his chest, now covered by leathers instead of armor.

I thrashed blankets around until I was completely covered, despite the fact that he never looked below my eyes.

"How the fuck are you in my room?"

His face had looked angry since he arrived. "Your druids don't have enough magic yet for wards."

I didn't move. Unsure if I needed to run or not.

He tracked my quick glance at the door. "That would be a mistake."

Bet.

Refusing to feel any shame, prioritizing my safety over

exposing myself, I bolted for the door, only to be slammed up against it.

No, I was no longer in my room.

I was in an unknown land, naked, and at the mercy of this demon pinning me to a tree.

I smelled the coppery tang of blood before I was forcefully turned around to stare up into hateful celestine eyes. His hand was already gripping my jaw painfully tight, and tightening it more as that sneer grew on his face. The other hand remained on my shoulder and didn't move.

Green eyes of pure jade looked over his shoulder, smirking at my anger. Anger I forced to hide the fear. He didn't touch me, but I knew the branches currently tying me to the tree belonged to him.

Blue eyes turned into blazing fire. "You really thought you could outrun us?" he said before bringing his mouth to my ear, whispering, "We've been scaling these woods for twenty years, little girl. You will never outrun us. You will never be able to hide for long before we find you, and we will *always* find you."

I snarled back, ignoring my body's response to his closeness. "And what do you plan to do with me?"

His grip on my jaw tightened, and forced me to face him. "Whatever the fuck I want. Do you understand?"

I snorted. "Are you going to rape me? Because I can guarantee there are things I will never willingly do with you."

He smiled, and it wasn't friendly as he flaunted his emerging serrated teeth. "No Princess. Me and my people would never stoop to the traditions of Dhadren soldiers." I blinked at that. He took a step back, releasing my chin while the other male surveyed me being tied to the tree, unabashedly.

Then I noticed where I was, where he had somehow taken me.

"How that fuck are you in my dream?" I snapped.

They both smiled, but it was the blonde demon that spoke. "That isn't just your dream, Little One. These are our forests."

Indeed, the trees looked nothing like the ones in Ghaldir. They were tall enough that it made sense how long it took me to fall to the ground in my dream, and thicker than two of Ghaldir's willow trees combined. "Where am I, and why the hell am I here?"

The blonde one kept smiling, while Conláed sneered, but neither of them answered.

"ANSWER ME!" I shouted at them in anger, failing to hide the panic in my voice. They heard it, and started laughing.

I could feel the heat rising in my cheeks, and I searched for the familiar roiling of power within my gut. If I could channel that power, whatever it was, I wouldn't run away before smacking them around a little bit. Because fuck them, and fuck this.

Nothing.

Absolutely nothing rose to the surface, and the part of me that was ready to ball like a baby? I mentally reached into my mind and choked that bitch. Abso-fucking-lutely not, could I shed a single fucking tear in front of these assholes.

I bit my cheek until it bled, hoping it would either calm my nerves, or force me to wake up.

It did neither.

Conláed's nostrils flared, as if he scented the blood I spilled in my mouth, and grabbed my jaw again. Once he did, blood mixed with saliva dripped down my chin. The other male, who's name I still didn't know, tracked it as it fell.

Conláed forced me to face him. "You will not hurt yourself. Do you understand? You agreed to a bargain ensuring you will be there for whatever I need, and I cannot have you hurting yourself." I saw the blood trailing down his large hand and wanted to look, but this asshole's magic forced my eyes on his. "If anyone gets to fucking hurt you, it's me," he growled, and a second growl grew behind him. Conláed rolled his eyes. "Or him."

My eyes widened, now able to turn to the other, noting the sparkle in his green eyes at the thought. Conláed was an asshole, but something told me the other was the rapid animal he kept on a short leash. He laughed loudly, and I wondered if he somehow heard my thoughts.

"Be ready for us," Conláed said before releasing my face, and then licked the blood off his hand. "Because I'm coming for you. Soon. And you *will* uphold your end of the bargain."

"When?" I breathed.

Branches were removing themselves from my skin, unbinding me. Con grabbed my shoulder, still not looking below my face, and I appeared back in my room, alone.

CHAPTER
TWENTY-FIVE

ÁINE

I sat in my bed until the sun rose, unable to fall back asleep. It took me longer than it should've to notice there wasn't a trace of Conláed's scent in my room. Thank the gods. That would be one less thing I'd have to hide.

I couldn't get those bastards out of my head; couldn't stop trying to piece everything together. My dreams were of *their* forests—but how?

I had spent most of the day after breakfast sleeping, if you'd call tossing and turning all afternoon sleeping. Paranoia was causing my brain to stir in a panic, so I forced myself out of bed and dragged myself to dinner.

"You look like shit," Maeve said from across the table in the dining hall. Isolde, nowhere to be seen.

"Where is Isolde?" I asked, ignoring her comment.

She stabbed her meat with a fork. "Visha's." And then she took a bite much too large.

"You're awfully concerned with her comings and goings as of late," Liam crooned, earning a glare from me.

Keira smacked him in the arm.

Sloan sat beside me, and ate in silence per usual, sipping from her wine.

I took a bite from my food, avoiding the topic entirely. Of course I was concerned. She was unpredictable with her comings and goings, just as much as her moods. Last night she bit my head off and left because I made a comment in the heat of the moment.

I looked down at my food, because if I were honest with myself, I would admit it wasn't just a comment. I'd been trying subconsciously to connect with her, even if I didn't want to. To make things worse, our newfound powers and magic returning made my feelings stronger, more uncontrollable.

It didn't make sense, and it did.

The possessive feelings weren't my own, but it was almost like an instinct I couldn't ignore. Perhaps some distance for a while would be wise, at least until I could sort that out.

A few hours later, we were readying our horses and equipment just outside the castle gates. A few at a time, horses were being brought to us from the stables.

Isolde was already late.

I shook my head in irritation, snapping my glaive onto my back. Looking over at Liam on his horse beside Keira, still in his weakened form, I practically huffed. He was going to get himself killed if we couldn't figure out how to make him his normal self. I paused at the thought. What if he didn't have one?

There are stories of lands with those called humans. From what I've gathered, our state in the curse was equivalent to them, except they would've died quickly from dehydration.

I looked over at him. What if that's where he's from? How could he have randomly appeared in our kingdom one day, with absolutely no memories of a past life?

He caught me staring at him, and frowned at my expression. I shook it off and mounted my horse.

Maddox's eye was fully healed, but the mace left freckled scars around the side of his face. I thought it made him look more terrifying. I patted him on the neck, ready to leave at any second.

Isolde appeared in the corner of my eye, approaching her horse beside Visha. I furrowed my brows. Why on earth would she be escorting her here? I shook off the possessive emotions that I *knew* couldn't have been my own, and we rode out.

We had been gone for some time, nearing the Cult of Assassin's castle.

A pained noise escaped my father, causing us all to halt.

"What is it?" I asked.

"There's a painful tightening in my chest."

My eyes widened. Could it be his heart? Did the curse affect him enough that breaking it wasn't enough? Had it been too late?

"Something isn't right," he breathed, practically ripping the chest plate from its hooks, gripping his chest tightly. "I can't tell exactly what it is, but.." He looked behind him. Back towards home.

Isolde softly asked, "Could it be Mira?" I stopped breathing at the thought of her *understanding* that tightening, because I felt a tightening around her constantly. If that meant what I thought it meant, she was absolutely screwed, because I would have to slaughter the entire council and likely the High Court to ensure she was safe.

He left no room for negotiation before turning on his horse, and bolting towards home.

We weren't a mile from the castle before I could practically taste what smelled like burning rust. We smelled it in Carsen's cell and on our hunt for his trail. Further unnerving all of us.

Liam hadn't said a word, but I saw the exchanged glances between him and Keira. Whatever thoughts they exchanged with their eyes, clearly about what they thought we were going to find, *terrified* me.

They knew I kept looking at them, searching their faces for answers. And immediately tried to compose themselves for my benefit. Which meant they thought something was seriously fucking wrong.

If anything happened to my mother, there wouldn't be a force strong enough to stop me from ending those responsible in the vilest and slowest of ways. There wouldn't be a kingdom brave enough to face my father's wrath. The King who once saved my mother, who immediately knew of her abuse and how her own parents turned a blind eye.

The castle portcullis was already being lowered, awaiting our arrival. The smell of the air that escaped from within the castle walls made my breathing stop.

Blood.

CHAPTER
TWENTY-SIX

LIAM

Whatever lies within this castle, whatever tragedy we could smell from out here, I wonder if it was something I could protect her from. Indeed, if there was a threat, these people would've either taken care of it or died.

There was no panic ensuing from danger. There was nothing. No one said anything. Their faces looked at us worried and confused, and they looked at each of us to find answers.

They were told nothing. They knew nothing.

Which meant it was really fucking bad. I didn't dare think any more about what I thought might have happened; what Keira and I were silently communicating about what could have happened.

We remained silent for the entire trip. Even now, while

the King did the same as he jumped off his horse and took off into a sprint, ignoring any of the people trying to catch his attention.

He had to know. Just as I would need to know if there ever was a thought that something might have happened to my queen.

I was instantly left behind as the towering giants I lived with disappeared into the depths of the corridor meant for the highest chains of command. I made my way up the staircase as I heard it.

The King roared in what I could only describe as unimaginable grief.

I swore under my breath as tears began to run down my face, already knowing without confirmation.

When I reached the hall that held the door to the King and Queen's chambers, the hall filled with dead soldiers. I saw our comrades leaning up against the walls. The horror on their faces made me want to dive into myself and hide from the truth that would hurt.

The truth that would break us.

Keira's gaze met mine, trembling, communicating with her eyes that we were right. My breathing became heavy, hearing Alaric's cries. I needed to protect this family. That was my one duty I felt within my blood.

And their Queen is dead.

The guards that were scattered all over the floors proved the enemy was counting on the Kingdom's most powerful players to be gone. Depending on our absence, the only roadblock strong enough to defend against them is to come into the stronghold.

But how?

No one would've lowered the gates. Someone would've had to fly in here, or magically appear like those with more power could do.

When I looked inside the room, I saw that Áine had barely reached the doorway. Her face was grave with confusion and denial, like she couldn't believe that what was in front of her was anything but an illusion.

Seeing her and Alaric's faces broke me to pieces. The Queen looked so small being held in her husband's arms, as her cheeks caught his tears.

He was shaking her, repeatedly begging, *"Stay with me."*

At those pleads, I heard Áine's breath catching in her throat.

Sloan approached him with a blanket to cover the Queen's bare and mutilated body. He snapped his eyes aggressively towards hers. She said the blanket was to keep her from getting cold. He allowed her to cover his wife.

At the sound of a loud thud, I turned to see Áine's knees slammed to the floor. She didn't make a sound as tears were flooding down her face. Her eyes looked like her soul was trying to shield her from the truth, trying to force the denial that it couldn't.

She lowered her hands to the ground and bowed her head, trembling. She began moving as if she would crawl toward her parents, but the King whipped his head towards his daughter with tears in his eyes, shaking his head as he whispered, "No..." not wanting to see the despair on his daughter's face.

Isolde and Maeve scooped their arms under each of hers, and Áine let out a scream I hadn't heard since I first met her. That blood-curdling scream filled with agony and grief that foreshadowed blood.

Alaric looked at his daughter with so much guilt, as if his entire soul was about to shatter. There was nothing we could do but stay in this room of despair that promised different people would leave it.

I waited for it.

Waited for the promise of blood made by that scream. That otherworldly wrath concealed within her.

The temperature in the room increased rapidly as she screamed and screamed. When I looked up at her eyes, they beheld flames. Her skin was steaming when Maeve and Isolde hissed in pain, letting her go. I turned to the King, who was looking in the same eyes I saw and watched as his daughter set her whole body on fire.

I caught movement from the window behind Alaric, but when I tried to see what it was, it vanished.

I turned my head back towards the scene unfolding, hoping the castle wasn't melting to the ground. Maeve was wrestling a blanket over Áine to swaddle out the fire, but it burned to ash. Maeve screamed out in pain, now covered in burns. Áine whipped her head towards her, noting the pain she had just caused her, and the flames dissipated.

"Do you hear that?" Isolde asked.

Alaric's face whipped towards Queen Mira's. Looking back and forth between her face and her chest, like he sensed something different that I couldn't. The entire room went quiet. Alaric's face was full of panic and hope.

"She's fucking breathing!" Keira shouted as she ran into the room. How she could've heard that from the hall...

"EVERYONE GET THE FUCK OUT!" Alaric shouted. "Get the god's damned healers in here! NOW!"

I ran out into the hallway. My breathing was heavy and all over the place. I wanted to help, but as soon as I left the room, they had already vanished with their preternatural speed.

I stood there looking down at the hall's floor filled with blood and corpses, turning over their bodies and checking for pulses. Not one.

They were back only minutes later, with Visha and two healers ready with supplies. They started their work immediately, shouting orders to everyone about how to position her and provide anything else they would need. Their bedroom chambers turned into complete chaos.

I waited in the hall to give them privacy. I didn't need to be there. No matter that Alaric took me in as his own, giving me a room within the same halls as his family. Despite the constant mistrust in his voice when he spoke to me. That was betrayed by everything else he'd done for me.

Since the curse was broken, the hot poker in my soul that called all the shots was fading. Ever since I was thrown onto the ground after being struck stupid by the physical changes of my comrades, there was less of that foreign voice telling me to go to her, to keep her safe. I was a lost mess who had no place here.

I passed another massive puddle of blood and looked over to see Marcus. The male who brought me to my room for the first time. The knight who didn't treat me like I was a peasant with mental challenges. Other kingdoms would've thrown me outside. Now, he was dead, too.

Sweat was dripping down my face as the temperature

around me rose. I turned towards where Áine might be, but a ball of fire blew past me, flying in the opposite direction of Alaric, screaming her name.

I whipped my head towards where she went, knowing I wasn't near fast enough to catch her. Even if I could, I could do nothing to stop her. The logic was there, telling me it was pointless. The hot poker was lessening its demands for me to protect her. But this went past all of that. The princess who brought me inside these walls that provided me with a home was about to do something foolish and possibly get herself killed.

I took off as fast as I could with dire determination to do the right thing for my family, following that pull.

CHAPTER
TWENTY-SEVEN

ÁINE

There will be blood, and I will not stop when those satisfying screams choke on it.

I will not stop when every last one of them no longer has a face.

I will not stop when the fires from my soul burn them to ashes.

I will not stop until the offense of sharing the same soil as my mother is remedied.

CHAPTER
TWENTY-EIGHT

CONLÁED

I saw my mother when I saw the pain in that room. I saw what I feared every single day. I understood the helplessness in her eyes as she saw what she thought she could've prevented. The helplessness I felt when calculating if and when I would ever be strong enough to save my own mother, still locked in chains at my father's feet.

I wanted to take this pain away from her, only to unsee that look on her face. I didn't know this girl. I didn't hold any affection for her, but her face terrified me. What would become of my face if something like that happened to my mother? What would become of me? That thought alone should be left unanswered because it wasn't a fucking option. The resolve I felt at that vanished as I felt her magic exploding for a second time.

When I first felt it, I stayed on the cliff outside the castle a bit longer, just in case a naïve princess attempted to run into the night seeking vengeance.

This time, it was raging and unfaltering. I waited for it. The time was here to make myself known to Alaric and his people. We needed this alliance for the war I had planned to wage for many decades now. I wouldn't be strong enough. I was male enough to admit that. Even if I gained alliances with some of the demons not under my father's thrall, it still wouldn't be enough.

We needed them. We needed *her*.

I heard the yelling and prepared for what was coming.

If she got out, I would make sure she was back in her bed by morning, sound asleep. I rolled my eyes at the shouting guards, thinking there was any chance in hell of stopping her. The portcullis was beginning to rise.

An explosion reverberated throughout the land, vibrating under my feet. I watched as a ball of raging fire and fury blasted through the portcullis, unwilling to wait for it to rise before her.

She screamed at the pain it caused and got over it quickly before she ran in the direction they all returned from. She was fast, but I was older.

I stopped a good few feet before her, so she didn't tackle me and try to rip my face off. She started to growl loudly as she halted before me. Her eyes didn't leave mine as her mind assessed a plan of action for evading me, but her eyelids lowered when my spell began to work. It took moments before her flame went out, and she fell fast asleep in my arms as I caught her.

I slipped my other arm under her knees and started

back towards the castle until I heard a fast movement. Alaric appeared right in front of me.

His current facial expression was the reason I never let anyone close. The reason I never sought a companion for myself. I would never accept a future where this could become my fate. I would fight for my people alongside my brothers. I would fight to free them from tyranny so others can live a quiet life with their companions.

"Conláed," he said as he stood in front of me, while I was still carrying his daughter.

I gave a slow nod, indicating that I was not a threat despite his hatred for my people. He looked ready to rip out my throat.

"She's asleep, but she'll wake in a few hours," I assured him.

If he had any retort or fight reserved for those like me, it was still in that room where a part of him died.

He walked up and gathered his daughter into his arms, not looking at me as he turned away. Not saying a word, he carried her at a heartbreakingly slow pace back towards where Liam stood outside the gate, back to his home. A home still filled with the blood of the queen and the smell of magic belonging to our common enemy.

My eyes trailed from Liam's to the girl standing beside him. She was stunning in her armor with her dark hair in a war braid, and her dark skin set her apart from everyone in this wretched place.

I felt a roiling in my gut when I noticed she was standing beside Liam, both of them coming after Áine, and wondered if that was the girl.

CHAPTER
TWENTY-NINE

ISOLDE

"MORE HOT WATER!" Visha screamed at me.

I ignored the pain in my chest that made me feel like I was dying. I stumbled around the large bed that belonged to the King and Queen, intending on running to follow Visha's orders.

No matter what, the Queen *could not* die.

That would destroy Áine, and ruin any pretense of normalcy now that our curse is broken and we all have a future.

I didn't make it to the doorway when Áine's face stopped me in my tracks.

The freckled face filled with manic hatred.

Not towards me.

No.

She was staring at the floor still covered in her mother's blood, and I knew what was about to happen.

I slowly reached my hand towards her. "No... Áine, please,"

She exploded.

Fire pulsed in waves off her skin, lapping around her skin until she was the epitome of rage.

The shockwave of that power threw me back and onto the floor, only to look back up and find that she was gone, and Alaric was screaming after her.

I wasn't thinking when I abandoned Visha and took off after her. I didn't think about the fact that they needed all the help they could get, not when Áine was about to do something so tremendously stupid.

It took no time with my new abilities and my new legs to reach the gates, not finding her until I reached the outside of those gates, and saw the trail of embers in the air.

She was just across the field, not moving.

I narrowed my eyes, ready to run and catch her somehow without getting burned. Not that it mattered.

I would gladly allow my flesh to be marred if it meant she was safe.

My breath caught in my throat.

Standing in front of her was an obnoxiously tall male. Even from here, I could see that he was gorgeous. Maybe even more so than Liam.

I didn't recognize his armor, didn't know where he came from, but they looked at each other like they knew each other.

I bristled, and the urge to rip him a new asshole was crawling out of my skin. I lost control when she passed out in front of him, and he caught her, but just for a moment.

Because Alaric was now by them, taking Áine from him, without any fuss.

What in the fucking hell is going on? And who is *that*!

I barely noticed that Liam, now shorter than me, was standing beside me, looking just as panicked.

Conláed, Alaric called him, infuriating me more.

I understood that obviously there would be many that Alaric knew, but Áine had been here her whole life. How does she know him?

Alaric turned his back to the male, and was now walking towards us when I caught the stranger's eyes.

They glowed blue in the night and were the most gorgeous I had ever seen.

And they were looking right at Liam before staring daggers into me.

My teeth were grinding to dust when I contemplated what that look meant.

Did he know about us? Was I getting in the way of something he wanted? Or did he already have her and didn't like sharing?

My chest was heaving at the questions hammering into my head, staring back at him without fear. I barely registered that Alaric was nearing us when the stranger vanished into thin air.

Liam and I waited in silence while Alaric approached carrying a sleeping Áine.

He stopped in front of me, looking with eyes of exhaustion and anger that I deserved. "Go home," he ordered, and kept walking, not waiting or bothering with any response I might give him.

Not that I really could, since he was the fucking king.

But still, I whirled my body around to try and convince him to let me go with him and help.

Liam put his hand on my shoulder. "Not now. She'll be ok in the morning." His eyes noted the burn marks still on my skin that haven't healed yet. "You should have Visha look at those."

"She's a bit busy with the queen, at the moment."

He didn't have a response for that.

"Besides, I just ditched Visha to chase after a woman who will never love me. I don't think they're going to be quick to help me right now."

Liam's eyes shot wide open. "Do you?"

I couldn't fake the deadness of exhaustion in my stare, aiding me in not giving anything away, even if my words just did.

"No," I said before leaving him at the gate.

CHAPTER
THIRTY

ÁINE

I awoke in a groggy state, back in my bedroom...

I jerked my body into a sitting position, remembering everything that had happened before I fell asleep in front of that male. I saw the flashes of what had been my parent's chambers before I completely stopped breathing.

A deep, throbbing pain started from deep within my chest. I reached my hand up to grab it and forced air into my lungs. I struggled to breathe and my chest heaved rapidly when I heard a boot scuffling on the other side of my door.

How long was Liam there this time? Where was my father?

The scuffling turned into the sounds of a chair croaking and sliding, and a knock was at my door. I didn't respond. I didn't want anyone in here while panic of reality settled in causing my breathing to go haywire. Not while the panic was threatening to consume me completely.

"*She's alive.*"

My sobs exploded at the sound of my father's voice. The door opened, and I was instantly in his arms. He held me through the broken sobs that raked violently through me.

Why would anyone do this? What could have warranted it? There was no warrant. None of it made any sense. Nothing could ever make sense of it, and I would make sure they regretted it.

"She's alive, Áine. She hasn't woken up yet, but she's breathing."

Rage was rising to the surface. My sadness was consuming, but my rage knew it and said *fuck that*. Instead, there would be blood.

My father and I dined alone that evening in the study, where the three of us would have tea together for hours, chatting or reading silently.

We said nothing as we picked at our food, barely able to eat anything. At one point, Liam came up looking for us, but we ignored the knock at the door. Unwilling to be around other faces.

He didn't mention me taking off or who found me earlier that day. He didn't say how I got home. I didn't ask, not particularly caring. I made sure I hugged my father before bidding him goodnight.

I returned to my room where my weapons and armor were waiting for me.

I waited until everyone would be fast asleep; waited until it was past closing time at The Broken Inn when others would be stumbling home. Waiting until there wasn't a sound throughout the halls. I knew they were all anticipating what I was currently about to do, that they would try to stop me.

Knowing their hearing was now as good as mine, I opted for leather, leaving the armored plates wrapped in sheets and packed into a bag. I would suit up after leaving the castle without any ears nearby.

I wouldn't blaze through the gates this time, alerting anyone in a hundred-mile radius of what I was doing. Certainly not the mysterious curse-breaking asshole who stopped me many hours earlier. I didn't have time for his tricks.

My mother suffered a fate I had saved Maeve from all those years ago. I wouldn't be satisfied until I was submerged in a lake of their blood, then setting it on fire to remove any sign they ever existed.

I knew it was the Cult. Whether it was initiated by Carsen or whomever, I *knew* they did it. In my parent's quarters, beneath the smothering scent of blood, was another. The faintest scent of smoke and rot.

I opened my window earlier in the day so I wouldn't make a noise opening it now, even going so far as to leave my boots in my bag. Placing my bag across my back, I heard footsteps in the hall and froze. Whoever it was would have to nap in my room for a while if they barged in. There was no jumping in the bed pretending to be asleep, not with our hearing. Someone heard me in my room, someone expecting it.

It could've been any one of them. I waited several moments, anticipating their decision upon learning I was clearly awake at an odd hour.

Footsteps started again, away from my door and went east. It was probably Sloan or Liam then. I tried to catch the scent, but the incense I burned to throw off what was happening in here completely overpowered my senses.

I heard a door open and shut but no sounds of bed movement. I continued to stay still in case they were tricking me, and then I heard the sigh. Sloan.

Then the door opened and shut, followed by a body climbing onto a bed. Getting out of here was going to be tricky. I slowly entered the balcony, looking for any of my family prepared to stop me. No one.

I leaped onto the roof next to ours and went from roof to roof until I reached the castle walls, finding the narrow pocket on the east side. It was a part of the wall with enough stones sticking out to climb, which I often did as a child to sneak off and play in the forest.

I made it down the wall and quickly put my boots on. I would wait until I made it further before bringing out the noisy armor plates. I would've left them all together if I didn't think I would need them for this potential suicide mission.

I didn't want to die. In fact, I planned not to, but I had a power within me that was strong. I would unleash my flames in their stronghold, burning every single last one of them alive.

I gritted my teeth hard when I heard someone's throat clearing. I slowly turned to see Maeve leaning on one leg with her arms crossed.

"I knew there was no stopping you," she mocked. I saw the straps and then realized she had a bag packed as well. "They tried to argue with me on it, but I knew eventually you would find a way out. And someone needed to be here waiting so you wouldn't be alone. If anything, I'm grateful you made it out on the first day, so I wasn't stuck out here every night waiting for the inevitable." She was smirking. "I may not have Keira's stealth skills, but I have the arrows to watch your back."

I waited a moment before responding. "And there isn't going to be a rescue party waiting for me in the forest?"

She snorted. "Liam is probably not too far away. I imagine he had the same thoughts as me. He has been walking the grounds all day, so his stench is everywhere, making it hard to tell where he currently is. I'd probably head around the bend first before entering the forest in case he's waiting out here, too. Unless you'd rather deal with him."

I considered the situation and decided I definitely did not want to deal with him. He wouldn't be able to stop us as he is, which still hasn't changed. He would end up coming with us and becoming a liability unless we knocked him out instead.

"Around the bend, it is." Which took no time at all. I could get used to this power, but I imagine I would have to if our enemies had the same advantage.

Liam was waiting for me in the forest, where his scent had become bolder than where we were by the castle walls. Thankfully, he couldn't smell us and eventually would head back to the castle.

Maeve opted for her leathers, and I considered abandoning my pack. But Liam might find it, or worse, Conláed might still be out here and find it. The last thing I could recollect was him catching me as I fell to the ground. Whatever powers he had, I needed to steer clear. If anyone is capable of killing me out here, it's him.

CHAPTER
THIRTY-ONE

LIAM

Áine was, without a doubt, strong, but if our safety relied on her stealth skills, we'd be fucked.

Even with my human ears, I could hear that she was obviously packing armor into a bag instead of opting for leather. *No one* picks armor for sneaking around.

I know how ridiculous it is that I'm out here, that I couldn't catch them if they ran or could do anything if they decided to render me unconscious. But I'd follow them just in case. She wouldn't die while I was still breathing.

I waited in the trees, keeping my eye on the wall she used to climb down as a child. Then there she was, trying so hard and failing to be quiet, struggling to get her boots on when Maeve walked up with her arms crossed.

When I saw that they decided to go around the forest, I jumped down and cut through, intending to meet them when they curved back.

I knew it was a long shot and that they'd probably be long gone by the time I arrived. But if her safety and survival relied on the moment I arrived, I would bring her back to her father before he realized she was gone.

I made it a mile into the forest before I reached my horse that I tied to a tree. Kept her far away so preternatural ears wouldn't hear her. She was a beautiful painted mare that refused to break like the others. Wild and barely domesticated. I chuckled at that. I lived my life surrounded by wild and barely domesticated females. I wondered what it would be like to marry a woman more docile.

No, I needed to know that if we were ever apart, she would destroy any enemies that dared harm her. I couldn't live with myself if she couldn't. I couldn't go through what the King was facing.

I shook my head at the thought. I needed to focus on the task at hand.

I rode on for almost an hour and slowed. Their stronghold wasn't far from here, and I needed to find Áine. She and Maeve moved fast, but they might not be far, likely hiding somewhere spying and devising their best plan of action.

I made it to a cliff overlooking the Cult of Assassins' stronghold, keeping myself hidden as much as possible while scouting the area for my friends. I heard nothing coming from behind the walls, which meant they hadn't made a move yet or were captured.

I waited to let the panic settle, breathing in and out louder than I should to keep myself hidden, but I couldn't freak out now.

I kept telling myself they couldn't be captured, but then

I remembered they were both the loudest among our group. *Shit.* I looked around, looking for a way in, and then I heard feet shuffling behind me. I jumped up, ready to fight, before I saw their faces. Maeve looked irritated, standing behind Áine, staring down at me with a cold expression.

"What in the actual fuck do you think *your* being here does for anyone?" Áine snapped. I narrowed my eyes at the wounded animal, clearly trying to make me angry and leave.

"Over my dead fucking body am I letting you get yourself killed and carrying your body back to your father," I snapped back. She wasn't getting rid of me that easily.

"I suppose I'll have to carry your dead body back then. Because only one of us is likely to end up dead tonight, and I can't babysit you," she snorted, trying to convince me she felt anything other than worry. Her nostrils flared, and she breathed deeply to keep herself in check.

"You came here on a suicide mission without thinking, and you're going to lecture me on stupid decisions? I've been babysitting you for fucking *years*, Áine. If you're that worried, then let's go home, where your father is a wreck and would lose his fucking mind beyond saving if he knew where you were." I waited for her to reveal that my words hit any targets, but she looked as if nothing could touch her. It was like prodding a dead carcass.

Maeve stepped between us, but before she could speak, their eyes widened, and I saw black.

CHAPTER
THIRTY-TWO

ÁINE

Regret wasn't an emotion I often felt. Still, seeing Liam here completely human-like and at the mercy of those so much more powerful, I snapped. I should've opted to find him in the woods first, knocked him out, and left him by the castle gates. Maybe I'll knock him out now and tie him up high in a tree for us to grab him when we're done.

I smelled it before I saw him start to sway, a familiar smell from the last time I tried to run out here and passed out. I started to get groggy after both of them were already on the ground.

Motherfu—

CHAPTER
THIRTY-THREE

CONLÁED

I knew I should have stuck around a bit longer. That girl would likely escape their hold on her for revenge soon enough. Right before I came home, I saw her eating a quiet dinner with her father. Or at least giving the appearance of eating, but they were together. So, I decided to come home and rest. Bathe even.

Drak was in the study, reading. Something that took up most of his time. Damien was out, likely at a tavern, looking for company or someone to warm his bed. It was privileges like these that we fought for. For this haven that we found in disarray after escaping Rodgärd.

I waited a few hours before setting out for the falls to bathe. I preferred it late into the night when there wouldn't be anyone meandering around the forest. I would relax under the stars since I couldn't sleep, anyway.

I entered my chamber, gathered my solvent, and then made my way down the halls.

"Con." I heard Damien from behind and turned. "We need to go back. Now." He looked nervous.

"What is it then?" I asked, trying to not look irritated when I just wanted to feel the waterfall beat down on my back.

"I was just outside the castle, tracking *that* lingering scent from earlier, but I could smell Liam all around the forest. And her scent trailed around it, headed towards the cult, and Alaric is losing his shit. I wanted to follow the trail but thought to grab you first. If it's me her father see's, he won't hesitate to execute me."

"Drak!" I yelled furiously down the hall, tossing my solvent through a nearby doorway. Clearly, he had heard everything since he was already approaching.

We landed on the cliff outside the castle, with only an hour or so left until dawn. I could smell Liam's scent fading into the forest, and Áine's not too far off in the same direction. There was another scent with her. One of her comrades, likely.

I heard shouting from within the castle, moving through the damaged portcullis, still boarded up until they could properly fix it.

The King was ahead of them on his horse, with three of Áine's friends at his side.

Shit.

Damien wasn't kidding. If the King saw us, he'd likely kill him on site. That is, if he still carried the strength from before he and his people were cursed. All three of us could end up killed, and this would all be for nothing.

"We should follow them," Drak suggested. I agreed. We'd silently escort them to the stronghold and get those idiots out alive. This whole plan was inching closer and closer to going to shit.

I was ready to pull Liam out yesterday when the curse was broken, but I decided to allow them a moment to grieve. Now I was just ready to kick his ass and completely throttle that beast of a beauty that keeps putting him in these situations.

"We'll go as backup. The King is strong, and these assassins are likely to be dead upon Áine's arrival if she unleashes her flames."

"You might want to strengthen that spell to mask our scents with him around," Damien suggested, not wanting anyone to lose their head around the King, who already wasn't mentally sound.

I closed my eyes, taking a deep breath. I needed to prepare myself mentally for the approaching bloodbath. It could all be for nothing. We could come to their aid and still end up being denied their assistance later. Or executed.

CHAPTER
THIRTY-FOUR

MAEVE

This was a terrible idea. This was a terrible and disastrous fucking idea. I knew I would never be a warrior who made decisions like the rest of them, but this may have been the worst thing ever. I should've thrown a complete tantrum, trying to bring her back inside the castle, alerting everyone to what was happening so they'd help me. I sure as shit wasn't strong enough to stop her. So, I tagged along to ensure she made it home safely.

Now here we were, in a large shady dungeon-like room hanging on chains from the ceiling, and Liam was with us.

He was going to die.

There was no way these people, who had access to something strong enough to knock us all out, wouldn't kill him instantly.

I looked over slowly, my head feeling heavy from the

forced sleep. Áine was beside me, starting to stir a bit, and Liam was beside her in a deep sleep.

Men covered in black robes with hoods walked in, smiling.

I knew what that meant.

The last time I saw looks like that, Áine lost her hound and repeatedly stabbed one of them in the face. When we met Liam, who came from nowhere.

Áine's eyes widened at their arrival and then looked at me. She nodded her head slowly, trying to assure me that we were going to be okay. That it was all going to be okay.

The smell from the cliff was heavy and saturated on our chains. We were completely weakened. I saw the flame flicker in Áine's eyes, but it went out immediately. They were somehow able to completely subdue us.

We would be lucky if all they did was rape us. These were the people Keira escaped from. Whatever horrors she faced before finding us, we would channel her strength to get through this. At least long enough until help came.

Unless Liam told no one and came straight to us...

Fuck. Fuck. Fuck. Fuck. Fuck!

I had to get us out of here, somehow. I felt strange fingers slide down my arm and flinched. The one beside me chuckled, and the others echoed, surrounding me.

I felt the scream building in my chest. It exploded when I felt a knife slice across my back.

"Maeve." Áine was looking at me with sorrow and guilt, shaking her head. Her face jerked back as one of the men slapped her.

"Shut the fuck up, *Princess*. Carsen said we had free rein to do whatever we wanted with you," He snorted, then looked at me. "I can't thank you enough for bringing more to share."

Áine vomited all over him, and he screamed in anger before his fist met her face. He grabbed her face, continued the assault, and knocked her clean out. I could thank him for not allowing her to remain conscious while these men were groping and prodding me.

I closed my eyes and thought of my friends as I felt blades of flesh and steel puncturing me.

CHAPTER THIRTY-FIVE

ALARIC

I could smell him. Leaving the castle, following us, and now here. I could fucking smell him. That sinister magic was oozing from his pores. If Conláed was behind any of this, his clock was ticking before his meat suit would be missing bones.

I dismounted my horse, signaling my army to remain behind me. They had a barrier surrounding this castle, preventing me from hearing or smelling anything from within.

This plan of Keira's was horrible, but it was all we had. I picked her up off the back of my horse, still gagged and bound at the wrists, and brought her to her knees beside me to face the assassins she had run from many years ago. Whom we've protected her from since we found her.

Sloan and Isolde were nearby, ready to utilize the element of surprise by any means necessary.

I wasn't leaving here without my daughter. They weren't leaving without their friends. It was an assumption that they were captured, but I smelled them up towards the cliff along with that magic. Magic similar, but not the same as Conláed's. Then their magic disappeared, and these men were still out here breathing. She was in there with Maeve and Liam.

"We have someone you might want," I declared, using the deadness I felt in my soul with each word. "Take this one. *Play* with her however you want... and return the princess. Now." I nearly vomited at the thought of handing Keira over to them, but I had to trust in my captains.

One wrong move, and I couldn't keep my magic reined in any longer.

It took everything not to break eye contact with the piece of shit in front of me when I felt Conláed arrive. He was on that cliff watching us, and the scent of fear radiated from him and the two others.

The black-robed scumbag in front of me tilted his head and snickered. "And what makes you think I'd prefer that lowborn, traitorous piece of trash? I think she looks better there, right on her knees at your feet."

I kept my shit together and smirked. They would not win today.

He began laughing under his breath, slowly rising in

volume, as two assassins walked up. Each one had a firm grasp on Sloan's and Isolde's hair. My breathing grew into low pants, failing to rein in my panic as I saw them look up at me with regret. There was nothing these kids could do that would disappoint me. They were perfect. They were good to Áine and would continue to do so when she wore the crown.

"Both you and your trash come before us now, or I slaughter all of your little children," he demanded while lazily waving his hands towards the girls.

I kept my mouth shut. It was a tactic I taught Áine. When you thought your mouth would make the situation worse, you stay quiet and let them dig their own graves. She would do that with her mother growing up when she got into trouble. Mira would lose her shit and give up the fight every time, cursing me in the process.

"I'll even sweeten the pot," he crooned. And I tried to prepare myself for any vile filth he was about to spew from his mouth. He was only egging me on to do something stupid, never planning on setting anyone free.

He lifted his fingers to his mouth before crossing his arms over his chest. "I'll let you keep Keira as your own personal pet. Yeah? You wouldn't even have to share her with anyone. Your daughter can go home safe and sound and you'll have your bed warmed again."

The fire in me was practically its own being, begging for me to let it loose as he continued to not shut the fuck up.

"I wouldn't wait too long to answer, dear King. Your daughter's safety depends on it. What a terrible way for your wife to die. Shameful. I would hate for that to happen to anyone else you love," he added.

I wouldn't let him win. Wouldn't even tell them Mira survived despite their best efforts. *Let me in this barrier, you piece of shit, and let's see you talk then.*

"If it hasn't happened already..." he crooned.

I looked past him and saw Sloan and Isolde's eyes widen in horror as they slowly turned towards the castle door, as if confirming everything he was suggesting.

Sloan looked back at me with rage, and my fire consumed me.

I picked up Keira and flung her into the air towards my army, and then my power exploded.

My daughter was powerless and in their grasp, enduring gods know what. My family was being ripped apart and destroyed from within.

My fire was damaging the barrier enough so that I heard Áine's screams.

I screamed with her, losing control over my power as it destroyed everything and everyone nearby.

The barrier dissolved. I watched the chatty one's eyes widen in fear, and that made me smile as I punched my fist through his chest and ripped out his heart.

CHAPTER
THIRTY-SIX

DAMIEN

It wasn't an hour prior to now that I was stuck in that dream again. That incessant fucking dream that no amount of alcohol could help me evade.

Dark swirling shadows danced along the ground, leading me away from my current path. This was the first time in a while that I had seen something different in this dream.

So I followed them.

Despite my brisk pace, the tall trees blurred in my vision, and then transformed into familiar willows. I knew where I was being led to.

I awoke in my bed with resolve, then vanished to that wicked land.

I stood on the cliff that overlooked the castle and the fields around it, focusing my sight and listening to find her.

My head whipped to the right. Liam.

His scent was in this forest, but nowhere in sight.

I appeared on the field and remained still, but there wasn't a sound. There was, however, a faint trail of her scent and another leading around the bend. That's when I knew something was horribly wrong. I swore vehemently

That fucking idiot snuck out in the night to seek revenge, and took a friend with her. And now Liam, in his weakened form, was headed in that same dangerous direction.

Standing on a cliff with our scents spelled, we watched as Alaric was failing to negotiate with these *people*.

My vision caught to the side, and noticed the two captains they dragged. Both were bound and gagged by materials that I recognized. Materials made to negate magic.

One of them was the girl, and for a moment, I was perfectly content with letting her die here.

Con was now staring back and forth between me and her, and I saw understanding on his face. His lip curled at her before looking back to Alaric, who looked ready to explode at any moment. A terrifying thought for anyone near.

I heard the threat in that prick's voice, and what he was implying. My blood was boiling, but he was likely bluffing to egg on the king. Perhaps he wanted to die.

My eyes shot open as I watched a confirming look on one of the bound captain's face. My claws shot out of my fingers when I saw the other girl thrashing around in anger and terror.

Fast movement caught my attention as Alaric, who was glowing, just threw the girl he was holding far away from him.

Then he erupted.

That overwhelming power of the sun that threatened to melt and burn everything and anything in its path, including the barrier.

I could now hear her screams.

Something unfamiliar threatened to take over my consciousness, my body, and consume me with the urge to blaze forward and save her.

CHAPTER
THIRTY-SEVEN

ÁINE

I tried to open my eyes, but there was an unbearable pain demanding I keep them shut. My head was ringing. I didn't need to touch my face to know the swelling was significant, not that I could, since my hands were chained to the ceiling.

I opened my eyes to assess the situation. Peering down, I saw that I was naked and covered in cuts and bruises.

I was in pain... *everywhere*... and recoiled at the realization of what happened to me while I was unconscious.

I will not fear.
I will not panic.
I will not lose control.

I repeated that mantra in my head, grateful for not being aware of what happened when it did, until another realization sank in.

I snapped my head towards Maeve. Her head was

dipped, facing the ground, and her body slumped forward. She was also missing her clothes... and had stab wounds all over her body, with flies buzzing around her.

I couldn't hear her heartbeat. I looked down and saw that we were submerged in a pool of blood. Her feet were oddly angled as they dragged through what I assumed was her own blood. More than hers...

I listened for what felt like minutes, waiting for a heartbeat, but it never came.

I whispered her name.

Nothing.

I glanced to my left and saw Liam was still unconscious, but alive.

I called her name again... and still nothing.

"No..." I whispered to no one.

Maeve was gone.

I screamed, and a power akin to my own erupted from above us. I couldn't stop the scream that escaped. There was no more fight left in me.

These monsters destroyed and nearly murdered my mother and then did the same to Maeve, who was now dead.

Robed assassins came rushing in, hitting me, and telling me to shut the fuck up.

Why did they even keep me alive?

They grabbed a shred of my clothing off the ground, soaked in the blood of others, and shoved it in my mouth.

I wanted to spit it out, but preferred it to any possible alternatives.

I wanted to fight every single tear falling down my face that I knew would only please them.

I had no fight left. I deserved this. I got my mother hurt. I got my friend killed. All because I thought it would be fun to emasculate some asshole in a bar.

Their black eyes and rotted teeth... The shadows wafting off their skin... I couldn't think of a worse nightmare.

My eyes narrowed when two of them walked over to Maeve's body. Knives kept getting shoved in and out of my body, but I couldn't focus on the pain when I watched them getting closer to Maeve, touching her.

A chuckle sounded from my other side. My head whirled towards Liam, only to be forcefully turned back by a hard slap.

I turned again, and when I looked at Liam... beside him, I saw rotted teeth smiling behind a hood. A hand had been brushing through Liam's hair, right before that hand ripped off Liam's shirt.

I cried out in fear for him behind the disgusting rag in my mouth, too scared to spit it out lest they put something else in it.

They enjoyed my cries, which became apparent when all of them laughed. I could feel the blood pouring down my skin as I heard breathy laughs to my right, where Maeve was.

The shadows that flowed from them, unlike the ones in the forest, reeked of carrion and found their way into the puncture wounds. I could feel my vision darkening, and my consciousness fading from whatever the fuck these shadows were doing to me.

I will not fear...

I screamed, unintentionally choking on the blood,

because the pain from those shadows was beyond worse than any blade.

I will not panic...

I slammed my eyes shut, focusing on my power.

It was my father's, wasn't it? Surely it should be more powerful than the binds!

I heard clothing being removed. Pants. I kept my eyes closed and prayed to every god imaginable for that beautiful asshole to rescue me, or at least put me to sleep, so I didn't have to be aware of what was about to happen to me again.

To all three of us.

One of them gripped onto my hips, and I sobbed until I felt his hands release their grip... and I watched them as they fell and submerged into the blood on the floor.

I looked up, and he was in shock, staring at his severed wrists, before looking at me in confusion... right when the tip of a sword came out of his mouth, spraying blood on my face.

Over his shoulder were familiar celestine eyes of pure rage. The rag fell from my mouth.

He was here.

He was here.

He was here, and he brought two others, one of which was the blonde demon. His chest was now heaving, with fire in his eyes and talons shooting from his fingers.

While one was subduing the surrounding men, the other, the one with the eyes of pure emerald, went straight for Liam. He untied him, wrapped his half-naked body in his cloak, and carried him over his shoulder.

He was here.

He didn't say a word as he walked up to me and

unchained my wrists, helping me as I stumbled, feet sloshing through the blood.

When I got my balance, still naked, I stood up straight to assess what was happening. The magic in the forest smelled like his, but it wasn't.

He looked like he might speak and then decided against it. Then he and his men walked behind the men, who were all grouped together and tied up.

I looked up at Conláed in question before the corner of his mouth slightly lifted, not matching the rage in his eyes. He nodded towards the monsters kneeling in Maeve's blood. "Do it." he ordered.

I searched inward for any fire waking up from being released from the chains, but it was only a flicker.

He seemed to understand because he held his hand out, palm facing up, and produced fire atop it. If he offered me strength, I wouldn't know how to take it.

Slowly, the fire floated from his hand and toward me. My body absorbed it without my control.

His flames were so much different from mine. All chaos and no form. I felt it go free in its new host, free and wild.

I looked at the monsters on the floor while I remained standing in my naked and brutalized body. Their shaking turned uncontrollable, trembling as they began begging.

I looked over at Maeve's body and then thought of my mother. How Maeve left this world feeling what I felt, worse. How my mother felt, almost having left this world.

I turned back slowly to the pleading infestation before me. Tears were flowing down my angered face, completely unable to hold back and completely unable to care. I held out my hands, palms facing the ceiling, before I hesitated.

His celestine eyes remained on mine, and he snarled, *"Do it."*

It wasn't permission. It was urgency. I needed to do this now, and he knew it.

I watched as slowly, *ever so slowly,* their bodies burned alive from the inside out.

The smell was atrocious, but I kept a smile on the last face they'd ever see.

Eyes melted from their sockets, their blood ran black instead of red, and the fire surrounded us, scaling the walls.

I couldn't stop.

When their bodies turned to ashes, I looked up, and Conláed instantly appeared at my side, still fixating on my eyes. I smelled the magic before I started to fall back asleep, falling into his arms again while the dungeon crumbled around us.

CHAPTER
THIRTY-EIGHT

CONLÁED, SEVERAL MINUTES PRIOR...

Damien swore under his breath, choking on it, and I didn't have to look back to know he was transforming.

The King was about to rain down hell upon everyone here if we didn't get off this hill and do something to help. If he destroyed the castle, it would capsize and kill everyone inside, including his daughter and Liam. And whoever the fuck went with her.

Power shot out around us, swaying the trees in its path, and I began to smell a tremendous amount of blood.

"He broke the barrier."

I could hear the storm of her heartbeat. I could smell the blood, the fear, and the magic that must be cutting off their powers. And I could smell pungent male pheromones.

Anger surged through me in waves of violence. My

brothers were bristling, growling, and we were ready to slaughter every single one of them in there. Even Drak.

Alaric's battle cries did not relent. He landed right in front of the two women they held captive, ripping out the hearts of their captors behind them.

A hundred of them, more, poured out from in and around their castle, pushing Alaric and his men back. He screamed, fiercely cutting down everyone in his path to save his daughter. His fire erupted again in a smaller surge, taking out at least thirty.

We vanished, appearing in the nearest tower. Six were in this room. They began running at the sight of us, understandably so.

Damien breathed in deeply, gathering his power before branches shot through the ground, the windows, impaling everyone, suspending them in the air. He sent a wave of fire, leaving nothing but ash in its wake.

I heard the scream the same moment he did. And then I heard it forced to a muffle.

They knew he was going to come for her. They didn't plan to make it out alive, and they were abusing the little power they had before death. This wasn't a suicide mission for Áine.

This was *their* suicide mission, likely at the spelled order of someone much more powerful.

That scent of magic was powerful, seeping in from the barrier or from beneath the castle. It led us to the door, to the scent of her fear and panic. To the men surrounding her, as one of them had his hands on her hips.

With a wave of my hand, his hands severed from his wrists and fell to the ground. I was there in an instant and shoved my blade up his spine and out of his throat. I was so blind with rage I didn't even notice the ones beside the other female, *or* the ones looking predatory around Liam.

A rag soaked in blood that wasn't hers fell out of her mouth. Her eyes were searching mine for any hint that this was an illusion.

She didn't break her gaze as I waved my hand, severing the chains binding her magic. She didn't look away as I made sure she could still stand, then stepped back.

This beast of a beauty was wounded and broken, and I feared that if I looked away, she would crumble and drown in the blood of her friend. We hated each other, that was the unfortunate truth, but now... Now she looked at me with something different in her eyes, reverent even.

She looked intently at Damien carrying Liam, who was still asleep, then at Drak, who gently carried her dead friend.

Her nostrils flared as her chest heaved. Her back straightened as she looked back towards me and to the evil pieces of shit we forced to kneel before her, unashamed of her bare body that had been defiled and mutilated.

I watched as she learned the wild nature of my fire and let it consume her fully.

She hesitated, infuriating me. I fought everything to hold back and let her have this justice she deserves. If she doesn't destroy them now, there would be nothing to stop Damien and I.

"Do it," I snarled at her.

I looked to my men when she smiled cruelly at the lowlifes beneath her. I saw Damien's eyes sparkle as I knew mine had.

If the rest of the world outside this room was being set on fire, and we all died tonight, at least we had this. At least *she* would have this.

I looked back at her, and my face slackened. She had been immortal for two days and yet had enough control to slowly melt all of them at once. Every single one.

She smiled maniacally as she made them feel every ounce of it and set them on fire, leaving nothing behind. The smell would've made any average person vomit their guts up.

Fire scaled the walls of the dungeon, a dungeon that was already on its last legs.

I walked towards her as she began to sway, picking her up as I spelled her back to sleep. I removed my cloak and covered her exposed body. Damien had Liam, who was still fast asleep.

We appeared in the courtyard where there were still so many of them surrounding Alaric, but it was the last of them.

Behind us, the castle caved in on itself, destroying any potential lingering life inside.

Alaric saw me carrying Áine as he sliced through someone's torso. Her body jerked before settling back to sleep.

My brothers and I whispered a chant, and the remaining fifty or so turned to ashes.

Alaric didn't take his eyes off us. There was fear in his eyes for his daughter and hatred for us. I only heard my own feet as I approached him. "She's alive, as is Liam."

I wondered if my saying his name would set anything off. It did, but only for everyone else surrounding him with their widened eyes. I bet this motherfucker knew who Liam was... *Remembered* him, even.

"And Maeve?" The blonde captain demanded before resting her eyes on the one Drak was carrying. Her eyes widened in horror, not hearing a heartbeat, and tears filled her eyes as she slowly looked up at Drak with an accusatory look.

His lip curled. "She was long gone when we arrived only minutes ago, right after your king broke the barrier."

I heard her breathing heavily before she thanked him, and he bowed his head slightly.

I turned back to Alaric. "I can take them home, have Drak gather my strongest healer to meet us at your castle, if you'd be alright with that instead of her riding home. We would be there in a matter of seconds. She is badly wounded, and I worry for his weakened form." I jerked my head in Liam's direction. "He was dosed with the same amount of magic as them, and he still hasn't wakened."

Alaric continued to stare daggers into me through his furrowed brows.

I shook my head. "I am not your enemy."

"You expect me to believe that? You think I can't see through this façade of yours?" he sneered.

"If it is a façade, then you should trust that even then, I wouldn't hurt her. I've proven that several times already."

He stared at me for several more moments before looking at his people.

"Sloan, you're in charge. Lead the army home," he demanded as he started towards us.

"That's not a good idea," she responded. He turned on his heel towards her in shock that she would say that in front of his men. "She is in a delicate state. I think I should be the one to go with them. I'll be the one making sure she is bathed and assisting their healer with her wounds."

He looked at her, considering, and then sighed, nodding in agreement.

A commotion was growing louder from within their army, and I could hear feminine rage within them making its way toward us, and then there she was.

The gorgeous girl who had raging golden brown eyes on a face covered in blood, shoved past everyone, and stared at me with hatred, *accusatory* hatred.

And I don't think it was in regards to what happened to Áine.

"Get your fucking hands off her," she snarled like a rabid beast and stormed her way to me, but Alaric grabbed her arm, stopping her.

She looked like she was about to thrash her body, disobeying the king in front of everyone, something many would be executed for. I could let it happen, let her die, but we needed their trust before anything.

But, I didn't do anything. No. That fucking bond has become a second being within my soul, driving me when it wants.

I watched the girl's upper body start to twist, and I couldn't spell her to sleep.

The blonde captain, Sloan, was there in an instant, and punched her so hard in the face she slumped in Alaric's hold, fast asleep.

I blinked, these females were nothing like the ones I grew up with.

Alaric passed Isolde's body, now stirring, to another

soldier, and mounted his horse. He stared me down once more. "If you touch her, I will remove your hands and send them to your mother."

I heard Drak growling behind me, but I nodded. For now, I'd allow it.

His wife, his daughter, and her friend were all violated, and only his daughter seemed to make it out alive. He was allowed to be a prick, and I believed his threat.

Sloan, and the surrounding others looked between me and the King in confusion as he rode off. He didn't tell them about us, then.

Interesting.

Drak handed over the fallen soldier to another and held his hand out for Sloan. She raised her eyebrow that held a state of what the fuck.

"If you're coming with us, you need to hold on," he said, looking away in irritation before she smacked her hand onto his, causing his jaw to flinch.

I narrowed my eyes at that before vanishing.

We appeared in Áine's room and I immediately walked to the bed to lay her down. Damien placed Liam down beside her.

Sloan was staring each of us down.

One by one, with her chin high and lip curled, she looked into each of our souls like she contemplated how to slaughter us all by herself. Like it was in her power to do so. Power that we could now feel radiating off her.

"Grab your healer. I'll get her cleaned up," she ordered.

Drak was smirking when he looked away and left with Damien. They went first so I could tell her what we saw when we found Áine. "You should know that things happened before we arrived."

She said nothing as she stared at me contemptuously, waiting for me to continue.

"It looked like any female's worst nightmare. Your fallen friend had suffered the worst of it, but the princess barely made it out alive," I continued, and she raised her chin higher, if possible.

"And she has you to thank for that," she sneered. Not a hint of gratitude behind it.

I stayed silent for a moment, considering my next response. That lasted all but a moment when I remembered that I didn't fucking answer to her. I vanished while holding her stare.

When I arrived back home, they were waiting for me.

"We need to release Liam's spell before he wakes up, and let him wake up here. Not there, in the middle of that disaster," Damien insisted.

"I agree with you, but I think we should wait until the aftermath of all this calms. They won't hurt him, Damien," I said in an assuring tone.

He snorted, thinking me delusional.

"Go get Lira. She likes you better," I ordered.

His demeanor shifted. "No, she just likes the way I fuck her. She actually kind of hates me."

"Well then, hand her cash and the promise of a good

time. And hurry. We have shit to do." And that was that.

Alone with Drak, I had to ask. "Did she hurt you?"

He smiled. "She would send a lesser male screaming, that's for sure."

I nodded, unable to find humor in any of it. "Good, we need that kind of strength on our side." I turned towards the bar cart to pour two glasses.

Drak sat down in one of the leather chairs as he had a drink. "You think the Princess will agree to working with us?"

I sighed as I sat next to him. "She doesn't have a choice. She made a bargain."

"And Alaric?" he added.

I looked at the floor before downing my drink, reaching back for the decanter I had brought. "I think we saved his daughter's life. Twice."

"Three times, and you two saved her. I was just there for the ride." He was clearly trying to make two points here.

I sighed, heavier this time. "I don't know, Drak. I can only hope. At the very least, we're off his kill list. I might be able to sway Áine beyond just the bargain, which might honestly be the key here now." I wasn't feeling the most enthusiastic about it, but that could be from the heaviness of what had just happened.

Drak remained silent, just listening to me.

"She's intelligent, *at times*, cares about her people, and I think she might be able to kill everyone if she wanted. Not that she knows that yet."

"But," he interrupted.

"But she was just assaulted."

"Raped. You can say it, Con. That's what happened."

I winced at his words. That girl was going to wake up, and her entire world would be on fire. "We don't know that for sure. They could've done... other things. We could've arrived right before it happened." I prayed as much, anyway. Not fully believing my words. Not at all, actually.

Drak finished his drink and poured another. "Con, that girl had her heart completely ripped out of her chest and watched as her enemies played with it. She's not going to be any help to us tomorrow, and she's not going to be any help to us the day after. We have to come up with another plan," he insisted with urgency in his voice.

He was right, but I haven't heard anyone else come up with another idea.

"Let me know when you think of something better than the fucking Dhadren," I snorted, downing the rest of my drink before pouring another.

"I have many times insisted we go to the Demon Realm, but you won't listen, not with that trance you're currently in," he accused. There wasn't any nastiness in it, but I still wanted to punch him.

"You can hit me if it makes you feel better, but we all see it. Everyone but you," he chided, smirking.

I wanted to argue, but I didn't have the energy. I set my cup down, so I wasn't inebriated in front of the blonde predator we were about to share a room with again.

I heard Damien's voice in the halls followed by Lira's annoyed tone coming closer.

They paused, opened the door, and silenced before he bowed his head, alerting us that all was arranged and we could go. Drak and I stood and readied ourselves to dive back into the bear's cave.

CHAPTER
THIRTY-NINE

SLOAN

My throat tightened when I saw three of the most dangerous looking men I've ever seen come out of the stronghold carrying Áine. I didn't trust them and their too-perfect displays as knights in shining armor. But they saved her and Liam.

I wouldn't think about Maeve today. I'd allow the tears when I knew they wouldn't be back soon with the healer. I needed to make sure my gratitude was known without groveling.

Also, without being a cunt, an in-between I was never good at.

I rinsed the rest of the soap out of Áine's hair while I had her leaning on my arm like a baby; like my arm wasn't already about to fall off. I picked her up and carried her to the bed that I had covered in towels.

Whatever spells were placed on that castle or in that

dungeon, it was causing her healing to slow significantly. None of the deep cuts were closed, but they were clotting, at least. At the slow rate of it, they would certainly scar. They needed to be stitched up soon if those males would hurry the fuck up like they promised.

I swallowed my nastiness before they came back. *Gratitude, Sloan.*

I placed a warm nightgown over her body. Not constricting and would make it easy for a healer to do their work. I braided her wet hair after adding in oils. As a female, she didn't take care of herself in the ways most were beaten into their skulls to do. Her ends were always dry and breaking.

It wasn't until we were teenagers that I tried to make her braid it into a protective style against the plague in the air, killing us. If we were going to die, our hair wouldn't look bad in the process. She couldn't braid for shit though, so I would do it. Or Mira.

All done. Like nothing terrible had ever happened to her.

I clenched my jaw, swallowing down the sorrow flooding my face, threatening to unleash tears. I sat beside her, just in case she woke up and needed to kill anyone else.

We couldn't risk her life now. The Queen would ring my neck if she knew I let Áine do half the stupid shit she's done. I was always comfortable with her recklessness, whether fighting a stranger, bringing them to her bed, or both. But still, I was always nearby to ensure she wasn't murdered.

Until the day she saved Maeve.

She changed so much that day. The beginning of understanding the responsibility of others. The dread when you let someone down or when they died on your watch, like Minsi. They were the reason she followed the path of leadership and not just warmongering.

A few tears escaped, and I heard the blonde monster clear his throat.

I jerked up, wiping my face before turning around. His face was that of steel. Cold and sharp. Though he swallowed audibly while looking at my face.

My face would've given it away if I hadn't already when I wiped my tears before turning around. I hated crying. My entire face became flush like Áine's and wouldn't calm down until several minutes later, and I dunked my face in cold water.

The third one, who looked like he enjoyed torturing people before breakfast, was with a beautiful young woman holding a pack.

"Which one should I inspect first?" she asked the room.

I said Áine's name at the exact moment the sadistic-looking fucker said Liam's. He curled his lip at me for daring to suggest Áine was more important.

The one with long black hair cleared his throat and instructed her to check Áine first.

My staring contest wasn't over yet with this one.

"And who the fuck is Liam to you?" I preened.

His jaw flinched, but he said nothing, seeming to not want to give anything away. I looked at Liam and then back at him. My immediate thought was brothers, but Liam looked so small in comparison, and I'm pretty sure this fucker was a devil.

"They say your name is Sloan," the healer interjected.

I nodded at her.

"Good, will you be so kind as to assist me with Áine? Maybe walk me through some of the injuries?"

I looked at the one Alaric called Conláed, trying to keep the contempt in check. "I wasn't there. He knows more than I do. You should ask him."

He didn't hide any contempt on his face when he stared back. "Drak, Damien, please give the three of us a moment."

Damien snorted as he led the way. The bigger blonde monster, Drak, I assumed since the name fit, shut the door behind them. Which was ridiculous. They'd have to leave the castle entirely to not overhear us. And then, as if they heard my thoughts, they vanished. That, or they didn't want to listen to what Conláed was about to say.

"I wasn't there either, Lira, so keep that in mind when I tell you this. When I arrived, her body was suspended from the ceiling by chains. Chains that were spelled with magic to keep her powers away. There were men surrounding her, repeatedly shoving blades into her skin in the many places I'm sure you noted moments ago. Another man was in front of her and grabbing her while he was about to rape her. He didn't, but he was about to before I murdered him. Although, I have a strong feeling I only saved her from what she had already been enduring before we arrived, since her friend was already dead, and the condition of her body was a duplicate of what I found of Áine's. She'll need to be checked everywhere for infection, and the wounds need to be sutured since she isn't healing like she's supposed to."

I ran to the basin and vomited violently.

"Then she absorbed my flames before wielding them to burn them alive," he added when I rinsed my mouth out.

I turned my face towards him. "You did *what?*"

"*She,* wielded, my,"

"I know what the fuck you said, asshole. I didn't know we could do that," I said as I looked over at her on the bed, still sound asleep.

"Not all can. It only works if your powers are compatible," he added with irritation to his voice. He was clearly over me being here.

I snorted at that and then realized what he just said. I turned on my heel before walking up to him. "What are you doing with her?" I asked, keeping my chin high.

He stared me down, revealing nothing.

I held my head high and told him, "I owe you a debt." And he blinked at that. "Despite the obvious ulterior motives, you saved Áine three times already. You have my gratitude." I kept my voice controlled and firm.

Nodding, he replied, "I would've done it for anyone." Attempting to be humble. It was a good joke. I'd give him that.

I looked him over before saying, "I doubt that." and walked back toward Áine.

CHAPTER
FORTY

ISOLDE

I woke to my body bouncing atop a horse. Someone had thrown me on it like baggage.

Looking up, Keira's eyes were now peering down at me in judgment. She pursed her lips before returning to look straight ahead. "Don't get any ideas." she murmured, but I was already off her horse and running ahead of them.

I ignored the King's calls, ensuring I slept in a dungeon tonight.

But it didn't matter, because my mate was in there.

She was hurt and in so much more pain than I could ever fathom, and that fucker carrying her didn't look innocent in the slightest.

I ran past the gates, and was immediately thrown on my ass.

Looking up, Visha was standing beside five guards. "You're coming with me."

I snarled. "Get out of my way, *witch*."

She smirked. "Under the King's orders, you're coming with me before you become a threat to yourself."

I snorted. "Under the King's orders? He hasn't even arrived to give those orders!"

She said nothing for a moment, not acknowledging my outburst. "Come with me now, or the guards will carry you."

"She *needs* me." I stood on my feet.

"She will kill you. And that's the last thing she needs, don't you think?"

My eyes widened in horror. "She would *never* do that!"

Visha shouted right back. "She wouldn't know she did it until she looks down at your burnt body girl! Are you so stupid you can't even think straight in a crisis? You're a captain!"

I fisted my hands at my sides. "Get out of my way, before I make you."

She snorted, "Pathetic." She nodded at her five guards before turning her heel.

My fist met the throat of one until I was being dragged by arms under my own.

Moments later, I'm thrown into a cell I knew I'd be sleeping in.

Visha was locking the door as I slid down the wall, contemplating my life choices. "You will remain here until you can calm down and stop acting like an animal."

I rested my arms on my knees, silently looking straight ahead at nothing.

"Are you hungry?" She had the balls to ask.

"Fuck off."
She turned around and did exactly that.

CHAPTER
FORTY-ONE

LIAM

I smelled it while trying to force myself awake. That magic and its overwhelming scent of burnt rust.

I could feel consciousness sparking through me, protesting whatever the hell was keeping me under.

Forcing my fingers to move first, a pain shot up my wrist. Which meant I was tied up. For how long, I didn't know.

I tried to open my eyes, but they refused. Everything was so heavy. I heard male voices, then Sloan's, and then another female voice I didn't recognize.

They went silent. Did they know I was trying to wake up? How long have I been out? And where was Áine?

I forced a noise in my throat that turned into a groan. One of the men picked me up like a child and carried me out of whatever room we were in. *Áine's...*

It smelled like Áine's room. I jerked my body, trying to

force consciousness through whatever bullshit was wrapped around my mind.

"Calm down. You're safe," the man carrying me said. There was something familiar about his voice that made me believe him. Probably more fucking magic.

I barely choked out Áine's name in question.

"Alive, and also safe. The healer is there now."

"*Maeve?*"

Silence.

He kicked open a door, *my* door, and put me on the bed before grabbing my chair to sit. Probably my babysitter, then. Who the fuck was this guy? Friend of Alaric?

I tried to sit up and failed. "Where is Maeve?" I asked him again.

He hesitated to speak for a moment. I was about to get loud.

"She's fine. In her room with another healer," he lied. He wasn't even trying to hide it.

"Tell me where she is. Now." My scratchy throat was ruining my authoritative voice.

He quietly chuckled at that, tilting his head. "And who do you think you are to be demanding *anything* from me?"

"Who the fuck are you? I've never seen you in my life, yet here you are, on one of the highest floors of the castle's quarters. Are you a friend of the King? Did he call you here for aid?"

He threw his head back and released a deep laugh. "God's no! That man would rather see my head on a spike." He smiled at that, which unnerved me.

The King and his kingdom have all been here for a *long* time. There hadn't been any visitors from distant lands, long-lost relatives, no one.... He resembled no one, but inside my soul, where the hot poker used to reside, something told me to dig deeper.

"Do I know you?" I dared to ask him.

"Go back to sleep, little Liam. You'll have the answers to all your questions soon enough," he said. He looked exhausted and worried, like he hadn't slept well in years.

I was getting pissed. I had been sleeping for too long already. "I asked, do I fucking know you?" I choked out, still failing to sound like the alpha here.

Still smirking, he shook his head before answering. "We met a very long time ago."

There was something about the green in his eyes that was familiar, but I knew I would've remembered someone who looked as terrifying as him. Unless it would've been a memory I lost before meeting Áine.

Panic flushed through me, and I forced myself to sit up. I had to catch him if he ran. *Come on, legs. Wake the fuck up!*

He swore before storming out.

I tried to run after him, falling off the bed and onto the floor like an invalid. I couldn't get up. This was so pathetic. This was why I couldn't save anybody. Áine was right. I had no business trying to be the hero anymore. I was their liability.

I heard the man who stormed out call for Con. *Conláed... Great. Just fucking great. Of course, it's him, and these must be his lackeys.*

I was still gripping the mattress, trying to pull myself up and failing. Whatever they dosed me with was powerful.

I heard mumbling getting closer.

"We can't risk giving him another dose. He's... weak." He paused for too long before saying the word weak.

I heard Conláed mumbling, but couldn't understand it. He seemed to be trying and failing to keep the other one from being too loud.

"Then fix it!" he snapped, not even trying to lower his voice. A strain in his voice sounded like this was the continuation of an earlier argument. "Let's take him then. Let's take him home. What if it happens *here*, and they kill him?" he urged Conláed.

"Fuck!" Conláed snapped, "Fine. But we need a plan because we can't drag him out of here kicking and screaming if he's awake."

"I'll knock him out. He can forgive me later," the familiar voice responded. They knew me. This wasn't a trick. At least I prayed it wasn't. I needed to know. I couldn't be left in the dark anymore. I swung the door open, leaning on it to keep myself upright.

"I won't kick and scream," I said to them. They widened their eyes at me, contemplating what to say next, what was safe since they knew more than me. They looked at each other for a moment and then nodded.

"Ok. You need to wait in your room. Damien will be outside the door here, keeping watch. Pack your bags." Then he, Conláed, walked off before I could respond.

"Are you sure?" the other one, Damien asked me.

I lowered my eyes briefly before looking back up at him. "They don't need me anymore."

CHAPTER
FORTY-TWO

ÁINE

Quiet. It was too quiet when my eyes slipped open. The voices I heard in and out disappeared. Sloan wasn't here anymore. I stared at the ceiling, seeing flashes of their faces in and out.

More silence. Everything in and out of my mind was quiet. I smelled him and the two who were with him. They had been here. I smelled Liam in my bed, probably also needing healing, or they didn't know where he slept.

I smelled the assassins. Their scent was in this room.

I jerked my body up, looking around and found no one. It was coming from a discarded piece of black clothing, a cloak, shoved in the corner of the room. I stood up too quickly and immediately fell, vomiting all over the floor.

I slowly stood back up and walked towards that cloak. It also smelled like the male who rescued me. He must have covered me in it before carrying me out. Like the powerless liability I was.

The smell of those monsters was all over the room. It was in my bed. It was coming from the bathroom. I walked out the door and into the hall in a gown that Sloan must have put me in... and didn't think twice before I set the room on fire.

My bed, all my books, everything. That scent would forever linger on all those things. And I couldn't deal with it. That smell needed to be gone.

I felt the flames vanish. I looked back and saw that my father had put it out. He said nothing. Didn't look at me. The disgusting and pathetic excuse for a daughter.

I used the remaining flicker of Conláed's flames that still resided within me like a napping tiger.

I kept the fire contained within the room and walked away. My father was swearing under his breath, not understanding why he couldn't extinguish it.

"Áine! Put this out now!" he demanded, but I felt nothing. No urge to help him. I wanted that room, and everything inside it destroyed.

I made it to Liam's room and opened the door. He wasn't there, but I still smelled him. I found a folded piece of paper on the dresser, held down by an inkwell. I saw his drawers were slightly open and empty. I went inside and read the note.

Please do not worry. Liam's mind was held down by the magic keeping him asleep. Magic that was strong enough to incapacitate an immortal, and too strong for him in his weakened state. The healer we brought with us was not skilled in this situation and feared destroying him. We brought him with us to see the most skilled of healers. We promise to bring him back when he is better and finally awake.'

No signature. No magic. Just their smell. I fought the urge to set this room on fire as well.

I went to Sloan's room. The only place I felt safe enough to sleep more. I rinsed the foul taste out of my mouth, crawled into her bed, and fell asleep.

I heard a knock before someone came in. I jerked myself up, fire threatening to erupt within me.

It was just Sloan.

"Your room has been redone. It took a while since they had to wait for the fire to go out," she informed me.

I didn't want to go back there and smell them.

"If you'd rather stay here, I don't mind sleeping in your room for now. I just came from there, Áine. The smell is gone. Only the incense I had burned for you," she said in what I assumed was supposed to be her comforting voice. I much preferred her bitchy one.

She clearly didn't want me in her space. I didn't blame her. I would also find being around someone as disgusting as myself difficult. I got up and walked out. She didn't look at me or say anything else.

I felt sick. I bet Liam left when he also realized how

disgusting I was, not wanting to be around the reason important people died.

He probably won't be back.

When I returned to my room, I took in the mattress on the floor. Where there used to be rugs, there was flat, charred stone. An entire wall of built-in bookshelves that held hundreds of my favorite books. Now, there were only ashes. Gone was the intricate four-poster bed I was gifted after I bled for the first time. A gift from my mother.

I looked over and noticed that the window was now locked from the outside. How ridiculous. Like I'd go anywhere. Like anyone will want me now. Unless they thought I'd jump...

If I killed myself, I'd set myself on fire if I thought I could burn, not leaving a body behind for them to clean up or for my father to see.

If fire wouldn't work, I'd go deep within the forest and allow the beasts to eat me.

In the bath chamber, I watched the water fill and thought about drowning. But that would be an even bigger mess for them to clean.

I started to undress and then smelled him. I whipped my head towards the window. No one was there, but the smell still lingered.

I was alone.

So completely alone.

I soaked the sea sponge with soap and began scrubbing the dungeon off me that I still felt on my skin. It wasn't coming off. The smell of those... It wasn't coming off. The scent of a powerless and despicable woman wasn't coming off.

The fire inside me was overheating, bringing the water to a boil. I stood and smothered myself with the rest of my solvent. It was too soft. It wasn't cleaning deep enough.

I jumped out of the tub and punched the wall, causing particles of stone to fall. I picked up the sharp pebbles and embedded them into the sponge.

The door flung open, and Keira came in, looked at the hole in the wall, and then at what I was doing. Anger and shame flooded through me. Fire began to lap my skin, and I screamed.

"GET THE FUCK OUT!!"

She fell back, stumbling over her feet, and ran out, slamming the door behind her. I smashed the rock in front of me into tiny bits and put them into a bowl with the solvent. I mixed them together and began scrubbing.

The smell needed to go away. If it didn't, I would die. Let the beasts eat me and shit out the scent of those males where it belongs.

I looked at my blood in the water and saw the pool of blood in the dungeon, the blood in my mother's bedchamber.

He shouldn't have let me kill them so quickly. I should've kept them in their own cell, peeling their flesh off their bones one by one for days.

I sat in the tub, staring into the blood water until it ran cold, watching as my cuts slowly healed. What a fucking *waste...*

CHAPTER
FORTY-THREE

LIAM

I wanted to leave a note for them. One from me. But Conláed rejected it, not explaining why, either.

They were all gathered in my room before Damien grabbed my arm, and we disappeared, landing in a field.

A *valley*.

Damien let my arm go as I took a few steps forward and took in the sight before me.

We were surrounded by snow-capped mountains.

I only remember seeing them in sketches, having never seen them on our lands. It was the most beautiful sight I had ever seen.

I turned back to see them now chuckling at my reaction.

"I told you he loved it here, Con. Now you'll never doubt it again," Damien said, still smiling.

The behemoth named Drak snorted. "Welcome home Liam."

I was so bewildered. I knew my face was demanding answers. Why are we here and not in the small castle right behind them?

"Liam," Conláed said, stealing my attention. He looked sad. No... that was guilt.

"How the fuck do you know me?" I demanded, choking back tears. I knew my entire world was about to explode.

"I'm sorry," Conláed said before raising and flicking his hand at the wrist.

The void where the hot poker resided, relentlessly telling me to protect Áine, erupted.

My body exploded in pain. I could feel the shifting of my bones beneath my flesh. It was unbearable. I screamed in pain as I felt my limbs being stretched. Like I had been held in a torture device. These strangers spoke as if I were someone dear to them, like family.

Like they didn't force me to forget everything about myself for years, thinking I was a nobody, completely alone and a complete burden to others.

Like I wasn't questioning who I was every single day and wondering why I was abandoned...

Like I didn't just spend my entire being watching over some spoiled fucking princess for them...

I was on my knees, howling in pain at my body reverting to its natural form. I looked up at Conláed with pure loathing in my eyes, heaving through the pain.

The guilt never left his stupid fucking face.

"You might want to leave," I snarled. "Before I rip out your fucking throat."

CHAPTER
FORTY-FOUR

CONLÁED

I was ready for it. I had been dreading this since the day I sent him down there. When he wasn't fully aware of what he signed up for. I couldn't tell him it would erase his memories, since it would risk keeping the entire spell contained. It would've been for nothing if he accidentally reverted back to his true form before their curse broke.

The fury in his eyes was that of heartbreak. I broke his trust. I would never understand the depth of emptiness he felt all those years, surrounded by strangers.

I watched as his body transformed. His old tattoos representing his people and command were overlapping and burning through the ones he got in Kilhorn.

Drak stepped in between us, facing me and demanded, "You need to go."

I snorted, trying to hold back tears. "I'm not running away. I deserve this."

"We are equally at fault here, and we don't have time. We can handle him here. You need to check on her. Now."

I looked back at him. He painfully and slowly lifted himself up to stand, never taking that loathing look off his face.

"I'm sorry," I pleaded before vanishing and landing on the cliff near Alaric's castle. Letting the tears fall now that I was alone. I'm going to be paying for that one for a long time.

After giving myself a moment to get it together, I had another to go to and watch fall apart. Also, my doing.

I appeared right outside her window, peering in to see that she was alive. I saw her in the bath chamber, readying it herself this time.

I took a deep, shuddered breath, trying to fight the guilt from seeing the deadness in her eyes. Even when in so much pain, she was so beautiful.

She stood so painfully still as she stared at the tub filling up. She pulled her nightgown over her head, and I stopped breathing.

I vanished before I lowered myself further. Alaric would know I was here soon, if not already.

I forgot to spell my scent away before coming here. I landed on the roof, sniffing out Liam's room to see if anyone was in there, and went in through the window. Áine's scent was faintly here.

The note was gone, so her scent could've been from her taking it, or it could've been lingering from the last time they shared a bed together.

My teeth were about to chip against each other before I heard something crash and reverberate through the walls.

My heart rate dropped as the possibilities flooded my mind. I listened to make sure I heard her heartbeat. It was beating erratically and she was panting heavily.

I heard someone barging into her room before Áine screamed. I exhaled a sigh of relief. She wasn't dead or dying.

Sloan was in the hallway when someone came out with her heartbeat thundering.

She was pushing out words through her heavy breathing. "She punched through the stone wall and had rocks in her hand, and she was trying to shove them into her bath sponge. I have no idea what the fuck she was doing. But her body was glowing red when she screamed, so I did what she said and got the fuck out of there."

I smelled blood and winced at what I assumed she was doing. I was overstepping. I shouldn't be here, which I was about to rectify when Sloan kicked the door open.

Worry and anger were written all over her face. She couldn't decide between fighting me and going to her.

"You want me dead? Get in line. She needs you *now*," I snarled at her. I could get on her level *real* quick if she wanted to play that game.

"Leave," she ordered before shutting the door.

CHAPTER
FORTY-FIVE

SLOAN

I only made it as far as outside her door.

What was my plan here? Drag her out by her hair and beat the despair out of her? I leaned my back against the wall and slid to the floor.

I'd sit here and clear my temperamental mind before barging in there. I had never been assaulted. I knew nothing of her pain and needed to handle this carefully before she added another ghost to the pile.

Complete silence came from inside, only her heartbeat that would periodically become erratic and then stop. She was losing it, and all I could do was sit here with my head up my ass.

I stared at the wall, zoning out for several moments, recalling when Conláed carried her out of that crumbling castle. In those moments, he didn't look snide and full of ulterior motives, but of a commander carrying out his nearly fallen soldier that he refused to leave behind. He reminded me of her.

When I found him in Liam's room, it disappointed me that he came alone. I knew he was here for her. It doesn't take an idiot to notice what he wants, but I didn't trust him. If his always being there at the right time wasn't enough of a red flag, Alaric knew him. From the looks between them, it wasn't a good thing.

Áine hadn't gotten out of the tub, and it was probably an hour since I'd been sitting here. That water had to be freezing by now. At that, I decided I was over the staring contest with the wall.

When I opened the door, I heard her growling. A warning.

"Is the wounded beast done with her blood bath?" I sniped, forgetting to make a better plan to approach her before coming here.

"Get out." Her voice was guttural and empty.

"No," She wasn't getting rid of me yet.

"Get. Out. Now."

"I. Said. No."

She sized me up for a moment before she opened her mouth. "Look at that, there are people in the world who understand what that word means. If only they knew more of personal fucking boundaries," she spat.

I snorted. *Unbelievable.* "You are not going to spin me into the monster here. Monsters don't come in to make sure their sisters are still breathing."

"You honestly think I'd kill myself?" she asked unconvincingly.

I rolled my eyes, made my way toward the tub, reached

into the bloodied water, and pulled out the drain plug. She growled the entire fucking time, like she was threatening to rip my throat out with her teeth.

"Get up," I ordered, turning to grab a towel.

She just sat there staring at the red water falling, looking ultimately defeated.

"Áine."

"She's dead," she breathed. My heart cracked at the despair in her voice. In her soul.

"I know," I said in the most comforting voice I could muster.

"I killed her," she choked out before looking up at me.

"You did no such thing," I said firmly. "You can't,"

"Yes, I fucking did. My terrible fucking decisions all led to them being raped and butchered!" she yelled with her voice cracking. I had never seen her like this. So... broken.

I could smell Alaric in the hall and hear his trembling heartbeat.

"My mind didn't think about the safety of anyone. The only place it's been was picturing the ways I could humiliate or murder Carsen, or what that space-demon asshole would feel like inside me."

I forced my face to remain unflinching. She needed strength that she didn't have.

She cackled and looked up at me with wide, vulnerable eyes, begging me to tell her what to do, and then laughed hysterically.

She lost her grip on herself. "I am nothing but that of lust and violence. A complete disgrace of a princess and daughter. I'm a complete waste, and you should just leave me alone and not bother."

She stood up straight and snatched the towel from my hands like she didn't say the most self-deprecating shit she could have.

I wonder if it was because she knew her father was outside the door listening or if she just now picked up Conláed's scent from outside the window. If Alaric cared that he was out there, he didn't dare barge in to confront him.

She put the towel around her and headed towards her armoire, and then her window was forced open. Alaric was here instantly, thinking the worst of Conláed, only to find Liam on the threshold.

'*Gods fucking dammit...*' I heard Drak snap from outside.

Liam changed, and not like us, but like them. He was one of them. He had the fae ears, sure. But beneath his skin lay a bluish hue. His body was now covered in tattoos. Runes and others of a language I didn't recognize.

Alaric snorted.

Liam looked at him and then at me, but this time with pure contempt, before looking back at Áine, whose face went slack at his changes. His entire aura was different.

"Get dressed. We're leaving," Liam demanded, not taking his hateful eyes off Áine.

Alaric stepped beside her to face him. "You are, yes. She's not going anywhere with you with that look on your face."

Normally Áine would've lost her shit if someone spoke for her, even if it was her parents.

Liam didn't even look at him. Something happened.

"You're not..." I whispered. He whipped his eyes to mine. "... are you? What happened to you?"

He looked back at Áine, who remained frozen. "The prick outside is what happened, who I'll deal with later. Right now, I need to speak with Áine, alone. Get dressed. I'll be back in five minutes," he said with relentless venom, disappearing before Alaric could object. He growled violently before leaving the room. He didn't have much of a fight within him, either.

"Áine."

She didn't look at me.

"Áine, he might not know what happened," I told her, thinking that might be what he wanted to know.

She didn't flinch. She just put her legs into her pants and pulled on a tunic.

"I know why he's here," she said, still not looking at me.

"If you don't want to talk about it, I can go in your place," I offered.

"You will do no such thing," she said firmly.

"Are you sure?" I asked carefully. That made her jerk upright to stare me down questioningly.

"You have never asked me that fucking question in your life, Sloan."

I couldn't say anything else but, "Okay."

I waited with her before he came back to get her. I was startled when he grabbed her wrist, and they vanished. I refused to leave here until he brought her back in one piece.

Or at least in the same pieces.

CHAPTER
FORTY-SIX

ÁINE

"What the fuck happened?"

I narrowed my eyes at him. That was not the attitude I expected after bringing me to the cliffs overlooking the ocean. The same sea that used to be black.

I took in his new appearance, ignoring his question. Something stalled his transition, and I wondered if it was perhaps because his was more drastic. I barely looked any different. Just taller and with minor changes to bone structure.

He looked like he had grown two whole feet. His skin was slightly darker with the faintest hue of blue, with new tattoos similar to Conláed's. His muscles were more prominent, but beyond that, his eyes seemed to hold something ancient. Ancient and furious.

"I asked you a god's damned question."

"And who the fuck are you really, to think you can order me around like that?" The words had authority, but he heard it as I had. My voice was lifeless. I was exhausted. I wanted to curl up in the grass and sleep to the sound of the waves.

He nodded to himself, answering some internal questions that irritated me.

"What is your real name?"

"Liam."

I frowned.

"Has your father not told you anything?" he sneered.

"No. He's been busy trying to save my unconscious mother, who was nearly beaten to death. You think that excuses him enough?"

All venom and promised violence disappeared from his face as he looked me over.

"You can take that pitying look off your face right fucking now before I rip it off," I snarled with lowered brows.

He closed his eyes and took a deep breath.

"Tell me everything," I demanded.

"I only know that you and Maeve were badly hurt, and that I was asleep the entire time because I was still weak, unable to burn through the magic as fast as you. When I woke up, I was in your bed with everyone in the room, and Damien carried me out. I'm assuming before I became fully conscious and saw the state you were in. I never saw it. They wouldn't let me." He spewed all that out so fast, while never moving his gaze away from whatever pebble was in front of him.

"Maeve is dead."

His eyes snapped up to mine, and his face became that of disbelief and anger.

"How?"

I said nothing. I didn't want to be reminded of her horrors.

"HOW?!"

Silent tears ran down my face. I looked at the hill further down the cliffs, where the ground was still black from her pyre... He followed my gaze and saw it himself.

"She didn't make it out alive. She never made it out of that dungeon."

"But... but she's immortal."

"The chains suppressing our magic prevented her from healing. She bled out until her heart stopped."

I stared out at the ocean. Now blue and magical, and she only saw it once. I heard his footsteps getting louder, and then he pulled me into an embrace. I swallowed the cries I wanted to scream into his chest, the anger I felt at myself, at never being able to see her again.

I tried to shove him off, not wanting to feel those emotions anymore, but he was too strong. He squeezed tighter, and I started to crack. Right before I felt different hands on me.

With every ounce of preternatural strength I had, I shoved Liam, sending him flying. I saw him crash several yards away as I bent down.

I placed my hands on my knees, only to lose my footing and fall to the ground. I could hear the sounds of steel puncturing flesh, louder than the waves of the ocean, and I screamed.

I smelled the rot of the dungeon mixed with copper.

I heard my name in the distance, but nothing turned off the sounds haunting me, paralyzing me. I felt the pain grow in my throat, all the way into my chest, as I screamed and screamed to drown out the noise until everything went dark.

CHAPTER
FORTY-SEVEN

LIAM

I sat on that cliff in silence, watching the sun slowly set while Áine lay passed out in the grass beside me. I spelled her to sleep when I realized where she was in her mind, and no amount of me slapping her or screaming her name would help.

I shook my head at the situation. I needed to take her back and hope Alaric didn't see her current state and skin me alive.

And I needed to get back and find a raven-haired fucker.

I gathered her up, appearing back in her room where Sloan was waiting.

I must've been blinded by fury to notice her room was completely destroyed.

"What the fuck happened in here?" I asked as I placed Áine on her bed, her bed that was now on the floor. I could see the burn marks barely hidden by a fresh rug.

"She woke up one morning and set it on fire. Is she alright?"

"No," I sighed heavily. "I spelled her to sleep. Which she desperately needs. She had some sort of flashback out on the cliffs and wouldn't stop screaming."

Sloan looked down at Áine, who was fast asleep. Her bottom lip trembled slightly before she cleared her throat. She turned towards me with a face full of questions, but said nothing.

I turned back to Áine. Her eyes were surrounded by black smudges that I couldn't tell were bruising or from lack of sleep.

I didn't turn back to Sloan as I turned away.

"Look after her."

I left, arriving right where I knew he'd be. Sitting on the roof, right above her bedroom.

Too fast for him to deflect, I grabbed him by the throat, and we vanished to the cliffs, hopefully out of earshot.

I slammed him into the ground before he kicked me, and I went flying for a second time today. I growled in frustration. Growled at the gall of this prick if he thought he had a leg to stand on.

He didn't make a move, only stood there waiting for me. He knew what was coming for him. I appeared in front of him, jumping up and kicking him with both feet. He fell off the cliff.

I waited for it. Crossing my arms until I felt a gust of wind behind me. I ducked, but there was barely any effort on his end. Hardly any force behind that jab. I spun low and brought him down too easily.

"You're pathetic."

He said nothing, making me even angrier.

"Fine." I lunged at him, throwing him to the ground, and started throwing punches. "You want to feel sorry for yourself? Get the shit kicked out of you?" He took every single hit. "AHHH!!!"

I couldn't fight like this. I threw him across the field. I stood my ground, waiting to see what he would do. I didn't deserve to feel guilty for this prick.

"You have *no* gods' damned right to throw a pity party! Get off your ass and fight!"

He struggled, but finally stood. He sighed deeply and then ran for me. I shook my head, ready to completely not give a fuck, and beat his face in.

Alaric appeared in between us. Looking out into the distance of the ocean, he was utterly unphased that he was standing right where we were about to clash.

Power exuded from him, causing the ground to shake. We stood there silently, waiting for whatever was coming. He looked at Conláed briefly before turning to face me.

"Both of you get the fuck off my land," his voice was monotone. Completely void of life. "Before I kill you all." And then he vanished. Not needing the confirmation that his threat would hold. We've known what that power is capable of, and he knew it, too.

Conláed was staring at the ground, face filled with regret. I snorted and got him the fuck out of there before he risked getting himself killed.

That privilege was reserved for me.

CHAPTER
FORTY-EIGHT

ÁINE, ONE WEEK LATER...

Though we've been freed, the trash never stops being trash. On the outskirts of town in my hooded cloak, I took it upon myself to patron the foulest of the taverns we should've burned long ago. I still considered it while I surveyed them.

I've become long past drunk. I could feel it in the heaviness of my head and the rage that only seemed to be increasing.

I've been forbidden from leaving the castle to seek vengeance again. Not until my mother woke up, my father ordered. Her waking up is now top priority while I wait in this shitty fucking bar to find my next prey.

It's as I said, the worst of the worst slither their way in here. All I have to do is drink myself numb until some asshole messes with someone else's drink and follows them out of the bar with predatory eyes.

Little do they know the worst predator is among them, and while I twiddle my fucking thumbs, unable to help my mother or even be in the same room as her, my rage is happy to settle for the scum who wander here.

I can smell the foulness of the bathroom from across the tavern, see little black dots moving on the walls in my peripherals, and smell the chemically altered herbs wafting off the staff. The only thing stopping me from setting this place ablaze now was that everyone would separate and start going to the nicer taverns.

Like mine, the one I was currently avoiding. Where a beautiful, tanned, and curvaceous captain was always looking for me. She would have to wait. I know what she wants, what she has only ever wanted from me.

Not now. Not until I know for sure that her being near me doesn't put her in danger.

My head jerked towards the door. A muffled shout came from somewhere out there. Again, it sounded. My chair flew back as I hauled ass towards that familiar voice.

Nearly ten men were surrounding Isolde in an alley. Four of them were groaning on the ground. But she couldn't take all of them. She was overwhelmed. And when I thought about what they wanted to do to her…

Screaming ensued for a second until each of them choked on their insides, bubbling in their throats. I kept the flames going until every last trace of them was ash. Isolde was looking at me like I was a ghost, body shaking from terror, disbelieving that she was now safe.

She stared at me, unmoving, unspeaking, for several moments before I turned to leave. I heard her footsteps follow, and I stopped.

"Go home, Isolde."

"No." She struggled to keep her voice firm.

I sighed in defeat as her footsteps neared. Her nearing scent, that usually soothed me, was now unnerving. A hand slid around my waist, and for a second, I was no longer standing outside with her.

I whipped my body around and shoved her away. I could feel the heat on my skin, see the difference in my heightened state of senses and sight, and knew that my eyes were blazing with fire.

Her eyes widened in fear as she took me in, not getting up from the ground. I tried to calm my breathing, but I felt like I would erupt at any moment.

"Go home Isolde. That's an order."

I left no room for debate as I returned to the tavern of hell and found a waitress smelling especially pungent with those herbs I had no business ever touching. She gave me a knowing smile, confirming my suspicions, and nodded her head for me to come sit with her.

I snarled at the piece of shit currently sniffing my fucking cloak, warning him to fuck off as I sat down.

"What are you drinking, love?"

I looked her over. "Something stronger."

Her brows rose in surprise, and then she slowly leaned on her elbows to speak closer to me.

She whispered, "I know who you are, and I'm not losing my head for giving you something you shouldn't be taking."

I smirked. "And you should? Listen lovely, if you don't help me out with something I need, I'm going to explode, and everyone in here is going to die. That's not a threat.

That's me telling you to hurry up because I can't contain it for much longer."

Her frown was laughable, but she noticed the steam rising from my body. I only worried my clothes would melt off.

She straightened and waved her hands in the direction she started walking. "Come on." Urging me, she walked towards a back doorway, one that led to a storage room.

I followed and found that the only storage they kept here was pest traps and air-tight containers of assorted herbs, which looked in no way like natural herbs anymore.

Bundles of green now spiked outwards with crystalized rocks. I watched in horror as she prepared them to be consumed, and not by eating them.

I neared consciousness again to her screaming at me. Apparently, I sank to the ground, no longer able to get back up, and set fire to all the little pests they failed to get rid of.

Fire was climbing her walls and threatening to leave the storage room from hell. With more of a thought than should've been necessary, I willed the flames to douse. I could feel it.

I could *feel* it, I thought over and over as I stared at the back of my hand. That power. That unknown fucking power that couldn't have just been fire.

I was being lifted by the surprisingly strong waitress.

Whom I now noticed was a beautiful goddess. Her chest, those hips, and legs... I wanted to *devour* her.

An aggressive male voice sounded from my right. My body jerked and twisted towards it. If he came near her, he'd die. Except he was already asleep on the ground, like I had knocked him out cold. *What?*

More voices sounded, each more aggressive than the next, and I wanted to burn them all.

My arm was nearly yanked out of its socket as the apron-wearing goddess dragged me outside. No. She had my hand, and we were now walking up a stairway.

The goddess looked over her shoulder at me, smoldering with obvious intention, and my body heated. Her eyes widened. "Please don't burn my house down, princess!"

Oh shit.

"I'm sorry. I keep overheating." I'm still not sure how to control it.

She gave me another knowing look, assuming overheated meant something else. Maybe it did. I smiled when I saw her ass jiggle.

I closed the door behind me and turned to find her inches away from me. Fear. I felt fear, but not for her. There's no way I could do this while I was still broken.

"Don't touch me."

She narrowed her eyes in confusion.

"On the bed. You don't touch me. *I* touch *you*."

Yes. I could do this. The first time would be challenging, but if I could push past the flashbacks, my life could start to go back to normal.

But, what if I couldn't? What if the flashbacks never go away, and I live the rest of my miserable life abstinent because I would never get those hooded cultist monsters out of my head? Was there magic to destroy that part of my memory?

She was sitting on the edge of her bed, looking up saccharinely.

"Do you have any more here? Or do you keep everything at the tavern?"

She raised a brow and then walked to a drawer beside her bed. "No, I have some here." She grabbed her own personal stash and kept looking back at me. "Are you okay?"

"Yes," I lied. "This power keeps surfacing."

She nodded. "It's probably your fathers, right? That's got to be scary to know that kind of power lies within you. To know you could level lands. Raise nine hells on earth..."

I was barely listening. Noises were coming from outside, and I neared the window, but no one was there.

She laughed silently under her breath as she kept working, and I heard that fucking noise again. I pulled the curtain open just a crack to see, but there was no one.

The worst sensation came over me when I closed the curtain and it brushed against my arm. It felt like hundreds, *thousands* of bugs were crawling all over me.

My breathing hitched.

She noticed and walked over urgently. "Here love. Calm yourself."

I took it again and gone were the bugs. All the sounds went quiet again. I opened my eyes, and there she was. The goddess... if a bit hazy.

"I'm doing what you said," she crooned as she backed onto the bed and sat. "I won't touch you until you tell me to. But gods, that will be difficult. You might have to tie me up."

I smirked as I knelt between her knees and began taking off her shirt. "Let's hope you can do what you're told, and I won't have to."

She laughed loudly. "Love, I am *terrible* at doing what I'm... *fuck.*" I started on her chest, pulling her pants off next. I shoved her onto her back, giving her the proper chance to follow orders.

She tasted like... nothing. I worked her and worked her. She completely soaked my face, and still, I could taste nothing. Could *feel* nothing, even if she clearly could.

"Won't you at least take off your cloak?" she pleaded.

"No," I rose to say firmly and resumed.

She whined in frustration at my answer, even as her back arched. I slipped in a third finger, and her hands grasped onto my hair.

Pain.

I felt an innumerable amount of pain in my chest as I slammed backward against the wall, putting several feet between us.

"What the fuck..." she breathed. But I didn't hear her voice.

"I told you not to touch me," I rasped.

"All I did was grab your hair! I was about to come, for fuck's sake!"

I still couldn't hear her voice. I couldn't see her face. Only those hoods. With my boots still on, I ran out the door.

I heard a short-lived shout, but I was gone. I got the hell out of there before I killed an innocent life. The breeze was calling to me, and it would not go unanswered.

I ran as far away from the sounds of people as I possibly could. Far away from the life that everyone was pretending went back to normal. Like twenty years of castration and near death was nothing. Like their queen and princess weren't ruined.

I skidded on my feet, nearing the edge of the cliff. Rocks slid off and fell into the ocean as I barely resisted toppling over. I slid until I found myself sitting and listening to the roaring of the sea.

It was so loud, yet so quiet. I breathed in the beastly water's breath of fury, closing my eyes, grateful that the herbs were already wearing off. They didn't seem to last very long.

I leaned down further and rested my head on my arm as I continued to watch the ocean waves roar in the darkness.

I awoke on a hard floor, surrounded by a familiar scent. Those fucking herbs and... blood. And the waitress. I was back at her place and had somehow fallen asleep on her floor. Did I pass out and dream of the fucking beach? My skin started to itch again. Maybe it was just this fucking place. I began to sit up and took in the putrid scents I hadn't smelled in here before.

Drip.

Drip.

Drip.

I looked towards the end of the bed and found a hand dangling off the edge, dripping blood onto the floor. I swallowed down the fear as I stood up slowly.

Moaning...

Moaning sounds kept flashing in and out. And then... I saw her. I wasn't on the floor. I was on the bed, on *her* bed, and I was riding her, gripping onto her leg and rocking back and forth. She did what she was told. She didn't touch me, but her hands were fisted in the sheets. And then she was screaming.

Drip.

Drip.

Drip.

I saw her hand dripping blood again, but I was still trying to stand. No... My vision flashed again, and I was still riding her, and my head was flung back in ecstasy. Her screams became pleading, desperate, and... gurgling.

I looked down at her body.

Drip.

Drip.

Drip.

The blood fell from the limp hand. My hands were now lapping with flame, burning into the skin on her leg.

I screamed as I looked down and no longer saw a woman crying out in pleasure, but was screaming to her death from what I did to her body. What my body was doing to hers while I found release.

I screamed and screamed and screamed from the horror of what I had done until I erupted. Particles of wood whipped around me like a storm until my flames burnt everything to ash. Fire and ash and smoke enveloped me before eviscerating outwards. It was like a shockwave from hell, and I couldn't stop screaming.

CHAPTER
FORTY-NINE

DAMIEN

S plashing water on my face does nothing for the smudges surrounding my eyes.

They've been there for years now, and I hated that Con never got them. As if he managed lack of sleep perfectly.

I didn't, I just *had* to.

Ever since we broke the curse, those dreams have been a constant occurrence. Every. Single. Night.

And for the past week, I've been unable to see that face. She burns my vision awake and not. That freckled face coated in blood, spitting out something I never wanted to think about, and she was broken. Completely, and unwaveringly broken.

The book I read to help me sleep was about magic from different parts of the world. Odds are, there had to be a sleeping spell strong enough, stronger than Con's that would actually help me.

I found one. I tried it.

It didn't.

This time, the air within Castle Kilhorn was hazy. I'd never had a dream here, which worried me.

I walked through the gates like a ghost, and through it, there was no one. Not a single guard or citizen, like a dreamscape.

Following the tugging sensation in my chest, I made it down several alleys, looking for the filthy tavern Con and I had seen her crawling into late at night.

It came into view, and it exploded, knocking me on my ass. Wind was carrying dirt and debris. I covered my eyes, and then saw her. She was floating in the sky where the apartment looking building was, screaming, and she was surrounded by a whirlwind of wood and fire and wind.

I fought through the wind, slowly trudging my feet forward through the pieces of wood hitting me, through the stench of burnt flesh.

I stopped moving. This was a dream, and obviously I needed to wake the fuck up right now.

I bit my cheek until it bled, and jumped out of my bed.

With my boots *and* pants on, I appeared in front of the tavern, uncaring of unwanted eyes.

Perfectly intact.

The tavern, the apartment, everything was perfectly intact.

But I felt that tugging in my chest again and followed it. When I approached citizens too close for comfort, despite my hooded robe concealing me, I decided to appear outside the gates and away from any eyes.

My instincts led me right, because I was being urged towards the ocean.

I chased that feeling, running towards it until I saw a figure laying on the ground by the cliffs, rolling back and forth.

It was Áine, and she was asleep, likely still within that nightmare screaming.

"Fuck it," I thought out loud, and picked her up.

She was still shaking and thrashing in my arms when I took her to her room. I placed her on her bed and left immediately, because if Alaric found me in here, I was done for.

I glanced at her pained face with smudges around her eyes, felt it burn into my brain, before appearing back in the palace study.

I had already knocked back two drinks before Con walked in. He saw it on my face and didn't have to ask. Hell, he might've even been there and watched as I took care of it.

I wondered if he felt it too, that shift in the air. The shift all of this has made with us.

Should any of it make a difference in how we think or feel about her? No, likely not, but it did. I could see the shift in Con's eyes, just as I could my own.

He grabbed a glass. "I made sure you were spelled and made it out. You should really think about learning it yourself, Damien." his voice was exhausted and irritated.

"Things have changed, Con. I can feel it." I poured more amber liquid into both of our glasses.

"Nothing has changed except a small delay."

I looked at him like he was completely full of shit,

because he was. "And how long does your trusted intuition say this will take?"

He looked down. "I won't give her very long. She's strong, and will get back up from this in no time."

"We're lucky she hasn't tried taking her own fucking life, Con. You must understand how fucked *everyone* would be if that happens? If she succeeded?"

Irrational anger unfurled in his eyes. "She will *not* die. I won't allow it. Neither will you. We give her the space she needs to breathe for a moment, and then she's *ours*."

Ours, he says. Funny.

"Her life is more important than your need for revenge."

He snarled in response. "Don't you dare sit there and act like this is only difficult for you. You think I don't wish I could bring those fuckers back to life just so I can torture them for a century or two? I do. I really fucking do, Damien. But she isn't the first to go through something like this, and she certainly won't be the last if we don't move, and soon."

I looked back at my drink, smirking. "Such a hero you aim to become." I swirled my bourbon. "Careful not to turn yourself into a monster along the way."

He sighed. "I know."

CHAPTER
FIFTY

ÁINE

I awoke in my bed, fully clothed and smelling of woodsy whiskey.
No... Bourbon.
Sweet bourbon filled my nostrils, but I knew I did not drink that last night. None of the whiskey smelled this delicious.

I looked over my body. Not a drop of blood was on me, and it was apparent I didn't bathe. *Just a dream.* It was just a terrible, awful fucking dream that I would never forget until the day I died.

The beast must have brought me home. I just wish I knew from where... I needed to know for sure the dream didn't happen. That it was only a dream...

I ran across the hall to Sloan's room, even though I knew she was at least halfway through training by now. I needed to get back to that. But not before I borrowed her cloak and made sure I wasn't a murderer of the worst kind.

I gripped my chest and fell to the ground in an alley when I saw her apartment was still standing. That everything was just as normal and sleazy as it was before. I focused my hearing and I didn't leave until I confirmed there was a heartbeat in there. Then I went home to take a long, long bath.

I emptied the tub filled with bloody water and refilled it, unable to escape the initial urge to rub my skin off. When would *that* go away? Even if I could heal, there was no way this was good for my skin.

All refilled and fluffed with bubbles, soaking in oils and suds, I rested my head back. The sounds of people filled my ears. People that were too far away to be considered a nuisance. I was still adjusting to the fae hearing, but now, of all times, I just needed everyone to shut the fuck *up*...

I sank lower into the tub until my ears went below water, and poof. Nothing. No sounds, just the croaking of the tub beneath and the water moving throughout it.

I sank further, now completely submerged in the water. I held my breath for what felt like several minutes, but not once did I feel the depletion of oxygen. This was what I needed. This was heaven. It almost sounded like the water in the tub was singing to me. A soft hum of soothing rest and sleep. A lullaby that seeped into my veins, cooled them, and calmed my aching and crying dark soul.

I opened my eyes and lifted my head above water, now sitting up. I wiped the water and bubbles off my face and then frowned. The sunlight seeping into my room now came in at a drastically different angle from when I first got in the tub. My breathing hitched as I realized there was at least an hour's difference in time.

I had fallen asleep underwater and didn't drown. The skin on my ribs moved. I jerked my body, twisting to look, but nothing was there. Maybe it was the after-effects of the herbs. Like the throbbing ache in my gums and my back. Even my damn fingers. Maybe just touching it? Who knew? That shit was sketchy. I shouldn't have touched it if that nightmare didn't already do a good enough job of scaring me away from it permanently.

I looked down at my arms. Scabbing, and yet, it still looked filthy to me. There were new scars all over me. I looked at the few tattoos I did have and made a decision. I arose from the tub and got dressed.

"Where do you want them?" Griffin asked as he prepped the ink with magic to slow the healing, giving the ink the time it needed to set.

I looked at my right arm, currently empty. "Fill this one with these." I dropped one of the burned roses on the table, then looked to my left, which only had one space left. I showed him my drawing. "And this one will cover this area."

He raised his brow. "That's going to take all fucking day."

I grinned broadly. "I'm down if you are."

He snorted, then shouted to his assistant. "Spread the

rest of my appointments throughout the week. I'm getting paid big time today."

I rolled my eyes as I leaned back in his chair before the pain soothed me into another nap.

I walked through alleyways, avoiding everyone as much as possible as I returned to my room. I could hear the raucous laughter and shouting coming from the dining hall. Where my friends would be. Just right down that hall into those double doors, yet they seemed so far away.

I swiftly made it to my bedroom and stuffed my bag with candles. I snuck into my parent's study and grabbed two books. Two, in case I decided against the first choice. I swallowed the lump in my throat as I thought of all my favorite books I had burned in my rage and despair. Books that were irreplaceable.

The ocean was roaring at me in the near night. Sun setting, but not pitch black yet. I set out every candle I could find and fit in my bag, which was about fifty of them, considering I brought the big bag. I spread them out in a circle surrounding me and used my powers to light them. I smirked at the image. I looked like an ancient witch of legends.

I ignored the hunger pains in my stomach and drank the warm tea from the canister. And like a boring old lady witch, I opened my book, drank my hot tea, and read a story to put myself in a world unlike my own. With fictional character's pain, that was unlike my own. Pain that was seeping and oozing and infecting its way out of me.

I was already at the part I saw coming a mile away. The inevitable choice struck upon the main character while we, the readers, pretend she won't pick the most dramatic option. One that typically led to forced proximity to a potential mate or husband. Fuck that. Why is it *always* a fucking mate?

I heard footsteps and looked to find my father looking out at the ocean, holding a plate of food.

"Wow," he breathed. "Much easier to breathe out here."

He leaned over to hand me the plate of heavenly-scented meats, vegetables, and fruits. Could never forget the fruits since I was determined to now make my skin a priority.

"Thank you." and I inhaled my food. Not realizing it was my first meal of the day. How did I not faint at Griffins?

He narrowed his eyes on my arms. "Nice ink."

Among the many I've obtained in such a short time. Anything to cover the scars. At the rate I was going, it would be no time until my skin was more inked than not.

I nodded as I kept chewing, not wanting to waste the food by spewing it from my mouth.

He rarely spoke to me lately. I knew it likely had more to do with his pain than mine, but we still ate meals together, mainly in the study or the breakfast hall where it was quiet. We ate in the courtyard once, but we couldn't lift our heads without seeing pitying eyes.

Being outside of the room was torture. I saw my mother and Maeve everywhere. And every time I did, I saw their bodies on the floor lying in blood.

The last time that happened, a guard walked up from behind me, undoubtedly just walking by, and I turned to punch him in the throat. I felt like a rabid animal when I looked up and saw my father's eyes filled with worry.

He sat on the ground beside my circle of candles, bracing his arms on his knees as he stared out into the sea. He looked back and forth between me and the water, clearly needing to get something off his chest.

"What is it then?" I set my fork down and waited.

He paused and looked at the view for a moment. "Áine, are you happy here?" I rolled my eyes so hard it was almost painful.

"Did Sloan talk to you?" I asked accusingly.

He narrowed his eyes. "And what would Sloan need to talk to me about?"

I considered his tone and believed it. "She said the same shit the other day, suggesting I *fuck off* like other heirs do. Other heirs without responsibilities, though." I took a bite of my food.

"True, but I'm asking because you rarely leave your room, and when you do, you see the same shit I see. It's holding you back and I'm afraid you're wasting away here." I stopped eating at that.

"And what about you, father? If you see it, then are you not *wasting away* here as well then?" I countered.

He exhaled audibly. "We're not discussing me. This is about you."

I said nothing, waiting for him to say something I'm sure I wouldn't like.

He sighed, "Heavens, I'm just trying to see if you're okay."

"Of course, I'm not okay!" I yelled and immediately regretted it. "I'm sorry. I shouldn't..."

"You will *not* apologize," he said firmly, struggling to withhold tears.

Seeing your father in tears was paralyzing. They were supposed to be the strength in your life. The few times I had seen him cry, all of which within these past few weeks, it was devastating. It meant that something was truly wrong. Not something that your father pats you on the head and says it'll be okay. If he said that now, I wouldn't believe him.

"When you apologize, you show a sign of weakness. And lately I haven't found an ounce of strength in you. Not even when you put Sir Eryn on his ass."

"What are you trying to say? That I'm a mess? I understand that I am completely fucked up right now. You couldn't even understand half of how fucked in the head I am right now," I choked. I shouldn't be saying these things. I looked back down at my food. "The last thing you need right now is to hear how terrible I'm doing."

"The last thing I need, Áine, is my daughter to fall apart completely," he said calmly. "The last thing *you* need is your father losing his mind, trying to mend the broken pieces of our home. But I must know if you're going to be okay. I can't focus on figuring out how to wake your mother up, even if she is completely healed, with our only child setting rooms on fire."

He turned to face me with a renewed expression.

"I think it's time we talk about what happened that day in the forest."

"I don't want to talk about Conláed."

He frowned at that and then dipped his head before continuing. "You need to know what he and his men did that day and why Liam was here to keep you safe."

My eyes widened as I realized my father had given him his own name five years ago. "So, you knew him, then?"

He nodded while looking at the ocean. "I recognized him when you brought him here that day. Noted his human form, and assumed it had something to do with you, so I made sure to keep him close. It didn't take long to realize that his swiped memory and incessant need to keep you safe was likely a spell."

"So, you know what he is, then." It wasn't a question.

He nodded again. "And I'm sure it won't be long until he and his ilk come demanding a reward for keeping you safe all these years."

I narrowed my eyes in question, waiting for him to continue.

He shook his head before speaking. "Conláed's race is of the same who cursed us to this island to die, Áine. He is of a race that shouldn't even exist. They use seduction and greed for their own personal gains, and torture for entertainment."

I waited for more, but, "What are they then?"

"His race is of the Demon Fae. He in particular is half high elf, and half demon."

My eyes widened. I was told the stories growing up, told of their nature. They were considered an abomination, which I always rolled my eyes at. But I was also told of my father's battles against them and the elves. He waited for my questions, but there were too many to choose from.

"Long, long ago, the King of the High Elves sought an opportunity to strengthen their race. So, they made a deal with the demons to form an alliance for war, so long as they handed over a large amount of their women to breed with. Willing or not," he said grimly, nodding in confirmation of my expression.

"It's a very long story that stems from the lovely High Court, but the bottom line is that Liam, Conláed, his older brother Drak, and that fucking shithead Damien, are all products of that catastrophe," he confirmed.

"Then what would they be doing here if their people cursed us? Why was one of their own keeping me safe?"

He sighed. "Not all agreed to this... union. There were some who rebelled, who were then slaughtered. I imagine there are others who are still against it but say or do nothing out of fear.

"I also imagine that Conláed, being as powerful as he, in fact, *is*," he added venom to that. "He likely is forming some sort of rebellion to take the people for himself. Now if he is doing it from the goodness of his heart, or because he wants to steal the crown for himself, I have no clue. Which is why I don't trust him."

But... "You trusted him enough to take me home. You trusted Liam enough in our home."

"I trusted that whatever it is they are trying to accomplish completely depends on your survival and me being on his good side. Isn't that right, little Prince?" he crooned, but didn't look away from me.

I looked over, and there he was. Right at the tree line, trying his best to not look furious and failing. Then he vanished.

My father snorted at that and shook his head. "What a peculiar one. At least he's nothing like his father."

"Why have you never said anything? My whole life?"

"I should have." That was all he said.

I shook my head. "And yet, you don't have the slightest amount of gratitude for the men who freed us?"

"You think we didn't have a plan, Áine? We're the fucking Dhadren. They needed so much power to seal us here because of what we are. They couldn't just kill us. They weren't strong enough, and couldn't wait for their new abominations to mature and fight their battles for them."

"And your plan was what, exactly? Let our immortality kick in when the curse tries to take our lives? In case you didn't notice, half of our population is gone," I argued.

He gave a sad smile. "And where do you think their magic went, Áine?"

"I don't know shit about any of this. You can't expect me to make any assumptions."

"Magic from the original Dhadren gets passed down through the bloodlines. If one dies, it jumps to another, typically next of kin. The more Dhadren are made, the more new and forged power is crafted. However, if the population dwindles, the people that are left could have powers that are comparable to the Gods who birthed us."

My stomach sank, and I thought I might vomit. "So, you

counted on if enough of our people died, we would eventually be strong enough to break free?"

"It's not that simple. This isn't common knowledge. Most of our people don't even know about it, Áine. How do you think they'd feel or react to that knowledge? This isn't something set in motion for some escape plan. This is the power of gods that won't die. If the host is cut into several pieces, you have several slightly *weaker* pieces, if you'd dare call them weak."

And if all are killed but one, you have one piece of perfect power. Dangerous information, indeed.

"The problem with this... *backup* plan was how the curse played out. How it didn't go as they planned. They used some sort of conduit that I know nothing of, but... it was destroyed when they tried to steal power they couldn't."

"No one can take a God's power. That is for their will alone. It knew it was being taken against its will, so it destroyed the conduit, and hid. Inside you."

My eyes widened. That's why they needed me alive.

"I didn't know where it went until I saw you that day in the sky, but somehow, they knew. The day that power sought its freedom and dispersed amongst its people again. That's what that fire was that shot in the sky. It wasn't only fire, but since that's your power, I assume it only appeared that way until separated."

"I have so many questions."

"I know."

"Why me?"

He shrugged. "I suppose it chose you as a worthy container. Try not to let it get to that big head of yours."

"It chose me? As in... *it* decided I was to be a vessel?" I pleaded for answers.

He shook his head. "I have no idea how vessels get picked, only that those that are have nearly limitless potential. Potential to lead, and potential to detonate."

I turned to stare at the ocean. It made me uncomfortable every time this topic always found its way into any of our conversations. "Then what curse did they break?"

He sighed. "The curse... was that of god magic. It encased our entire land with death, like a blight, but the magic went away instantly. A curse that normally would never kill us. Something they would have to take our magic away first to accomplish."

"Then they broke it...."

"They broke it because the demon blood gives them an affinity for curses, and because of that, they likely found the rift first."

"So then, why did our appearance change?"

"The curse they used was the magic of the gods. There have been many stories told of gods who punished their creations for disobeying, or from just not being pleased with them, and so they took back the power that kept them alive and powerful, and left them to either rot or infest unwanted lands. Sometimes they were created for that very purpose. That's how many of us look older in such a short time."

My eyes threatened to pop out of my head.

"Our curse, Aine... was that of humans."

CHAPTER
FIFTY-ONE

CONLÁED

In the courtyard in front of our palace, at one of the many wrought iron tables, Drak, Damien, and myself sat.

"I think it's time we head to the demon realm now, while we wait." The understanding in their faces told me I didn't have to clarify what we were waiting on.

Damien grumbled. "So you want us to leave her in this state?"

Drak looked at him oddly.

"We can't just sit here and wait, Damien."

He shook his head. "We can't leave her like this. I don't trust her to be alone with herself. Not after the shit show I just saw."

"You're not staying," I ordered. "I need you *and* Drak in case shit goes south. We've never been to that realm, and they could kill us instantly if they wanted."

"Then why go at all!" he shouted, surprising me.

It was Drak who responded to his loss of control. "This was the plan, Damien. You *knew* this. If you want me to be at my strongest, we have to go there and break my father's curse on my power. It isn't something we have the luxury of negotiating."

I could feel his voice in the table, it was so deep. Only my father would be cowardly enough to neuter his own son's power. A selfish bastard who didn't want the threat of his son killing him or eating him in his sleep.

"We'll stay one more week, Damien. Watch over her, and if we see progress, we'll leave for the demon realm. It'll give Søren and Alastair enough time to prepare to lead and train while we're gone."

"Fine," Damien grumbled.

The Princess was digging her claws into his chest. I could see it right at this moment.

Maybe for a moment, I worried the same was happening to me, but his weakness in the way he speaks about her, reacts to conversations about her, only strengthens my resolve.

If *Damien* of all people is affected by this, then I need to step it up and set the example, hardening my mental armor.

Terrible things happened to good people just as much as bad people. And I have no doubt Áine is one of the bad ones.

I have no doubts that the girl Sloan knocked out is under the same fucking spell. And if the Ancients thought they were going to control us, to control each kingdom this way, I would prove to them that not only were they wrong, but they would be completely fucked by the time I'm through with her.

CHAPTER
FIFTY-TWO

ISOLDE

My lips were dry, sticking together every time I opened them. I ignored the glass of water Visha left for me in her cottage. She kept me here in a secluded bedroom, away from anyone who might need treatment from her, and away from Áine.

My foot shifted, making the chains clink together. She had chained my foot to the bed at night to make sure I didn't lose control and go after Áine.

Either Áine had no idea, or she didn't care enough to investigate. Regardless, I resented her for it.

Each day passed by, no training, no bantering with my Commander, whom I am still not allowed to see.

I wanted to kill the King for it, but I understood. It wasn't out of protection for me, but for his daughter and what hurting me would do to her.

And with each day, I thought about Maeve.

Before I buried that reality so deep within the pit of my mind, and then nothing. My mind was blank, not a memory or a voice. Just the chaotic screams flashing sporadically in the abyss.

I was drowning in my sorrows, and I so desperately wanted her to walk through that door.

Reaching my arm up, I looked at the burn marks that scarred. Not only was I not fireproof, but for some reason, my fae magic would not allow me to fully heal from it.

Because the gods hated me, Visha walked through the door, not bothering to knock.

She said nothing as she unchained my ankle and then leaned against the doorway.

I didn't bother looking at her when I sat up and fastened the chain back around my ankle.

She looked unaffected, like she was expecting it. "I have information on your family."

My jaws tightened, and I warily looked up at her. She unclasped my chains once more and walked out the door, not even checking to see if I followed.

Arrogant bitch.

She said nothing as we walked for several minutes through the courtyard, through the castle, all the way to her old cellar.

When we stepped over the threshold, the candles didn't light in my presence.

"It's because you're muted, *dull*."

Ok, whatever that meant.

She looked me over in disgust. "You smell like shit."

"Get on with it."

I followed her to a large table in front of a shelved wall full of books. They looked like ancient grimoires and tomes.

One of which had a large triskell figure on the cover, with several runes within each loop. Some runes I didn't recognize. It also looked like it was around longer than this castle.

She reached for it, following my gaze. "Interesting how you're drawn to the book we need."

I ignored it, and swallowed down the worry those words caused.

She flipped through several pages, each whipping up more dust than the previous page. The pages had yellowed, and many of which were completely unreadable. But the page she stopped at...

Dagny.

I had never heard that name before, but it clanged through my mind like a ricocheting arrow.

I didn't notice Visha had stepped away when she came back with a sheet of paper. I narrowed my eyes at the words on the top.

"The marriage record for your parents. Your mother's maiden name..." and she pointed.

Dagny.

I shrugged it off. "Am I supposed to recognize that name?"

She surveyed my face, my eyes, as if she were expecting a physical reaction of some sort.

Her eyes turned back to the book. "Dagny is a surname for a particular line of witches. Many of which were burned alive, and might be why your mother fled here, marrying to change her name."

Her words caused an emotion to flutter that I didn't recognize. I gasped when the candles all came to light.

She continued, looking around at all the candles. "It also means something important you need to know." Her eyes turned grave when they found mine, and she gently clasped my wrist. "Witches don't recover from fire. Your fae blood may help with the healing, but looking at these burns on you that are scarring..."

She was answering a question I didn't ask, and never wanted an answer to.

"So her power can kill me. Why does it matter? She wouldn't do that."

She glanced at the ground before speaking again. "No... but, if her body temperature rises for other reasons..."

My eyes shot wide open, and despite everything that's happened, the pain those words caused destroyed me. I spiraled internally over the horrible images in my mind.

I didn't recognize my own voice that now trembled violently. "Why are you telling me this?"

Her eyes were the gentlest I'd ever seen them. "Because I think now is the time you found that family. Across the sea in Oskela, where those witches still reside. Many of them have a coven the courts do not dare touch. Especially since they realize how essential their alliance could be in battle."

Indeed, I thought of the witch who was beside Carsen.

"Let her heal," she whispered. "She needs time, and..." I could *feel* the reluctance in her voice for whatever else she wanted to say, whatever it was that would likely rip my soul out of my chest. "And the King has ordered it."

"Why?" I snapped. Why was he so insistent about

keeping me from his daughter? What could I have done to cause such disapproval?!

I swallowed audibly at the idiotic thought. What *hadn't* I done to earn his disapproval?

Visha was pursing her lips, refusing to answer.

I didn't need one. I knew the day would come that they'd pick up on our feelings, on our joke of a relationship and forbid it.

Knowing Áine, she would undoubtedly honor it.

Her *unwavering* alliance to her father and her people... I snorted. Not an ounce of that would ever come my way.

Never had she seen me as a person, as someone who could love her. Not that I'd given her a true reason for it. At that thought, "When do I leave?"

I stared at the name in the book before I closed and held it to take with me. This was something I wouldn't ask permission for.

She nodded. "Now."

I blinked. "*Now?*"

She ushered us out of the cellar. "You can't be near her right now. Not while she is unstable. The faster we get there, the faster you can find out if there are any spells linked through the power of your family that will give you any chance in hell of being with your mate."

My feet nearly tripped over themselves halting, narrowing my eyes at her as she turned around.

"Oh, are we pretending now?"

"Do the King and Queen know?"

Visha took a step towards me. "Child, why in the hell do you think I, of all people, while the Queen still slumbers, am subjected to taking you to another continent?"

My breathing was labored. "They really hate the idea of me being with her that much?"

She snorted. "Of course. You're an irresponsible child who was given the title as captain much too early, and not once have you properly followed through with any order Áine has ever given you."

My chest was now heaving. First, in anger for the truth of her words, but secondly, for another emotion I couldn't place.

"*Even still,* a mating bond isn't something to interfere with. A king he may be, but you? You have an important part to play here, and to stay here means to fail, and failure is death. Do you understand?"

"No," I answered honestly.

She rolled her arms, lightly grabbing my arm and ushering me forward. "Of course you don't. I'll explain on the road."

I yanked my arm back, but kept walking beside her.

No longer would I remain the errant child that remains everyone's bother.

They expect me to return a different person, but with each step I took, I saw Maeve's face.

I saw the disappearance of the one thing that kept me here, that held me *down*.

No more.

A witch, she says?

Dagny.

The name clanged through my brain again.

It fed me resolve, and for the first time in a long while, I had ambition. A *goal*.

And if I find what I'm looking for, I'm not coming back.

CHAPTER
FIFTY-THREE

ÁINE

Another week passed, and still no word from Conláed or Liam. No more visits from Isolde, and then they told me it was because she'd left.

If I wasn't already in horrible pain, I might've managed this fine, would've understood her need to find herself and be free.

But now? Not being able to sense her anywhere, smelling her only to find she's not there, it was killing me.

Everyone tried to pretend nothing happened. No one mentioned Carsen, Maeve, or my mother.

It was as if the suppression was the answer for fucking everything, but it wasn't working for me. It built and built until I could feel it in my throat.

I climbed onto the roof, which still smelled of Conláed, and hopped over to watch the training from up high. When

I found a group of our soldiers from a reasonable distance away, I crouched down and narrowed my eyes.

Sloan had them completely under her control. My sister and captain, who was demonstrating the perfect representation of structured and diligent training.

And they respected her.

All moved together in synch, fierceness in their faces, as they imagined themselves actually in battle. Today was formation training, then.

She didn't show off, and wasn't being an arrogant asshole like me. Everyone was working. Not a single fucking one of those pricks was standing somewhere with their jokes about women handling steel.

I was ashamed of the feeling swelling in my gut, watching them. This woman, she was meant to lead. I did everything I could to defy my role in this kingdom, and it fucking showed. I was just a spoiled princess, being rebellious.

Sloan was the blood and bones of a true battle queen.

Everything I tried and failed to become. Flashbacks were threatening to consume me at the thought. Any heightened emotion seemed to trigger them these days. Having a full-blown episode on the roof was the *last* fucking thing I wanted to happen today.

"You know, you could join us," Keira said from behind me.

"Holy shit Keira…" I grabbed my chest and tried to catch my breath.

She laughed, "Did I scare you?"

"Obviously."

Another voice from far away started, "Are you ever going to get your ass down here or what?"

Sloan was looking right at me, smiling.

Well, shit.

Keira and I hopped down there. I was definitely dragging my ass.

When I approached Sloan, I put my hands behind my back in a warrior's stance and waited.

She snorted and said quietly, "You're the Commander, Áine."

I looked over at her, then shook my head.

"Today, you're the Commander."

She raised her eyebrow in concern and question.

I nodded. "With the work you're doing here, Captain, I doubt that will be your title much longer," I declared loud enough for them to hear. They nodded and grunted in agreement as I smiled my authoritative smile at her.

I wished so deeply for it to feel like a real one, but all I could see was the lack of Isolde's presence with us.

She stood up straighter. However, that was possible...

"Very well. We are about to wrap up the day with hand-to-hand combat." She turned towards the soldiers. "*My* personal favorite." And they all groaned.

No one could stomach getting punched by Sloan. Literally, she punched me in the stomach when we were younger, and I threw my guts up violently, unable to eat the rest of the day.

I stood with the girls as they all removed their armor and put away their weapons, coming back in only leathers.

I watched as Sloan had certain groups sectioned off and

lined up in pairs. Her leadership skills really were a feat to be admired.

"Áine?" Sloan caught my attention.

I looked up, and she had her hand gestured to one of the males who looked at her with respect. He was one of Carsen's men that I absorbed, one of them that didn't seem like an evil sack of shit.

"Right, you're the boss today," I smirked as I walked past her and in front of...

"This is Lionel. Try to be gentle with this one. He's one of the few decent and respectful males here."

He was beaming at her compliment as the others groaned at her audacity. She laughed.

I raised my arms and got into position, waiting for her command to start. I saw Lionel was nervous and hesitant with movement.

"Don't hold back Lionel. I'm not a commander or princess of anything out here."

"Easy for you to say. You weren't ever born in any other stature."

True.

"Just promise you won't laugh at me too hard when you knock me on my ass. I haven't trained in weeks. I imagine I'm about to eat some dirt, and I'm perfectly ok with that."

He gave a pitiful, knowing glance towards the dirt before nodding, unable to look me in the eye.

Great.

Sloan shouted. "Begin!"

We circled each other for a moment, testing each other out, but I threw the first punch and missed.

His fist met my rib cage, and I groaned.

He backed up, but I growled. "No backing down Lionel," I pointed at him. "It's your responsibility to make sure I leave this field a warrior again. You understand me?" I spoke with all authority, with no room for argument.

He nodded.

I dropped, swinging my leg out to disable him. He jumped up, evading my attack completely. When his feet met the ground again, they bounced, and he spun a kick towards my face. I blocked in time, but I was still thrown to the ground.

I laughed through the pain and excitement of the fight.

"Very good!" I praised him, erasing the fear he had on his face.

They were walking on eggshells around me, and the first day would be the most uncomfortable.

I charged at him in a sprint, and he spun his body perfectly to evade my attack, using his hands to turn me away from him. It was beautifully done, but I still had to fight the urge to vomit everywhere from his hands on me.

I was just struggling from flashbacks on the roof earlier, and now I needed to make sure I didn't lose my shit *here,* of all places. I needed to make sure that reaction died today on this field.

He swayed when I swung with more grace this time. Dipping his whole body into a duck as I swung wide, he clocked me right in the face. I landed face-first in the dirt.

"Áine!" I heard Sloan cry out in worry.

"I'm fucking fine!" I snapped, not needing her to add insult to injury.

I struggled against my aching body to stand, now weakened from not leaving my room. Hopping on my feet to shake it off, to shake off the wind getting knocked out of me and the flashbacks of that man hitting me while Maeve was...

Tears fell, and I wiped them off immediately. Lionel clearly noted it with a pitiful look, but I shook my head in warning. I needed this if I would ever return to my post here.

I was distracted, and Lionel pounced. I threw my hands up to block his blows. The moment he slackened, I jerked my upper body far to the right to land my first kick. He blocked it. Then I spun in the opposite direction, spinning my other foot as fast as possible to land on his other side.

He barely dodged it. One hand up to take the hit, the other gripped onto my hip to tackle or throw me to the ground. Whichever it was, it wasn't fast enough when a flashback came of that man's hands gripping my hips as he was about to enter me. Fear consumed me, and my hand punched through Lionel's chest.

No.

No, no, no, no, no.

Please tell me I didn't do this.

"Oh, gods..." Sloan said behind me.

People were covering their mouths in shock. Some were looking at me with disgust.

I watched as Lionel was choking on his own blood. That sweet face for such a skilled fighter. He would make such a good husband one day. He can't die. Please tell me I didn't do this!

I let go of his heart and took out my hand, holding him as we fell. I held him in my arms while my tears coated his face.

"Please..." I breathed.

He didn't take his eyes off mine, filled with understanding and forgiveness.

"No, don't you dare forgive me. You're going to be ok. You're immortal, right? Heal up right now and please, for all that is holy, punch through my chest too. If you don't, I'll never forgive myself more than I already don't." I kept talking, needing to focus him on me. Needing to allow him time to heal, but the hole was too big, and I nearly took his heart.

I laid him flat on the ground, his eyes never leaving mine, and placed my hands over the hole in his chest and did the only thing I could do. Prayed.

"Please, please, please heal in time. Please don't let him die. He still needs to grow up and become a commander. He still needs to become the best husband who protects his family. Please..."

The silence surrounding us was deafening. I listened to his heartbeat, and it was slowing down. I screamed.

"PLEASE!" I begged no one and everyone.

I laid my head on his chest, still covering the wound with my hands, continuing to plead for his life, for him to heal. I lay there for several moments, waiting for the inevitable.

I waited for the moment he was gone, and Sloan would drag me to my room, where I would slowly rot and die like the curse never left.

I was the curse.

These people needed me gone.

"Please..." I begged again.

I would leave. Sloan is the right person for these people. I would only lead them to die horrible deaths.

A hand was touching my back, too big to be Sloan's. I jerked my head up, and Lionel was looking at me.

His eyes were wide and alert, in shock.

I lifted my hands and saw that the hole was closed. The hole through his tunic revealed perfectly healed skin.

"Princess..." he breathed.

I looked at his handsome face and cupped his cheek, still not believing this was real.

"Holy fucking shit," Sloan exhaled beside me. "You can heal."

I can...

I can heal...

The relief that washed over me that Lionel wasn't going to die today at my hands, eviscerated.

I can heal...

I stood up, looking down at Lionel's chest.

I healed him.

He can grow up to marry one day and sire children who will have both parents.

I stepped back at the realization of how completely fucking worthless I was.

"I can heal?" I pushed the words out between the laboring breaths.

"Áine..."

"My mother is... Maeve is dead, because of me, and I can

HEAL?" I shouted, echoing through the silence of the training yard.

Everyone was looking at me with either pity or disgust.

I shook my head at all of them, and started to back away.

"No..." I whispered and then broke into a run. I ran to the gates that wouldn't rise fast enough.

I climbed the walls and jumped over, landing on my feet. I ran to the forest, cutting through the trees and their snaked branches as they cut up my face.

I tripped over the many roots that emerged from the earth. I could feel something in my leg snap. Not a bone, since I could still run on it, but not without pain. Pain I needed. Pain I deserved.

I kept running until I reached the lake and dove in. And because I couldn't swim, I sank all the way to the bottom until I reached the lakebed, now formed in large, colorful, crystallized stone, and screamed.

I screamed until the crystals were glowing red like the day our curse was broken.

Until the earth trembled and bubbles were forming around me, shooting up to the surface.

I didn't stop when the heat ripped apart my clothes. I didn't stop when I felt the painful shifting in my spine and rib cage, the vicious roiling in my gut, the sharp pain in my gums and fingers.

My mother is barely alive, and my friend is dead because of me. And I could've saved them. If only someone had said something. Something about it being possible to inherit the powers of both parents.

Did my father know? Of course, he didn't, or he would've been begging me to save her.

The water vibrated around me as I screamed, and I didn't stop when I heard and felt the stone crack beneath me.

What a fucking waste to have such beautiful power, passing it onto your child, and they can't even save you when it's their fault you're hurt.

I screamed until I couldn't anymore. Consciousness was beginning to slip away from me.

Good.

At least if I died here, the beasts that live in the water would have dinner for their younglings, who likely aren't entirely useless.

I snorted at the thought as my power exploded over and over until everything went black.

EPILOGUE

DAMIEN

The portal looked like an airborne sinkhole.

The edges would literally cave in to give a wider view of where we would arrive.

There were no birds, no magic that could send a message alerting them of our presence.

You were either welcomed here, or you weren't.

"Damien," Con called. "As usual, you remain quiet. Drak will handle the negotiations." Drak's face reflected all the excitement he held for that decision, which was none.

Even if we would finally, *hopefully*, find a means to set free the full capacity of his power, he had no interest in leading. He would never be able to hold a court or a land of people without scaring them into abandoning their homes.

Not any fault of his. His deep voice and general appearance reflected that of the monster you sent in to exterminate a village.

Con rubbed his chest, but shrugged it off. I furrowed my brows, but he shook his head. "Same shit," he answered my unspoken question.

We stepped towards the portal, through which we could now see the sky of the demon realm with its array of colorful moons, and then my knees hit the dirt.

A growl built in my chest, escaping my mouth in a loud, violent thunder of pain. I gripped my chest tightly.

Drak was beside me, cursing vehemently under his breath not knowing what to do. When I was finally able to open my eyes, I saw Con next to me, also on his knees and gripping his chest.

His eyes were as rounded as mine, and reflecting panic like I've never known.

To be continued...

ACKNOWLEDGMENTS

My husband and kids, for dealing with my crankiness from writing for hours!

My sister, who yelled at me every time I didn't write complete sentences.

My mom, who has been cheering me on forever.

My dear friend Jessica, my RBF twin and very first reader who told me, "Publish that shit NOW!"

My author group, Distracted Inklings, for giving me the support system to finish my work!

Rebekah, for your limitless knowledge on, well, everything.

Amber T., for all your advice, your charm, and that GORGEOUS FUCKING COVER YOU MADE.

Nicole, you and I are a duo no one will see coming, and I can't wait to read what you wrote right alongside me. This is our fucking year!

Amber P., for your help proofreading my shitty grammar!

Roxie, for your bubbly attitude that brightens mine and everyone else's day.

Veronica for being everyone's number one fan, pushing the negativity away when it comes creeping.

Kim, for your inspirational morning voice messages.

Cassie, for being my first and best beta reader, and for introducing me to our author friends when I knew NO ONE!

The local fire department when I had my house fire in December, and all my friends, family, and the booktok community who came together and sent me and my family help when we lost everything.

To the meaning behind my pen name, for I will always wield it proudly in the shape of a middle finger.

ABOUT THE AUTHOR

Rotting in Vain is Lady Kilroy's debut novel, with many others in the works. She has no degrees or awards. Only a brain filled with years of research and too much life experience to keep hidden. When music, witchcraft, and fantasy books are off the agenda, Lady Kilroy is running from sleep, writing with her author group, Distracted Inklings. Secretly a sucker for cheese, but has a head and heart for the darker side of things, and draws inspiration from her favorite dark fantasy authors, as well as from within. She is a writer of characters that are morally grey, emotionally complex, as well as badass FMCs who eviscerate gender roles and bathe in the blood of their enemies.

Made in the USA
Middletown, DE
29 December 2024